A FRIENDLY GESTURE

BY RAMSEY CAMPBELL

"**FOUR THOUSAND EIGHT HUNDRED. FOUR THOUSAND EIGHT. WHO'LL GIVE ME FIVE?**" As a hand at the back of the saleroom sent him a wave anyone less vigilant might have missed, Lyndley said "I have five thousand. May I look for more?" When a barely visible shake of a head brought the contest to an end he declared "This fine diamond-encrusted Victorian brooch sold for five thousand" and confirmed it with a rap of his gavel as discreet as any of the responses he was constantly alert for.

"Another sterling performance," Jacqui Havering told him once the afternoon was done. "Scenting your bonus?"

He was smelling her habitual celebratory vape, which grizzled the air in her office, and had to clear his throat to say "Just doing all the best I can."

"Make certain you're on time tomorrow. You've a consignment of books to appraise." Momentary pensiveness widened her eyes, which appeared to tug her small severe face blank. "Let's hope we gain value with age as well."

"I expect we'll find out soon enough."

"Thanks for reminding me, Claude." She sounded some distance from grateful.

"See you in the morning," she said as if he needed a memorandum.

He escaped the crowded downtown streets as soon as he could. Close to Haverings Auction Rooms (Est. 1898) steps led down to an urban canal. A pair of chefs crowned with caps like party hats waiting to be coloured in were sharing a pungent cigarette on the towpath. Ducks and their overlapping ripples converged on scraps of bread thrown by a woman in a wheelchair. A man with a metal claw on a pole was retrieving donations to the waterway— bottles, cans, a polystyrene bivalve, home to a sodden burger. Reflected sunlight groped at the undersides of roads while

Lyndley's footsteps roused thin echoes in the gloom.

He was nearly at the steps leading up to his road when a barge glided past him. A motorcycle bestowing a bounty of fumes in its wake as it roared across the bridge had caught his attention, so that he was scarcely aware of the elongated vessel until a passenger waved to him. He just had time to glimpse a silhouette through a window and return the greeting before the boat painted with a mass of reeds coasted under the bridge. Some caprice of the dimness and indirect sunlight made its reflection look more solid than it did, as though the boat was reflecting the submerged shape. As a barge decorated with cartoonish sunflowers passed it the bearded helmsman covered his eyes, no doubt fending off the glare of sunlight as he sailed into the open. Halfway up the steps Lyndley heard a muffled splash beneath the bridge, where presumably the reedy barge had jettisoned some item.

Five minutes' stroll along the avenue planted with saplings in wire tubes took him to the gentrified tower block, where the lift announced each floor on the way to the fifth with a resonant thump. He microwaved a compartmentalised supermarket carton and dined without a plate in the main room, where the view across the balcony beyond the table by the window showed him the canal stretching beneath streets and out of town. After dinner he watched a stridently energetic action film on the expansive sliver of a television screen flanked by shelves of volumes his subscription to a book club brought him, all of which felt like a break from the past that provided the auction material. When at last the film fell silent he watched an illuminated barge advance across the countryside while an unlit virtually indistinguishable vessel crept after it, and then he went to bed.

His phone woke him with an outburst reminiscent of a watchman with a bell. As he saw off his breakfast someone passing on the balcony waved to him, a gesture scarcely more substantial in the dimness than a waft of smoke. Once he left the suburbs behind, the upturned streets grew office blocks that reached deeper into the canal. The nervous buildings shivered with a drizzle that urged him to hurry to work.

"I've set out the books for you," Jacqui said not unlike a reprimand for arriving later than she had. The items on the table in the stockroom—novels and magazines close to a century old, boasting names such as Hammett and Chandler—raised his hopes, but every cover was tattered, and spinal injuries were rife. "I'll try for five hundred," he said.

"You think that's all we can ask for."

"I'll do my best to realise more, of course."

"I should hope so," Jacqui said and gave him a frown to contemplate.

The doorbell sent him to admit Fatima, who seemed troubled by a companion. "This gentleman would like a word," she said.

"We aren't quite open yet," Lyndley told him, then recognised the seller of yesterday's brooch. "But do come in, Mr Forth."

An untamed reddish moustache spanned Forth's fiercely piebald face. "I received your message about the sale," he said.

"We were pleased with the outcome and we hope you are."

"I've been informed I have reason not to be."

As Fatima retreated to the staffroom Lyndley said "Pardon my asking, but who gave you that idea?"

"I was contacted by someone who assured me they would have given me a higher price."

"May we have their name? Whichever of our competitors they were, that's utterly unethical."

"They aren't in your line of trade. They're a private individual." Forth dealt his moustache a furious tug as if determined to adjust its proportions. "Have you seen something more important," he demanded, "or just had enough of me?"

"Neither, I promise you. Someone didn't come in, that's all." Whoever had waved through the pane on the door must have been indicating they'd mistaken the place before dodging out of sight as Lyndley glanced towards them. "Then why didn't this person put in a bid?" Lyndley said.

HAUNTED PLACES • TORMENTED SOULS
AND THE CREEPING UNKNOWN

COVER IMAGE AND INTERIOR ILLUSTRATIONS: ALLEN KOSZOWSKI
PHOTO ART: NATU SHABBEY
EDITOR AND PUBLISHER: TOM ENGLISH

Nightmare Abbey 5 (Spring 2024) is published by Dead Letter Press and is copyright © Tom English and Dead Letter Press, PO Box 134, New Kent, VA 23124-0134. All rights reserved, including the right to reproduce this book, or portions thereof, in any form including but not limited to electronic and print media, without written permission from the publisher. Dead Letter Press has endeavored to source and credit the copyright of all stories, photos, and artworks used in this volume but would be glad to right any omissions in the next available issue. All stories, art, and film and television images are copyright © the relevant writers, artists, producers, studios, or publishers, etc. The publisher adheres to the "fair use" policy of using photographic imagery, artworks, and other material for critiquing purposes.

www.DeadLetterPress.com   ISBN-13: 979-8-9862307-7-1

DEAR ABBEY

MISSING

Bleached bones, red eyes, maniacal grin. Last seen wearing dirty, moth-eaten cassock. If found, please contact Nightmare Abbey.

HAVE YOU SEEN ME?

WITH APOLOGIES TO DICK HOLLER AND DION, *"Anybody here seen my old friend Abbey? Can you tell me where he's gone? ...You know I just looked around and he's gone."*

I can't say Abbey "freed lotta people." In fact, even as I write this, he's got some dude stretched out on the rack in our dungeon. (I guess I should go down there and release the poor sucker. Uh, maybe after I finish my coffee.) What I *can* say is, Abbey was always the life of the party around here—a real *gagster*, a genuine *cutup*—and without him haunting these unhallowed halls... *Well*, this place is like an empty tomb.

Oh dear! Abbey's sudden disappearance has made recent developments here rather bittersweet. Leave it to our demented caretaker to rain on our parade and dampen the festivities surrounding the arrival of our newest family member. No, I'm *not* speaking of Ramsey Campbell. He may be the guest of honor for this little gathering of literary spirits, but as much as I'd like to, he simply refuses to allow me to adopt him.

No, our newest family member, *Indy*, is a sixty-pound, two-year-old male Siberian Husky with a rowdy disposition and a huge appetite. This *indy*-pendent hound fills our sleepless nights with the sound of his claws clicking across the cold stone floors of Nightmare Abbey, his ungodly howls echoing through the darkened halls and decaying chambers of this cheerful abode. During the day, however, he spends his time gnawing on old bones. And burying things. That dog spends more time digging in the dirt than anyone I've ever known—including Burke and Hare. Why, only yesterday I watched Indy neatly dispose of a pile of brittle old bones in the abandoned cemetery behind the Abbey, where the ground is soft, the dirt loose from the many graves he's overturned since his arrival.

The Living Terror: hard at work on a little something he uncovered at Nightmare Abbey.

CONTINUED NEXT PAGE

And speaking of *Abbey*, our titular care-taker, I will continue to search for him. I have a feeling he's around here somewhere. If so, he's bound to turn up sooner or later. I'll find him, even if I have to move heaven and earth—*a lot of earth*. Meanwhile, I've hired a private investigator to search the grounds. I'm hoping he can dig up some clues as to the whereabouts of the bony old fellow.

By the way, I told Indy I was employing Sam Spade to locate my dear Abbey. That wisecracking dog of mine said I'd be better off using a shovel.

Okay, enough about the dog. But please let me know if you have any information regarding the disappearance of my dear Abbey. I really need the guy back home. If for nothing else but keeping the dog occupied while I finish this bloody introduction.

Oh yeah, introduction....

We have a great line-up of stories and articles for you this issue, from a host of stellar writers, and...

Wait a minute.

Here's a rather novel idea: why don't you just read the blasted Table of Contents? After all, don't you think I have better things to do than explain every little detail? I've got to feed this devilish dog of mine. This hound from hell, this canine from Carcosa, this...

Oh, how I love this dog!

W**f! Grrr! W**f!

Tom English[*]
New Kent, VA

[*]

4 · DEAR ABBEY

"They tried online but you wouldn't let them in. They think you waved the bid you got here through."

"I honestly don't think that can have been the case. We'd never turn away a legitimate bid."

"Those were their exact words. I assure you I'm not a liar."

"I wasn't saying you were. I mean, I'm sure you're nothing of the kind. If you give me their name I'll check with my colleague who takes remote bids."

"That won't be necessary, thank you. May I expect to see the bank transfer before close of business today?"

"I'll make certain, but if you'd like—"

"I wouldn't," Forth said and let himself out of the saleroom.

"Well," Jacqui said, a word that gathered weight until Lyndley turned to face her, "I wouldn't call that the best start to the day."

"I'm sure the Milnes will make it worth our while."

The set of all the Pooh books would have fetched at least twenty thousand pounds in fine condition, but the lack of jackets and the scattered scuffing reduced his expectations to a dozen until the auction proved him wrong. "I have twelve, who'll go thirteen? Yes, at the back... To you again, sir, fourteen, thank you... Against you at the back, may I say fifteen? Fifteen, thank you... To the front again, sixteen... Sixteen bid, sixteen..." This was the last, prompting a round of applause, some of which Lyndley liked to think was meant for him.

"I think you saved the day," Jacqui said at the end of it, and he could have fancied his sense of triumph was calming the canal and holding the upended buildings still. It enlivened the tastes of his microwaved dinner and lent strength to even the feeblest jokes in a television comedy show. It let him deduce the solution to a detective novel while continuing to enjoy how the tale led the reader to the eventual revelation. He was ready for bed when the view beyond the balcony detained him. The shadow of a cloud across the moon had fitted itself into the canal to crawl along it before merging with darkness that flooded the landscape. A filament of the mass of cloud must have produced the inexorable advance of the strip of blackness.

In the morning Jacqui greeted him with a grey exhalation, but her face suggested they had little cause to celebrate. "There's been a serious allegation," she said. "About you, Claude."

"Who's saying I've done what?"

"Invented bids on the Milne lot to inflate the winning price."

"I hope you know I'd never do anything of the kind." In the absence of an answer Lyndley pleaded "What are we going to have to do?"

"Nothing," Jacqui said before sucking in smoke to emit with the rest of her response. "Nothing about that with luck, but you'll need to make absolutely certain nobody can say you've behaved unethically."

"You're dismissing what the buyer says, though. You're believing me, not him."

"It wasn't the buyer who said it. That's why I'll be leaving well alone unless I hear from him."

A sense of having lost the trust he thought he'd earned made Lyndley blurt "Then who's been lying about me?"

"A lady who was on the back row. She says you kept taking bids from the back, but nobody there was bidding."

"Then she must want her eyes tested, because I can tell you someone was."

"I'd appreciate you not antagonising our customers. You didn't handle the fellow with the brooch too well. You came a lot too close to calling him a liar."

"I don't think I went anywhere near it," Lyndley protested, but her face made it plain she'd heard enough from him.

When he took his place in the saleroom he saw she meant to observe the auction. He craned over the podium or leaned from side to side to ensure he identified every bidder, but his mime of scrutiny fell short of placating her, and didn't appeal to some of their customers either. At least the clutch of crime fiction set off a competition between a trio of aficionados, and the lot sold for twice Lyndley's estimate. "Better than expected," Jacqui said as she locked the auction rooms, but he couldn't tell whether she had the sale in mind or him.

On his way home the buildings with their heads down in the canal began to tremble, and he could have felt the world had grown unstable around him. When he looked up to reassure himself the streets were staying still he glimpsed someone waving to an unseen friend—at least, surely not to him. If the gesture had looked somehow mocking, perhaps because its perpetrator had dodged so swiftly out of sight, that had nothing to do with him.

He was close to home when a barge painted with sunflowers nosed past him. The bearded bargee sent him a glance and then conveyed recognition with a longer look. "Evening," he called.

"Have a good one yourself."

The boatman seemed to feel he'd been sufficiently loquacious, and was almost at Lyndley's bridge when he looked back. "You want to watch out who you're making friends with."

"That's why I haven't got too many. I'm the choosy type."

"Who or what."

"I'm not much of an animal lover either."

"If you don't know what I'm on about, maybe you're safe. All I'm saying is don't encourage anything you might be sorry for."

"Take pity on them, do you mean? I do if I think it's deserved."

"Sorry you've invited it." By now the boatman sounded as though he was delivering a dogged lecture despite the obtuseness of his audience. "You shouldn't let them make you look," he said. "And don't go giving them any kind of comeback when it only brings them closer. You shouldn't even talk about them."

With a laugh too bewildered for mirth Lyndley said "You seem to be."

"Aye, and I've said enough." This appeared to silence the bargee, but as the boat inched under the bridge he called "Sometimes they just play tricks."

Lyndley was tempted to pace the boat while he learned what else might be involved, but he disliked the prospect of asking in the gloom. As the barge headed for the sunlight beyond the bridge he remembered how the boatman had covered his eyes while emerging from another tunnel—protecting them from dazzle, or warding off the sight of the other passing vessel? If he'd yielded to some boating superstition, that had nothing to do with Lyndley, who tramped fast up the steps to the road.

The man's vague ramblings weren't about to bother him. He didn't need to feel even slightly reassured that his apartment was some distance from the canal. Once the microwave rang its bell, a thin contemporary substitute for the dinner gongs he sometimes auctioned, he took the plastic tray to the table by the window. He was seasoning the paella to bring up the tastes—he didn't usually find the dish so bland—when someone passing on the balcony waved to him.

The hand he raised before he had time to look up or think brought him a soft thump of fingers on the window. They must belong to a child, since they were all that showed above the sill. Though he supposed the gesture was meant as a wave, they were writhing as slowly as slugs, a similarity underlined by the trails they left on the pane while they slithered out of sight. What had the disgusting child been up to? Lyndley dashed to fling the kitchen door wide, only to find the balcony deserted. When he finished cleaning the window and emptying the bucket down the toilet he didn't feel much like resuming his dinner.

The television failed to engage him, and the books he did his best to sample fell short too. He was reduced to standing at the window as if something out there required vigilance. The clouds weren't letting out the moon, which left him unable to judge whether an elongated smudge was lying low in the canal. Did it eventually withdraw under the nearest bridge like a snail into a shell? Once his eyes began to ache with peering he sent himself to bed.

The clangour of the phone alarm dragged him out of the last interlude of sleep he managed to achieve. He blundered through his bathroom activities and breakfast before hastening down to the canal. As he strode into the dark under a bridge on the outskirts of the town he saw a glove almost submerged in the water. The glistening fingertips appeared to beckon to him as a brace of ducks sped out from beneath the bridge. Their ripples must have disturbed the glove before Lyndley saw it happen. Had someone stuck the stuffed glove on a pole and then dumped the assembly in the canal? The twisted stick was buried in a vague grey restless underwater mass—attached to it in some fashion, at any rate. As Lyndley made for the sunlight the glove floated after him, groping at the air. Had it come loose, or was the entire misshapen submerged bundle crawling in pursuit? Rather than linger to ascertain the situation, Lyndley ran up the steps to the street alongside the canal.

As soon as Jacqui admitted him to the auctioneers she turned away, saying "Take care today."

"Why, what..." Lyndley blurted and trailed off.

"I was telling Fatima to be careful with the chinaware," Jacqui said, only to scrutinise his face. "What did you think I was talking about?"

"I thought you might mean—" His search for an answer petered out at "Keeping an eye on the bids."

"There's such a thing as keeping too much of an eye," Jacqui said and treated him to a demonstration. "I hope you didn't embarrass anybody yesterday, the way you were staring at people."

He stopped just short of pointing out he'd done so at her behest. He willed her not to watch his auction, and strove to ignore her when she did. As Fatima wheeled a trolley carrying a Meissen dinner service around the room he started at two thousand. "Who'll say two thousand one?" A hand jerked high and subsided on if not behind the back row, too swiftly for him to decide how much of a hand he'd seen. Rather than acknowledge the glimpse, he surveyed the audience. "Do I see two thousand one?"

A disconcerted mutter on the back row gathered words. "I just bid that."

When the woman's face tilted into sight as though the burden of her scowl had tipped her head Lyndley tried protesting "I didn't see you."

"Of course you did. He was looking straight at me, wasn't he?"

As a chorus of murmurs confirmed it Lyndley said "I meant I didn't recognise you."

"Do you only sell to your regulars? Is that your game?"

"No, not at all. Let me take your bid."

"I don't know if I want to bother now."

"Please do. By all means do." In increasing desperation Lyndley begged "Please repeat your bid."

Jacqui darted across the room to lean over the woman's shoulder. "Please accept my apologies for any misunderstanding. I'm afraid my auctioneer has been under a bit of a strain."

"Then he should keep it to himself." By no means instantly the woman added "Go on then. Two one from me."

"Two thousand one hundred I'm bid. Who'll say more?" Lyndley couldn't help feeling relieved when the woman was outbid, and she didn't trouble to show her face to signify defeat. For the rest of the auction he ensured he looked every bidder in the eye, but she didn't bid again, and nothing else sidetracked him. He did wonder if Jacqui's presence at the back of the room was keeping out an intruder.

As she locked the doors he risked saying "I didn't think today went too badly on the whole."

"Did you not."

"We made more than the reserves on the Wedgwood and the Meissen."

"How we do it counts as well. One of the assurances my family always sought to offer is discretion." Before making for the car park she said "I very much hope we didn't lose a customer."

Lyndley was dismayed to find he preferred not to walk home on the towpath, and the gestures he glimpsed in the streets disconcerted him too: people waving to halt taxis or waft away fumes or attract someone's attention—he assumed these were the reasons, even if he didn't care to look too closely. He felt surrounded by unidentified presences bent on making him look. Just one would have been too much.

He locked his door and drew all the curtains as soon as he was home. He reheated the paella but binned a substantial portion, having been distracted by persistent footsteps on the balcony. Sodden was the best word he could find for them, and he wasn't tempted to look. Attempting to watch television involved battling the temptation even once the footsteps ceased or at any rate grew stealthier, and books failed to divert him. Quite soon he went to bed. His inactivity made the air feel stale, and he opened the transom above the bed, although only an inch.

He wakened from a dream of walking in the rain, a dream apparently so persistent that he felt a drop fall on his forehead. The breeze that fumbled at the edge of the curtain beside the transom was carrying a shower. He blinked at the activity overhead for some moments before its nature grew more definite. He was seeing not a breeze but a hand the colour of the dimness, dripping greyish moisture on his face as it groped into the room. As he floundered off the bed and wrenched the curtain open, the hand slithered out through the gap that was still an inch wide, far narrower than the swollen intrusion had been, and a shape perching on the windowsill dropped out of sight with a plop like the fall of a sack stuffed with mud.

Lyndley slammed the transom and fled into the main room to take refuge in the armchair furthest from the window, only to spend hours listening for surreptitious activity outside. When the imminence of dawn extended him a hint of reassurance he sagged into sleep, and jerked awake in daylight to realise he'd left his phone in the bedroom. As he stumbled to retrieve it he saw the pillow was unmarked by the drips he'd taken for rain. Could the incident have been a nightmare he hadn't wholly left behind when he'd thought he was awake? Just now all that mattered was not having heard the alarm, because he was in danger of arriving late for work.

He struggled into yesterday's clothes and dashed out of the apartment, struggling to dig the buttons of his coat into their fugitive holes. The thump with which the lift greeted each floor sounded like a soft hand seeking admission. He stayed well clear of the canal while he jogged and intermittently sprinted through the suburb. As he reached the downtown shops a glistening hand welcomed him with a wave—just someone cleaning the inside of a display window. When he made to dart across an intersection a hand rose to accost him, and he recoiled before he identified a policewoman warning him to wait for the traffic lights. Who waved as he came in sight of Haverings? A businesswoman was warding off a magazine sold in support of the homeless. Some instinct to earn better luck made Lyndley snatch out a fiver to buy a copy, which he almost left with the seller when she lifted a grateful hand.

Haverings was open, but as he tried to steal past Jacqui's office she threw the ajar door wide. "You've decided to favour us with your company, then."

"I really am trying to do my best for the firm. The alarm let me down, that's all," Lyndley said and wished it were.

"I trust nothing else will," Jacqui said while her scrutiny gathered distaste. "I've seen you look a lot neater."

"I was rushing to be here. That's what I thought you'd want."

"That very much depends on what you're bringing." She took a step out of the office and halted, wrinkling her nose. "Had you no time for a bath?"

"Just a bit of a shower."

"And yet you found time to buy yourself some reading matter. You need to realise what your priorities should be." As she stalked back to the office she said "It's a blessing you won't be anywhere near the customers."

"That makes two of us," Lyndley muttered as the closing door sent him a whiff of her vape. He went to the podium well in advance of the auction and stayed there while the saleroom grew crowded. Was it exhaustion or Jacqui's vape that had scraped his voice rough? As Fatima displayed the first lot of the day he said and to some extent coughed "A fine Cartier gold vanity case. Who'll start at two thousand?"

Jacqui sent him a blink under a frown across the room. He knew he wasn't asking even half of the reserve price, but this was how it and he worked. "Two thousand bid," he was able to rasp at once. "Who'll say two thousand five?" A gloved hand sprang up at the back of the audience. "Two thousand five," Lyndley spluttered. "Looking for three." He found it on the front row, and then his effortful appeal for better brought a response from the back. As soon as the item was sold he would call for a drink of water. Had the owner of the grey glove shifted to a different seat, or was that another bidder? "Looking for four thousand," he croaked and was rewarded from the middle of the room before a grey hand wriggled up at the back. It wasn't where he'd previously seen the bids, nor was it wearing a glove. While the swollen appendage was indeed encased in grey, this was just its spongy skin.

"Can't you see it?" Lyndley shouted. "Why aren't you doing anything about it?"

As Jacqui sent him an admonitory stare he lurched away from the podium, brandishing his gavel, and marched down the room. Two women on the back row wore gloves, but neither was sitting where he'd seen the hand. "Where is it?" he demanded amid his coughs. "It can't have got out. Don't tell me nobody saw." Everyone was watching now, too late, as he crouched to peer beneath the seats and hammered the floor with the gavel to drive out the intruder. He'd searched under just a couple of rows when a hand seized his wrist so savagely he almost dropped the gavel. "Go home and take whatever's wrong with you with you," Jacqui muttered in his ear. "And make sure you get rid of it this weekend or I'll be advertising for another auctioneer."

In a bid to recapture professionalism Lyndley protested "But who's going to run the auction now?"

Jacqui snatched the gavel, bruising his fingers. "I'll just have to conduct it myself."

Lyndley fetched his coat, only to feel as if his battle to button it was a show he was performing for everyone in the saleroom. He lingered at the back to watch Jacqui's efforts at the podium, and couldn't hide a bitter grin when she barely achieved the reserve for the vanity case. When she twitched a furious finger to send him on his way, he did his best to strut out of the saleroom.

How many hands were gesturing in the streets, at him or otherwise? His mounting anger might have blinded him to some of them. At home he found he couldn't dine for rage, and there was certainly no point in seeking any form of entertainment. He could only loiter on the balcony to keep watch—for what, he was wrathfuly determined to discover. He'd stood with his elbows on the stony parapet for hours, and twilight had begun to dull all the colours of the landscape, when he saw an elongated patch of weeds drifting away along the canal.

It wasn't vegetation. The reeds were painted on the hull of a barge that was sneaking out of the suburb. The sight and the events of the day overwhelmed Lyndley with a rage too violent to have time for thoughts. He dashed out of the tower block and down onto the towpath to sprint after the vessel. Had it gathered speed? He hadn't caught up with it when the streets fell behind. As he laboured to maintain his pace he saw the barge slither into an extensive stretch of weeds outside a tunnel through a grassy ridge.

Was the barge about to hide in there, or would it use the reeds for cover? Either possibility infuriated Lyndley as he tramped along the darkening towpath. When he reached the reeds he peered between them, straining to see into the barge. The few portholes were so cramped and grimy they offered him no view. "Show yourself," he yelled. "Let's see what you look like." While this earned no response he could identify, the porthole closest to the prow looked as if someone had rubbed it relatively clear. Lyndley craned over the edge of the water, stretching out his hands to plant them on the hull while he endeavoured to distinguish the interior.

The reeds and the vessel had convinced him it was closer than proved to be the case. As he toppled through the vegetation he made a desperate grab at the roof. The impact swung the barge away from the towpath, and only a panicked leap saved him from plunging into the canal. The effort of managing to land on a bench at the front of the barge twisted his wrists. He staggered onto the diminutive deck, towards the open entrance to the elongated cabin. As his hands thumped the panels on either side of the doorway, dislodging scales of rotten wood, he was faced with the interior of the vessel.

No wonder the portholes hadn't let him see inside when the walls glistened with lichen and the low ceiling dangled other sorts of growth. Why was the view growing dimmer? Because, having floated out of the weeds, the barge had found a course in the middle of the canal and was drifting inexorably into the tunnel, where the distant exit looked hardly larger than the smallest coin. At least this had to mean there was no pilot, except that noises in the depths of the cabin robbed Lyndley of this reassurance. The softened shuffling and the equally pulpy advance of hands along both walls put him in mind of an amplified version of the sounds he imagined a snail emerging from its shell might make, a similarity suggested

by the objects swarming over the tentatively outlined shape. As Lyndley recoiled into the little space the prow afforded, the entrance to the tunnel shrank out of any reach. The darkness closed around him, and a silhouette leaned over the twilit reeds the arch framed to wave to him. It was no longer beckoning, he saw. It was waving a farewell.

The Oxford Companion to English Literature describes Ramsey Campbell as "Britain's most respected living horror writer," and The Washington Post sums up his work as "one of the monumental accomplishments of modern popular fiction." His awards include the Grand Master Award of the World Horror Convention, the Lifetime Achievement Award of the Horror Writers Association, the Living Legend Award of the International Horror Guild, and the World Fantasy Lifetime Achievement Award. In 2015 he was made an Honorary Fellow of Liverpool John Moores University for outstanding services to literature. Among his novels are The Face That Must Die, Incarnate, Midnight Sun, The Count of Eleven, The Darkest Part of the Woods, The Overnight, Secret Story, The Grin of the Dark, Thieving Fear, Creatures of the Pool, The Seven Days of Cain, Ghosts Know, The Kind Folk, Think Yourself Lucky, Thirteen Days by Sunset Beach, The Wise Friend, Somebody's Voice, Fellstones, and The Lonely Lands. His Brichester Mythos trilogy consists of The Searching Dead, Born to the Dark, and The Way of the Worm. His collections include Waking Nightmares, Ghosts and Grisly Things, Told by the Dead, Just Behind You, Holes for Faces, By the Light of My Skull, Fearful Implications, and a two-volume retrospective roundup (Phantasmagorical Stories) as well as The Village Killings and Other Novellas. His non-fiction is collected as Ramsey Campbell, Probably and Ramsey Campbell, Certainly, while Ramsey's Rambles collects his video reviews, and Six Stooges and Counting is a book-length study of the Three Stooges. Limericks of the Alarming and Phantasmal is a history of horror fiction in the form of fifty limericks. His novels The Nameless, Pact of the Fathers, and The Influence have been filmed in Spain, where a television series based on The Nameless is in development. He is the President of the Society of Fantastic Films.

Ramsey Campbell was born in Liverpool in 1946 and still lives on Merseyside with his wife Jenny. His pleasures include classical music, good food and wine. His web site is at www.ramseycampbell.com

KOLCHAK: THE NIGHT STALKER   I WALKED WITH A ZOMBIE

NIGHTMARE ABBEY

1

BIG PREMIER ISSUE
RAMSEY CAMPBELL
13 QUESTIONS and THREE TERROR TALES

STEVE DUFFY ☠ GREGORY L. NORRIS   JASON J. McCUISTON
HELEN GRANT ☠ DAVID SURFACE   ALLEN KOSZOWSKI
JOSEPH PAYNE BRENNAN   LYNDA E. RUCKER
JUSTIN HUMPHREYS   DOUGLAS SMITH
HENRY KUTTNER   ROBERT BLOCH
KURT NEWTON   A. M. BURRAGE
JAMES DORR

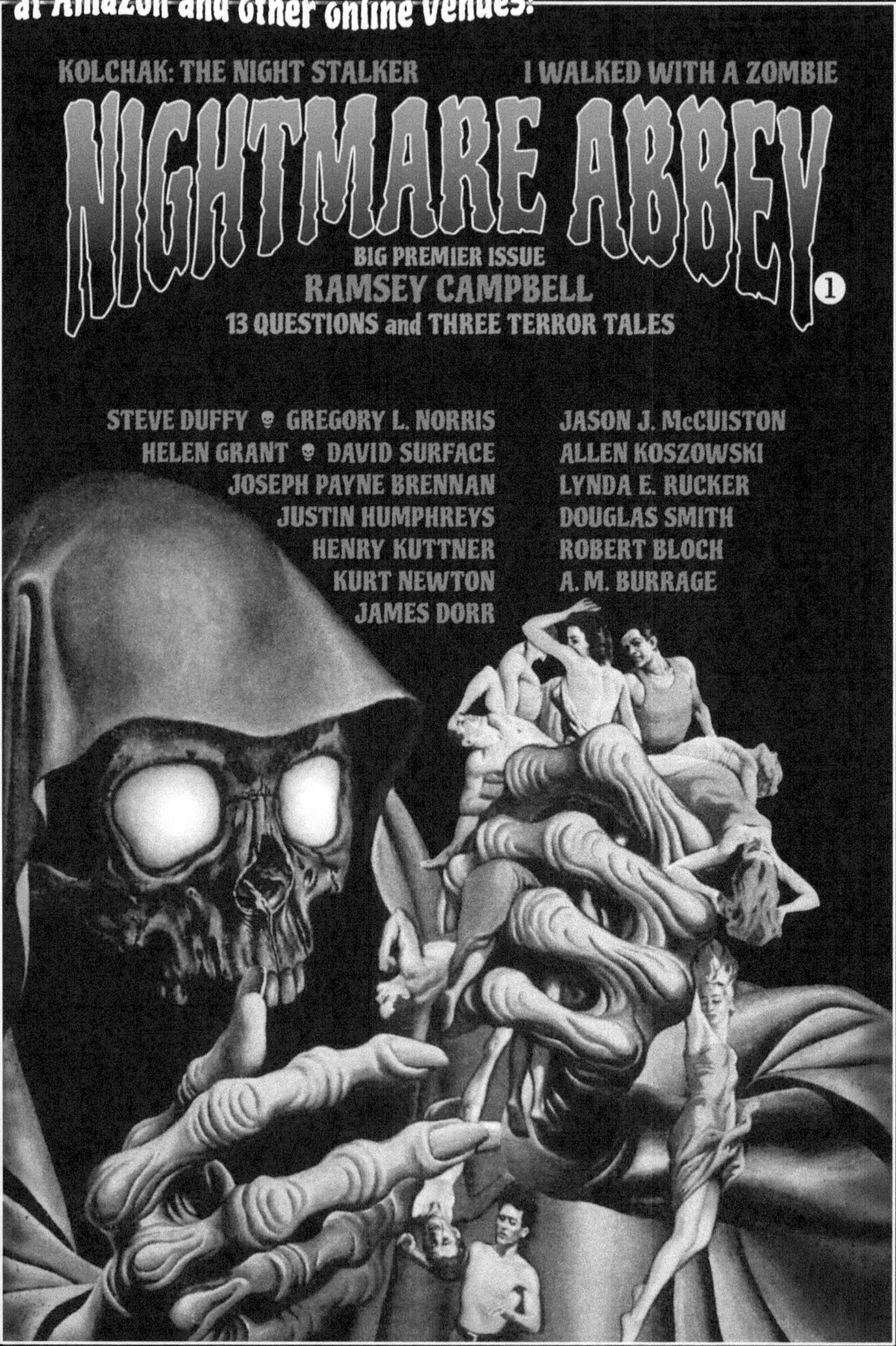

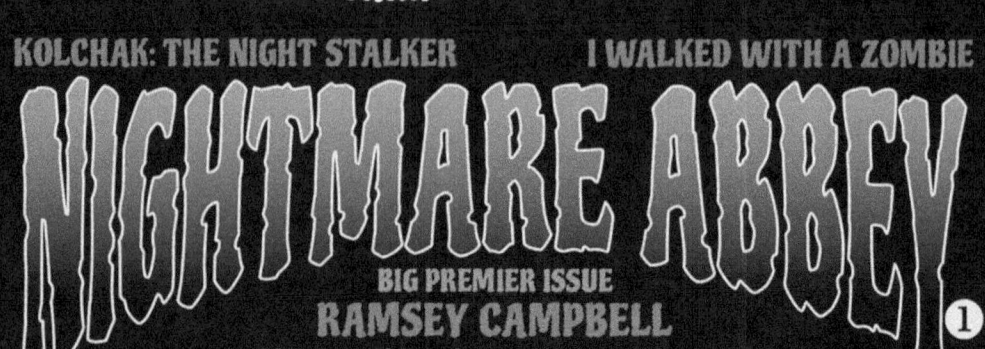

LUPINS

BY STEVE DUFFY

T HE BOY HAD BEEN WANDERING FOR LONGER THAN HE COULD REMEMBER, ALL YEAR LONG IT SEEMED. Orphaned and uprooted, he'd been sleeping in barns and out-houses, or else beneath the shelter of trees, or in the ditches at the side of the road. In all that land around there seemed to be no men but soldiers. When they passed in their columns through the villages, the women and children would hide. Nobody hid when the boy followed in their wake; they only stared at him with unreadable expressions, wishing him gone.

Some of the women on the farms gave him food in exchange for help with their tasks, herding the cows or digging vegetables. Otherwise, he might well have starved. They'd send him on his way once his chores were completed, tell him to steer clear of people whenever he could. But he had to eat, so he ignored their advice. On he trudged, into the heart of the unknowable summer, and sometimes at his back there was the sound of distant guns, now far away, now closer.

One afternoon, far from any habitation, it happened that he came across a track that led into a silent forest, a rough trail black as soot, worn down to ruts by an inexplicable volume of traffic—how many trucks must have passed down this lane to nowhere? For it didn't lead to a town, nor even a village: it brought him into a large clearing, where there stood a strange thing, a farmhouse with no farm. No cows, no chickens, no crops in the field, only a plain two-storey house and a farmer in the door-way, and all around them a tract of waste-land, weeds, and untilled soil.

The boy approached him warily, ready to run back down the track if he needed to—before he'd really taken in the farmer's face, he'd noticed the old army Karabiner slung from a strap across his shoulder. On closer inspection, the farmer, a heavyset man in overalls and dusty boots split at the sole, didn't appear to be angry. Then again, nor did he seem especially pleased at the pro-spect of a visitor. He just rolled a cigarette and silently assessed the twelve-year-old who looked maybe four years younger, grimy and disheveled, cautious eyes wide beneath his oversized cap. "Well?" he said at length.

The boy spoke, his voice hoarse from days of silence. Having learned not to beg men for food, since it brought him nothing but curses and stones, he asked instead, "Have you work for me, uncle?"

The farmer thought for a minute. "Can you weed?" he asked.

"Anything, uncle," the boy said.

"Not uncle," the man said, though he did not suggest another name by which he preferred to be called. "I asked you, can you weed?"

"Yes," he said, nodding very hard.

"Can you plant?"

"Of course." Taking things out of the ground, putting things in. This was not difficult.

"Then you can help me."

"Show me what you want," the boy said. "Anything."

The man struck a match on his thumb-nail and lit his cigarette. "First, let's see you weed."

He took the boy around the side of the farmhouse and showed him the unhealthy-looking tract on which it stood. Six barren acres on a gentle slope, hewn clear of trees but uncultivated in any way. "This is poor land, full of rocks and rubbish. We have to clear it before we can plant. Get rid of the rocks, get rid of the weeds. Understand?"

The boy jumped to it. He pulled the sleeves of his coat over his hands to protect the palms and started tugging at a thistle between his feet. The farmer watched him struggle with the thick roots, the spiky leaves, filthy fingers scrabbling in the dry dirt. "Put everything in a pile there," he said, pointing. Meditatively he smoked his cigarette while the boy labored away. After a little heap of weeds had mounted up, he said, "You're a worker, I'll give you that. You don't belong to anybody?" The boy shook his head. "Nobody will miss you?"

"No, uncle."

"Then you can clear the fields for me." He turned and walked back to the farm-house. Over his shoulder he added, "There'll be dinner for you in an hour or so. I'll find you gloves and a spade. And one more thing."

Doglike, the boy gazed after him in ex-pectation. "I'm not your uncle," the farmer said. "So stop that."

THE WORK WAS TEDIOUS and unremitting, seven days a week, but the boy was grateful for any respite, no matter how temporary, from his wandering. The farmer's wife would wake him early from his bed in the corner of the kitchen for a breakfast of maize porridge. She was a silent unsmiling woman with angry black eyes, and it never once occurred to the boy to call her "aunt." After his meal he'd head out to the clearing and set about pulling weeds from the gritty grey soil while his employer sat on a bench out-side the house and smoked, occasionally shouting advice or encouragement.

Sometimes the farmer would tinker with the engine of a rusty old truck he kept parked behind the house, an Ursus from the 1920s. Since he never seemed to start it up, let alone drive it anywhere, the boy guessed it was a way he had of passing the time, as another man might whittle or play patience. At the end of each day, he'd rake together the fruits of the boy's labor and make a bonfire. Priming it with petrol from a can, the farmer would spit into it as it smouldered, watching a ribbon of filthy smoke drift across the clearing.

There were other things besides weeds in the soil, but they could not have grown there. Bricks, whole and in fragments; they went in a pile of their own. Sometimes the bricks were cemented together, and some still adhered to concrete foundations. The farmer told him to work around these places, would speak of taking a sledge-hammer to them, though he never made good on this intention. There were strands of barbed wire, too, sunk deep in the ground like the roots of cruel vines. The boy tugged at them valiantly while trying to avoid shred-ding his flesh on the spikes. Everywhere on this plot there were odd crops, strange produce that would never find its way to market: charred posts, scraps of fabric, pots and pans and cutlery fused with rust. (And then there were the bones, but he didn't dwell on those, the bones...)

He wanted to ask the farmer about these finds, but he sensed that his questions would not be welcome. Did the man really expect to make a living from this land? It was like no smallholding he had ever en-countered, and he had grown up in farming country. It reminded him more of the town dump than a farm. What seeds had ever been sown in this soil?

One lunchtime he'd strayed away from the clearing where his work lay, curious to see what might be inside the forest that surrounded it. "Stop that," the farmer had roared, when he'd barely stepped in be-tween the trees. It was dark and green and mysterious in there, very quiet at the height of noon, nothing moving in the dappled light. He could see fallen trunks, all grown over with weeds and moss, and piles of shaped lumber, stacked more recently—they looked like railway sleepers. "Don't go in there," the farmer said, laying hold of him by the collar and dragging him back to the clearing. "There are mines in the forest, land mines, you understand?" With his mouth he made the noise of an explosion, threw wide his hands. "It's dangerous."

"Why mines?" the boy had asked, and the farmer said it was to keep the bad things away. So, a good thing, a cause for comfort. They must be safe here in the clearing.

A day of hard labor, then an evening meal served by the unsmiling wife. No one talked to anyone in that dismal parlor: the farmer sat with tobacco pouch and cigarette papers, spitting shreds of tobacco into the meager fire that burned in the grate; his wife darned clothes and swept the floors, never casting a glance in his direction. Alongside them, the boy, invisible, taking up as little space as he could, left alone to think his own thoughts. The room was spartan, devoid of heirlooms or mementos; there was not even a photograph on the mantelpiece. Maybe, the boy decided, the couple had no memories, or none that they wanted to cherish. He sympathized with this viewpoint, having almost succeeded in obliterating his own past, the horrors that had put him on the road.

The wife was always the first to retire for the night. Usually the farmer would sit up long after sunset, lost in contemplation of the hearth, the logs of unseasoned birch that burned away so quickly, filling the grate with a fine grey ash. Several times, the boy had helped him chop and stack more logs, practically the only job this feckless small-holder ever seemed to carry out on the land —until the day the trucks came; but more of that in good time.

Eventually the farmer would rouse himself with his own snoring; by this time the fire would generally be dead or dying. He'd lean forward, clumsy with sleep and drink, grunting as he stirred the shriveled embers with the poker. From his straw palliasse beside the fireplace, the boy would watch him, wrapped up in a scratchy old blanket that somehow smelled of dog, though there were no animals on the farm. The farmer would mumble something in a language the boy didn't recognize; it wasn't the one he spoke every day, but occasionally he'd heard the farmer and his wife conversing in it, when they didn't think he was listening. Then, without looking at his diffident lodger, he'd heave himself to his feet and take the lantern with him up the stairs.

Down in the kitchen, deep country dark would enfold the boy, and even the short summer nights would seem very long. Sometimes he'd hear the voices; again, though, let's not get ahead of the story. We'll come to the voices in time. They were faraway still, at this stage, a murmur at the edge of things; bearable, he thought, so long as they stayed that way.

He'd got into the habit of dragging his palliasse over to the hearth, for the residual heat that clung to the bricks. The farmhouse was newly constructed—it still smelled of wet plaster and sappy fresh-sawn wood, there was a dampness to the air that came from the structure not yet having settled— but the bricks, he noticed, were not fresh from the kiln. They'd been used before, gathered up out of rubble, knocked clean of old cement and relaid. Quite possibly the farmer that came before this one had been so unsuccessful he'd torn down his own house in disgust. Always, you see, the boy was looking for explanations: trying to find a scenario that would fit the circumstances of this strange farm out in the wasteland.

Though he was inevitably dog-tired, the boy did not always go straight to sleep, which perhaps is not surprising, thinking as he was deep thoughts such as these. Still, he was never afforded the luxury of a lie-in. Early to bed, early to rise, was the way of the farmer's wife. And then, one morning as he was wolfing down his breakfast mush, there came the sound of truck engines from the clearing. The farmer appeared precipitately from upstairs, pulling his braces over his shoulders, hopping clumsily into his boots, muttering "shit" to himself.

"Get out there," he told the boy, "stand by the bench, keep quiet, not a word out of you. Do whatever they tell you, don't speak unless you're spoken to." His wife was clashing crocks together in the sink, her face like thunder. Perhaps her anger was the reason for the fear in the man's face, for this new dynamic in the farmhouse kitchen. As the farmer, still struggling with his boots, steadied himself with one hand on her arm she hissed something contemptuous in the hard guttural language that they shared when they didn't want him to listen.

Leaving them to it, the boy went to the door. Parked up outside the farmhouse were four Borgward three-ton trucks, field grey camo paint blurred and softened with road dust, camouflage tarpaulins covering the cargo. The men in the cabs were dressed in uniforms, but he didn't think they were real soldiers; they weren't the blank-eyed hollow-faced men with rifles and packs and stick grenades that he was used to seeing march in ragged columns down the country roads. One of them, a fat red-faced man with a shaved head and Prussian handlebars, had stepped down from the cab to relieve himself on the front wheel of the truck. He shouted something at the boy in a hoarse throaty voice and the others all laughed. The boy smiled ingratiatingly and shrank back in the doorway.

"*Raus! Ahoi!*" the pissing man bellowed with his head thrown back, the flab at the base of his neck creasing in meaty folds. "*Komm her, du Scheißkerl!*" Sharing in the hilarity, the rest of the men took up the cry, *scheißkerl, scheißkerl.* The boy guessed this obscure greeting was meant for the farmer, not for him. The words themselves made no sense to him; all that registered were the sounds, the crunching percussiveness. He wondered whether the farmer's name might be Scheißkerl: after all, in the couple of weeks he'd spent on the farm, they'd never properly introduced themselves. It was something to look into.

He felt the farmer's hand at his shoulder, roughly pushing him out of the way. The red-faced man roared something else at him, and again the other men broke up in laughter. They conversed at a more normal volume for a few minutes while the boy, forgotten for the moment, watched them, listening for any more repetitions of the farmer's name.

After more mutual backslapping, the soldiers started to unload the contents of the trucks and lay them out on the ground. There were tree saplings, pines bound up in string netting, and there were trays and trays of seedlings, nondescript leafy plants looking limp and leggy from their journey in the trucks. "We need water," the farmer ordered, "lots of water, right away."

Nearby one of the sections of broken concrete foundation there was a standpipe, called the kitchen well. Now, eager to show the strangers how hard they worked here on the farm, he ran back and forth between the pipe and an old iron trough that stood outside the house with bucket after brimful bucket. As he toiled the men unloaded the trucks and disappeared inside the house, from where they emerged an hour or so later. The farmer stood in the doorway and watched as they drove away, then called the boy over to him. "It didn't occur to you to move the trough to the water?"

The boy stared at him vacantly. Things, he assumed, were as they were for a reason. It was not his place to change them.

"You Polacks." He cuffed the boy around the head, not very hard, more in play than anything. "Anyway! Trenches, so deep, then plant them this far apart," indicating with the toe of his boot. "Jump to it, quickly now."

"What are they?" the boy asked. They were like no crop he'd ever seen.

"Lupins," the farmer said, which conveyed nothing to the boy.

For the first time since the boy had chanced on the lonely black road to the farm, the farmer was showing some purpose in his actions—some urgency, even. Having told the boy where to dig, he set about making his own rows, working in parallel up the gentle slope. "Water," he'd direct, and the boy would wet the trench in preparation. Tenderly the farmer would deposit a seedling and bed it in, patting the gritty earth firm around the roots.

They dug more rows, kept at it until all the seedlings were safely planted. Stretching out his back, the farmer exhaled and said, "These will need watering, morning and night, not too much, not too little. Regularly, though, without fail. That's your job from now on. Special duties."

"What sort of plants are these 'lupins'?" the boy asked.

"Special plants," the farmer said.

Everything was *special* all of a sudden. "They come from the laboratory."

"Special how?"

"God in heaven, you ask a lot of questions. They're hybrids, the scientists have crossed them for fast growing and large crops. It's the new thing in livestock feed, scientific."

But they had no livestock, the boy thought. Which came first, the animals or the food?

"Mr. Scheißkerl?" he began tentatively.

The next thing he knew, a large and jagged rock had connected painfully with his head, knocking off his cap and sending him sprawling in the dirt. Struggling to his feet, blood running down his forehead, he blinked in the direction of the farmer, prepared to duck if anything else should be thrown in his direction.

"My name is Strebel," the farmer said thickly. "Strebel." He turned on his heel and walked away. "Don't ask so many questions."

THAT AFTERNOON, Farmer Strebel sat in the shade and drank his way through a crate of pilsner beer left by his guests, while the boy dug holes for the saplings. "All along there," he directed, pointing at the rocky trail that led up the rise away from the farmhouse. "Up the road to heaven," in a slurring undertone.

The boy didn't understand him but said nothing, loath to risk another rock coming his way, a thing he supposed might indeed put him on the road to heaven. Stamping his spade into the dirt, he encountered something that crunched against the blade. *Bones*, he thought, *more bones*; but no. Picking through the soil, he found a mess of broken glass, which he assumed at first was the remains of discarded bottles; perhaps the farmer had been disposing of his empties by lobbing them into the weeds. But the shards were thin and smooth and regular, shaped at some stage into perfect circles. He rubbed one of them clean of dirt and held it up to look through: it acted as a magnifier, and he realized that it was the lens from a pair of spectacles. But there were dozens of them, so many...

"Stop playing around," the farmer said, and burped cavernously. "Work, that's the ticket." While the boy toiled away he'd offer the odd word of advice: closer together, no, further apart, not in straight rows, this isn't bloody Versailles.

At close of day the boy had made diligent progress, and the farmer was mostly drunk. As the shadows of the trees slid stealthily across the clearing, Strebel levered himself upright, tottered a little and summoned the boy from the field. "Hard worker," he said through a belch as he patted him on the back. "A real peasant, this one. Good lad."

But when they entered the kitchen, the farmer's wife was sitting in her chair by the fire, and no evening meal was waiting for them. Strebel squinted owlishly at the bare table and grunted in indignation. He said something to his wife in their private language, but she ignored him; he slammed his palm on the tabletop, and she spoke a few words without turning in his direction. Lurching across the room, he made as if to strike her, but she rose in defiance, and the look on her face stayed his hand. The boy saw anger in there, and disgust, but most of all, he thought, contempt. Language had deserted Strebel: he made a belligerent gesture of dismissal, chopping the air with both hands, and staggered back outside.

After staring him out of the room, the farmer's wife refocused her attention on the boy. "Sit," she told him. "There's bread and sausage." As he bolted it down, she stood over him, and he felt her take off his cap with unaccustomed gentleness. Outside, Strebel was roaring drunkenly, though the boy couldn't make sense of the words. He asked the farmer's wife what he was saying, but she told him not to be so nosey. As if to make up for this rebuff, she wetted a cloth in the sink and blotted the dried blood from his forehead. He looked up at her with curiosity, and saw that a nerve was jumping in her face. "Thank you, missus," he said uncertainly. She shook her head and walked quickly to the stairs, leaving him alone at the table. Later, he thought he heard the sound of weeping from upstairs; a hesitant, grudging sound, as if the farmer's wife wasn't very good at grief.

After finishing his food, the boy peeked outside to see what had become of the farmer. All through the evening meal the sound of Strebel, cursing and arguing with himself, had been filtering into the kitchen, but now he lay sprawled on his bench, fast asleep and snoring raucously. There were still three or four unopened bottles of pilsner in the crate. Moving with exquisite care, the boy snagged one for himself and retreated round the side of the farmhouse to the lean-to where the farmer stored the fuel.

After struggling with the cap, he smashed it free against the rough brickwork, cutting the heel of his hand, though he barely heeded it, and drank deeply of the pale lager beer. It tasted weird, he thought; after another draught he decided it tasted fantastic. Long before he'd finished the bottle he was to all intents and purposes blind drunk. He lay with his back against the fuel cans, trying to clear his spinning head, and as his distended gut churned queasily in protest, he heard the voices, so much clearer than before.

Usually it was dark before they came, and he'd be wrapped up in a blanket on his palliasse in the kitchen, on the verge of being swallowed up in sleep. From that place of safety they were all but impossible to make out, and easy enough to dismiss in his customary state of exhaustion. Here, though, outside in the gloaming, the sound was sharper, more distinct, and there could be no evading it. What was this secret language? He thought he'd heard the farmer speak it: *to hell with this place*, he'd been yelling, *to hell with*—and then the word he couldn't understand. It sounded like the clatter of trains on a faraway track, *a-clinka-clinka*. He wouldn't dare to ask him what it meant. But the boy could hear it clearly now, as voice after voice took it up.

The susurration of a multitude, a dim invisible Babel. Mixed in with the voices was the shuffle of slow feet, and there seemed to be direction in it, as if that unseen host was heading away past the place where he'd been planting that afternoon, up towards the top of the rise. As a counterpoint to the sounds of that invisible crowd there came a high soft rustle, suddenly omnipresent,

everywhere and nowhere, as close as the rush of blood in his eardrums, as distant as wind in the far treetops.

If he could hear them, he thought in fuddled uncertainty, then couldn't he see them too? Around him in the gathering dark there did appear to be movement, of a sort: motion without form, the imperceptible shifting of shadows, wraithlike and fugitive beneath the sickle moon of summer.

He shook his head drunkenly, banging it quite painfully against the edge of a jerry-can. None of it was real, he wanted to insist. It was stupid, you could either see a thing or you couldn't. What you couldn't see couldn't hurt you, and it followed then that neither could it scare you. He felt his way around this syllogism, testing it for stability, but it seemed to have a flaw, because why then was he scared? Why was his skin crawling; why was he sure that behind him, around him, beneath him, there loomed something that threatened him but would always elude him, something he wouldn't dare to confront but which would still feed unseen on his very weakness, would only grow in potency while he cowered and sniveled in the dirt?

Unsteadily he pushed himself to his feet, whether to fight or flee he didn't know, just aware that he couldn't stay still. The ground shifted beneath him, undulating, giving way, no longer solid but collapsing into looseness and void. Vertigo forced the contents of his stomach upward, and all at once he was vomiting, helplessly and convulsively, turning inside out in a geyser of sausage, beer and panic before subsiding, spent, against the jerrycans with watering eyes and throat on fire. A minute or so of blinking and choking, and the world began to come back into focus; he could no longer hear the voices, and he wondered if that otherworldly throng had reached its destination.

In place of the voices there was a low throbbing sound which at first he took to be the drumming of his headache. He couldn't be sure, but if the sound didn't come from inside his own head, why then surely it was the rumble of a distant train, loaded bogies rattling on iron rails, somewhere off inside the wood, *a-clinka-clinka*. It might have been a soothing noise, had the boy's nerves not still been on edge. As it was, he listened to the dull monotonous clattering with fretful unease.

Once he thought he heard an explosion, far off in the forest it sounded, muffled by distance or by the singing in his ears. He remembered Strebel's warning about the land mines. Was that a would-be interloper, come to grief among the trees? The thought probably ought to have been reassuring, but when he finally fell asleep he was wondering who had laid the mines, and why, exactly. Had they really been placed there to guard them from the bad things? If so, why did they make him feel hemmed in and threatened: why was it that he didn't feel safe?

IN THE MORNING his stomach was a reef-knot of rawness and aching, but at least he wasn't the only one suffering. Farmer Strebel had spent the night out of doors as well, and between arthritic stiffness and a Wagnerian hangover he was barely able to set one foot in front of another. As for his wife, her unexpected solicitude of the evening before had entirely vanished. She seemed disgusted with both of them, and wouldn't even stay in the kitchen while they picked at their breakfasts, slinging their plates down on the table and stomping off without even pouring their coffee. The two cast guilty glances at each other, and sloped off outside like the miscreants they were. "Carry on with those saplings," the farmer told him, squinting glumly at the sun. "Jesus God in heaven, I feel like week-old shit done up in a sack."

Obediently he set to work. When he judged it safe, he took off his cap and held it in both hands before asking: "Is there a railway near here?"

Strebel glared at the boy as if somehow he was the proximate cause of all his misery. "See there?" He pointed off into the trees, at the strange overgrown track on the far side of the clearing. The way was all rank with weeds and knotgrass, barely navigable beyond where the eye could see from the head of the trail. There was a wild green stink of uncontrolled growth in there, distinct from the sour parched smell of the clearing, and a baleful humming of horseflies from morning to night. "You know

there's all that timber piled up down there?"

The boy remembered seeing the low-heaped wooden sleepers, strands of ivy winding along their oil-soaked lengths.

"That used to be the railway," the farmer said, grunting as he shifted his bulk in an effort to get comfortable. "There's nothing nearer than the junction now, the stop at Malkinia."

The boy wondered what could possibly have brought the trains here to the farm where nothing grew or ever had been harvested, and why they didn't come here any longer now the work of planting had finally begun. A twinge of pain in his head, where the wound left by yesterday's stone had scabbed over, warned him off pursuing the matter. He directed all his attention to the saplings. Heaped in a pile, the spectacle lenses he'd unearthed yesterday gleamed in the sun; that afternoon he made a little border with them, to keep the slugs away from the fast-growing lupins.

Life returned to its unexceptional routine for the rest of the month. Around a week after their first visit the trucks returned, bearing more trays of seedlings. This time the men had only unlabelled bottles of spirits to share: *duch puszczy* they called it, "spirit of the forest," a venomous 150-proof home-brew that rendered Strebel insensible within a very few hours. The boy knew his job by now, and had most of the planting done by the time the farmer regained consciousness.

As he labored in the hot sun, a pounding of hooves made him look up. Over the crest of the rise a stag came galloping, churning up the uneven ground. It was heading his way as if all the hounds of hell were behind it, and he was about to drop everything and run when something seemed to startle it. It broke away to the left and made for the far side of the clearing. It plunged full-tilt into the cover of the trees, and the boy could hear its trampling, splintering process receding through the undergrowth. Before the noise had died away in the depths of the forest, there came a flat crack and a boom all in one, loud and vivid, as if the world had been suddenly broken in two across the knee of an ogre. A column of black smoke rose above the treetops. The boy was so scared he scarcely reacted to this last shock. Instead he backed off in the direction of Strebel, woken from his sleep by the explosion. Owlishly, the farmer wagged a finger at him and slurred, "Told you so." He mimed the explosion of the land mine again, lest the boy had been slow to heed the lesson. That night there was venison for dinner.

The next few times the men came, it was more of the same. Each week they complimented Strebel on the fine showing of the new lupins, their purple-yellow variegated spikes already several feet high, pure energy bursting bright and bold across the clearing. As for the boy, though none of the praise went in his direction, still he felt proud of his achievements, of the way he'd husbanded strength and beauty into the world, here on this most stony and unpromising ground. It was amazing, incomprehensible, that anything could take root in such poor soil, let alone thrive, and he wondered if the lupins were themselves not some sort of weed after all, and therefore matched perfectly to this inhospitable clearing. If they could thrive, he thought vaguely, so might he.

Gradually, he allowed himself to believe that he was safe with the Strebels at the farm, all night-time noises and formless misgivings to the contrary. Even the voices were, in the last analysis, bearable. Idly, without much urgency, he wondered whether he'd feel the same when autumn came and the weather turned, how the clearing would look when snow fell and smoothed off the ground, leaving only the tops of the new conifers poking through. The lupins, he guessed, would have died back by then, or else they'd be harvested. Already he'd begun to look forward to their return in the spring.

But it was still summer when things took a turn for the worse: even the boy could see it. That last day when the men in the trucks appeared, there was no good cheer, no bonhomie, no alcohol of any kind. Instead, they took Strebel aside and conversed earnestly with him while the boy set about digging more trenches. Once, as he bent to the spade, a stone came whizzing past his head: "Not there," the farmer was roaring, waving him away from a turned-over spot of soil from which the edge of something large and circular was half protruding. Anxious not to annoy him still further, the boy retreated to a safer range, even though it meant a longer walk to and from the trough.

Through the afternoon, he could hear voices raised in argument from the farmhouse. More worryingly, although the trucks had long since departed, he could hear other voices too; they resembled those phantom sounds he'd got used to hearing in the night-time, but even in the bright sunshine he couldn't make out where they were coming from. They were at his back, around the corner, away off in the trees; nowhere he was looking and everywhere he wasn't. Miserably he labored away at the planting and the watering, in a constant state of apprehension now, wishing he could ask the farmer or his wife whether it was all in his mind, or if they heard the voices too. Supposing they could, well, that might make it better, he thought; more bearable at least, though it would still leave the most disconcerting question of all unanswered.

The shadows of the trees had almost reached him with their creeping fingers, and he was hoping the farmer would soon call him inside for dinner. When Strebel did appear, though, it was to do something so unusual, so very unlike him, that the boy simply knelt in the dirt and watched.

The farmer was digging, for a change. Over at the spot he'd warned the boy away from, earlier that day, the place where the circular shape was poking up from the earth. He had his spade wedged beneath the thing, levering it away from the soil; now he was prising it up and fumbling underneath it, tugging at something buried underneath. From this distance—halfway across the clearing—he couldn't make it out properly, this thing the farmer had found: a box? a bag such as a doctor would carry? Strebel was clutching it close to his breast, hurrying back to the house, when he stopped, as if conscious of the eyes on him (Did he hear the voices as well? They were especially loud just at that moment) and glared in the direction of the boy.

"Boy!" he shouted, and the boy

straightened up. For a moment he seemed lost for words, then: "You know where the lumber is stacked?"

The piles of old sleepers on the over-grown trail; yes, he knew.

"I want you to go and—" he appeared to be thinking on his feet here, searching unsuccessfully for a pretext—"yes, I want you to count the sleepers for me. Can you do that?" The boy nodded. "Good. Go on," gesturing at the head of the track, "do it now, right away. Take details in your head, do you hear? Special duty. Count every one, measure them and count them. Chop-chop," and with that he was gone, hurrying back inside the house.

This was so very uncommon that for once, the boy felt emboldened to disobey his orders, or at least to postpone their execution. Instead of hurrying off to set about the count, he crept silently across the clearing to the farmhouse. Standing on tiptoe, he could just about reach the kitchen window. Furtively he raised his head above the sill and squinted inside.

The farmer was sitting at the table across from Frau Strebel, and between them was the object he'd taken from its burial place. It was a small valise, he could see now, stained and soil-streaked, clasp opened, hinges wide. Stacked alongside it, neat as the rows of lupins the boy had been watering all afternoon, were coins in little piles, golden coins and silver, and thick sheaves of foreign banknotes, all counted out by the farmer and his wife.

The boy gaped like a yokel. Never in all his life had he seen more money in one place than would fit in someone's fist. This, laid out on the table; this was a fortune. And all the time it had been lying out there buried in the yard. Had the farmer misunderstood the whole business of agriculture, he wondered stupidly? Had somebody once said to him "put your money in the land, Strebel," and he'd grasped hold of the wrong end of the stick? Improbable, yes; but wasn't this whole business improbable? Farmer Strebel the capitalist, Farmer Strebel the moneybags, treasure-hunter, alchemist.

Amazement made him incautious: he overbalanced while stretching for a better view. Both the farmer and his wife heard him grabbing at the windowsill, and the last thing he saw was their heads turning in his direction. Rather than wait for the consequences, he took off for the trees. The shower of rocks that Herr Strebel launched in his direction from the doorway mostly failed to connect, landing left and right of him, but he dared not turn around. He didn't stop running until he was safely out of the farmer's range, dodging down the overgrown path that ran through the woods. Somewhere close by in the breathless green suspension of the forest, another of the land mines exploded, and he shrieked with terror and dived into the shelter of the trees, heading for the railway sleepers.

Here, he told himself, he would be safe for a while—from the rocks and from the farmer's ire at least—but the voices, the voices were so loud... The whole of the forest was alive with a crawling commotion, invisible, faceless, insubstantial as a breath of wind yet real enough, it seemed, to trip a land mine. He pulled his bruised and bleeding limbs into a fetal tuck and huddled against the heaps of lumber, trying to work out what to do for the best.

His life, he sensed, was spiralling back out of control, now that the phony comfort of the farm was exploded. Where could he run to now; what safe place? They moved so fast, the voices, surely they could overtake him. And then there were the mines, the purpose of which now seemed clear. And the farmer and his wife, they hated him now, so there was no way he could stay. Helplessly, he pressed himself against the sleepers while the shadows lengthened and the ghosts of language slid between the silent trees like evening sunlight.

Some time later—he didn't know how long, had no way of knowing, but the sun hadn't yet gone down for good—the roar of an engine roused him from his stupor. Had the trucks returned? He went on hands and knees through the weeds to the edge of the clearing, shutting his ears as best he could to those other sounds, which must only, he scolded himself furiously, be noises in his head.

It was the farmer's truck, the rusty old

Ursus. Finally, he'd got it going! It was huffing and shuddering alongside the farmhouse, smoke belching from the exhaust, and Frau Strebel was running to and from the kitchen door, loading it with bags and cases and armfuls of household junk. Over the engine's grinding he could hear Strebel's panicky haranguing, *hurry up, hurry up.*

The boy didn't know what to do. Horribly scared of Strebel in his current mood, he was more scared still of being left behind, and this bore all the hallmarks of a departure. He waited irresolutely until Frau Strebel had stowed the last of her belongings on to the truck, and only then did he dare get up on his feet and step out into the clearing.

But it was already too late. The truck was pulling away from the house with a lurch that almost sent Frau Strebel's goods bouncing off the flatbed. The boy uttered a high, wordless shriek and began running after it, not looking where he was going, waving his arms and breathlessly mouthing *stop, stop, wait for me.* The truck came to a halt, engine still running, and Strebel opened the driver door and hopped down. Thinking himself reprieved against all odds, the boy redoubled his efforts, but a wicked strand of wire sticking out of the soil snagged his ankle and he went sprawling in the dirt.

In the instant of his falling he heard a high crack, felt a whiz above his head. When he raised his head from the dirt, spitting the dust from his mouth and blinking his eyes clear, he saw Strebel standing by the cab. He was lowering his battered Karabiner rifle from shoulder height, squinting through the blue engine smoke in his direction. *He's shooting at me,* the boy realized with horror, and froze.

Without aiming, shooting from the hip, Strebel let off a couple more rounds. One went high above the boy's head, one dug up dust a few yards to his left. The boy felt his bladder let go, but he didn't move a muscle. The farmer raged inaudibly, threw his rifle to the ground, picked it up again, and clambered back into the cab. The truck began to move away once more, and the desperate balance of panic dragged the boy to his feet.

He made to run after the truck once more, bellowing now, galvanized by the action of anger and fear. "Wait! Wait! You Mister Scheißkerl-stinking-Strebel, wait for me!" One tottering step after another, his wet pants sticking to his legs, and all the while the weeds clutched at him, wound treacherously around his feet, as if determined that he at least should never leave the clearing.

But Mister Scheißkerl-Strebel and his wife were already disappearing from view down the track, gone already; and when the haze of the truck's exhaust had mingled with the dust kicked up from its wheels and settled on the early evening air, there he stood, miserable and stinking filthy, abandoned.

And yet, as he collapsed to his knees among the lupins with tears drawing streaks of incongruous cleanliness down his grimy cheeks, he did not feel himself alone.

BECAUSE THERE WAS NOWHERE else to go, he sat in the farmhouse kitchen bathing his wounds with water he'd heated on the stove. There was little else left in the kitchen but water and firewood: he found some unlabeled canned goods at the back of the cupboard, and opened a tin at random, hacking at it with a broken clasp knife until he pierced the lid. It turned out to be jam, which was surpassingly sweet, but he gorged incautiously on it and brought most of it back up within the hour.

He ran outside to be sick, and managed to reach the hole in the ground from which the farmer had retrieved his sack of gold. The hole was still part-covered by the strange circular lid, which he now saw was made of wood. He strained to push it upright, and saw that its underside was a clockface—just that, not a real clock, there was no clockwork attached to the back of it, just wooden hands on a wooden face. The time on this clock was always ten to twelve. In the boy's dog-tired confusion, it felt reassuring to know the time, so he propped the clockface upright with the help of the farmer's long-handled spade, so that he could see it from the farmhouse if he looked.

Half uncovered at the foot of the pit there was a skull, staring up at him with the bland incuriosity of forever. The boy might have been scared, if he hadn't been turning up bones and parts of bones all the time throughout the course of his digging on the farm, and so become accustomed to this jigsaw scattering of skeletal remnants. The clearing was all bones, after all; bones and barbed wire and ashes wherever the spade went in. Unable to suppress his curiosity, he'd finally broached the topic with the farmer a few days previously. Strebel had said, "It's the way of things. Anywhere you dig, there are bones in the ground. The whole earth's a graveyard. Old soup bones, most of them."

This, of course, was not an old soup bone, unless the clearing had once been the abode of ogres. Without knowing quite why, the boy reached into the pit, loosened the soil around the skull with his fingers, pried it from the ground. Had he ever been told of that long-ago Danish prince, or heard any stories apart from old grandmothers' tales of ogres in the forest, he might have speculated on the whoreson mad fellow that had lain there for twenty-three years, or even longer, or only as long as it took for the flesh to fall away from the bone.

As it was, he held the skull in his hands for a little while, regarded it as if trying to stare it out, before setting it reverently atop the handle of the spade that propped up the clockface. The cracked hole at the base of the skull fitted the helve of the spade perfectly, and he took this to be a sign. He pivoted it back and forth, as if deciding which view it might find most pleasing, before settling its gaze in the direction of the farmhouse. At ten to twelve by the clock, when night had fallen, he returned to the farmhouse and tried to sleep.

They'd left him a box of matches at least, so he lit a fire in the grate for a luxury, though the night was muggy and close. Out of habit he lay on his palliasse, though upstairs the beds of the Strebels lay, presumably untenanted. He had never been up those stairs, nor would he ever. Instead, he lay on the thin ticking of the palliasse, staring into the flames as they died and night came creeping through the kitchen. The fire licked out into embers, and he could hear the brittle sound of burned wood cooling to

charcoal, and beneath it a sort of hissing, which he took to be the brickwork of the hearth losing its heat. But it grew stronger as the redness of the embers died away, and with a dull creeping unease he realized that mixed in with it was that voiceless muttering that had enveloped him that day in the woods, the sound he'd heard around the farmhouse that night of drunkenness, a hundred thousand voices and no breath...

He rolled away across the rough brick floor, came up against the table with a thump, got to his feet and stared around. He knew there was no one there. He heard the voices. When the stone shattered the window behind him he thought he screamed —he must have screamed.

Most of the stone's force had been expended in breaking the glass: harmlessly it hit the floor and rolled to a stop at his feet. In jumping to sidestep it he cut his feet on the treacherous splinters, invisible in the dark. There were more stones, smacking against the walls of the farmhouse, rattling on the roof like hail, and then there was silence again. Even so, it took him a long time to approach the window, shuffling forward while standing on the bunched-up palliasse, pushing the broken glass out of his way.

Outside the clearing was quiet beneath the moon. Nothing and nobody moving; the only movement, the only sound, seemed to be here, in the room with him. The clock said ten to twelve; the skull had seen nothing, or at least would betray no confidences.

All through the rest of the dark hours he did not sleep, just sat in a corner of the kitchen and listened for the hissing whispering presence of nothing in the room. At ten to twelve, when the sun rose, he could see his own blood tracked across the floor; there were no other footprints.

At ten to twelve, he watered the lupins, according to the ritual.

That afternoon, around ten to twelve, he became aware of a throbbing throughout his body. When he took off his socks, more hole than wool by now, he saw that the skin around his cuts from the night before was an angry red. There was also inflammation at his ankle where he'd tripped on the barbed wire, and he suspected that if he were to look into a mirror—there wasn't one in the farmhouse anymore, Mrs. Strebel had taken it along with the rest of her meager possessions—he would see that the numerous grazes on his face were also inflamed. He felt feverish, unaccountably weak. And there were things at the edge of the forest he couldn't focus on—it was hard to focus on anything, he realized, his vision had begun to blur unpredictably whenever he looked too long in any direction—but he knew they were there in the lee of the tall trees, watching, silent for the time being, waiting for night. It was no longer certain that he was alone. By ten to twelve, when the sun set, the boy was curled up like a dog in a corner of the kitchen, in the grip of a debilitating fever.

HE WOKE, after how long he wasn't sure, from a succession of nightmare impressions, too insubstantial to be recollected yet too frightening to dismiss as mere dreams. Hours or days, he had no way of knowing: his guts were aching and his mouth was parched, so much so that he had to unstick his lips by moistening a finger with water. The fever, he thought, had broken, though.

It was ten to twelve by the clock. There was mist across the clearing, and the boy guessed it was the break of dawn. There were figures in the mist, but the boy thought that if he looked at them for long enough, they would disappear, or else the sun would come up and chase them away, and this turned out to be so. He wondered if the skull atop the stick could see clearly what he could not, and whether the insubstantial figures would be frightened off by its unblinking stare.

He spent ten minutes hacking open another tin, but it turned out to contain boot polish. Knowing he had to have something, he tried to fill his belly with water, but the sloshing inside his empty gut turned him nauseous, and up it came in a greasy colorless rush. He was so hungry! Pressing his forehead against the kitchen wall in frustration, he became aware of a vibration, deep in the whitewashed bricks. No, not a vibration; a sound. He turned his head so that his ear was up against the wall. Now he could hear it properly.

Voices, a language he recognized but could not understand. Now it was a murmur; now it was groaning; now it was screams, and he pulled back from the bricks that hid the screaming. He could still hear it, though, from every side of the room, and even after he barged head-down through the door and tumbled on the ground outside the farmhouse, his ears still rang with it. As if the voices had crept from the brickwork and entered his head, from which no amount of shaking or pounding would evict them. He prayed for the bark of Herr Strebel's voice, or even the minatory silence of his wife, but he couldn't hear a thing amid the howling.

By ten to twelve, he had decided on a plan of action.

The farmer had taken all the jerrycans marked "BENZIN" from the lean-to at the back of the farmhouse, but there were still some smaller round containers, which he knew were kerosene. Working as methodically as he could in his wasted condition, he went up and down the rows of lupins, sprinkling the kerosene as if he was watering them. The sharp stink made his head reel. The wooden clock too he drenched with kerosene; what was left over he sprayed around the farmhouse kitchen, then one by one he smashed each window on the ground floor and poured the fuel inside. For a discouraging moment he thought it was all in vain—no matches in his pocket!—but he tiptoed back into the reeking kitchen and retrieved a box from beside the stove. He had just enough sense left to step back outside before he struck a match.

By now the morning mist was burned away, and the fire was all but invisible in the bright sunlight of ten to twelve, but the smoke that rolled out of the flames was black and oily, and it caught at his throat like a strangler's grasp. Away from the burning field of lupins, leaving behind him the farmhouse roaring ablaze, he began to totter down the ashy road by which he'd first approached the clearing, an unknowable age ago at the beginning of the summer.

His head was down as he stumbled along, and only when he became aware of the sound of engines in the distance did he look up. He would have welcomed Herr Strebel, then; welcomed a shot from the farmer's carbine through his head. It might have dislodged the voices, which he could still hear faintly behind him, rising in the smoke from the clearing. But there was more than one engine, and as the rumbling grew louder he saw the first in a column of tanks trundling towards him. On the flat front of the first tank he saw a red star; atop its turret sat two soldiers with caps and rifles.

One of them waved to him, and he returned the wave shyly. The other slid down the smooth slope of the armor-plate and strode towards him, a smile on his face and strange words in his mouth. All the boy could think of was food and rest, so he kept on waving, anxious to ingratiate himself. What could he say that would help make a good first impression; what useful information did he have for them? His mind a stubborn blank, he straightened up as best

he could and swept the tattered cap from his bruised and scabby head.

"Masters," he managed, his voice like the bark of a bullwhipped dog from the back of a kennel, "welcome, masters." For as far as he could see, the clearing and everything left in it belonged to him now: he was its custodian, the last man standing, and he handed it over gladly, without hesitation, to these conquerors.

The soldier laughed. "*Nyet, nyet,*" he said happily. "*Towarzysz?*" as if he wasn't sure of being understood. "*Tovarich? Kamrad?*" The tone of his voice carried the message.

Saluting with his free hand, the boy racked his brains for the name the farmer had let slip in his cups, the name the voices had whispered every single night. What was it, the secret muttered name of the place, the word no one dared say out loud? It came to him, freight on a clanking rail, *a-clinka-clinka-clinka,* on and on into the woods; the voices whispered it in his head with their final graveyard breath. Shout it loud, and he'd be free at last. This would be his gift to the soldiers.

"Welcome," he croaked proudly, a smile cracking the corners of his thin parched lips, arms flung open wide. Behind him black smoke still rose from the blazing ruin of his kingdom, staining the high clear August sky. "Welcome to Treblinka."

Steve Duffy lives and works in North Wales. His most recent collection of weird stories, The Faces At Your Shoulder, *was published by Sarob Press in 2023; he's currently in the process of putting together his next. Steve was the winner of the International Horror Guild's award for Best Short Story 2000, and in 2015 he received the Shirley Jackson Award for Best Novelette. "Lupins" was inspired by the real-life policy of concealment intended to cover up the existence of the death camp at Treblinka; the characters, however, are entirely the writer's own invention. Between July 1942 and October 1943, Treblinka was second only to Auschwitz-Birkenau as a center of extermination: between 700,000 and 900,000 Jews were murdered there, along with some 2000 Romani people. Upon the termination of Operation Reinhard, the death camp, together with its fake station featuring a dummy clock-face and phoney train timetables, was torn down, and bricks from the gas chambers were used to build a farmhouse on the ploughed-over site. A former camp guard was installed in the farmhouse, with orders to tell people that his family had been farming the land for generations. The site was planted over with conifers and a specially selected fast-growing strain of lupins, in an effort to obliterate all traces of its former use.*

Allen K. '92 After Lee Brown Coye

BOUND

by Ray Cluley

WE BEGAN PREPARING FOR ELAIN THE SAME DAY WE heard of her passing, though it wasn't until the sun dipped behind the mountains and dusk began its flood of the valley that the girl came to our cottage.

"Help him, Ro."

Sylvia was still cramming what we'd picked from the banks and meadows into a tin kettle. She hadn't looked away from the work yet knew before I did that Aeron, burdened as much by grief as the body he carried, staggered the gravel drive. I watched him through the kitchen window. How slowly he planted one heavy foot in front of the other, as if reluctant to reach his destination. How he kept his eyes down on the distressing sight of his little girl rather than look at the house for which he was bound. Men rarely came to us anymore. Few believed in what we offered, and Sylvia was too old now for what else they'd once liked. I was still too young.

"Ro."

"I'm going."

I wiped my hands on a tea towel. They weren't as clean as I'd have liked for visitors, the beds of my nails dark with blood and soil, but they would at least be dry.

The spring on the back door announced me, and Aeron looked up at last from his daughter. His face, already a contortion of sorrow, seemed to collapse further at the sight of me, and I remembered too late that my apron was bloody. I untied it quickly and bunched it behind me to greet him.

"Did you walk, Aeron?"

I couldn't see his truck, but we were more than a few miles from his farm. From any of the farms, for that matter, and further still from town. All he said was, "My girl," and held her out to me as if I might take her from him.

"You have to carry her a little further," I told him. "I can't touch her."

He nodded, gathering his girl back to his chest. Her throat was swollen with what she'd eaten, her lips berry-wet and open for breath that hadn't come, but her eyes were closed. She could almost have been sleeping.

Soon, if the deal was agreed, it would be as if she had been.

Aeron had stopped, waiting for more instruction, and I directed him, "Round back," pointing toward a garden that was simply a section of the woods we'd bound to the cottage with lines of twine. I followed him, glancing into the kitchen as we passed its window. The flat-bottomed kettle boiled on the hob. Above it, dangling from the housing of the extractor fan, was the bundle of sticks

I'd peeled and knotted together with flower stems. They turned in the kettle's steam.

At the back of the house, Aeron stood with Elain cradled to his chest like he might shield her from the sight of what confronted them; I had dug a wide but shallow hole in the earth, and upon the turned soil lay the red meat of a skinned deer.

To relieve his arms if not his heart, I said, "Put her down there," and pointed to one of the seats taken long ago from Sylvia's old camping van. He placed Elain down gently and stood over her.

I was about Elain's age, I realized, and tried to see something of myself in her.

Her hair was long rather than short and practical. She was slight but not scrawny. She wore a Taylor Swift t-shirt, black and white with trees as if she'd dressed especially for this place before dying. The shirt was tucked into jeans that were clean, not grass-stained or torn at the knees. Her shoes were new. I didn't go to school, but she would have had friends there. I wondered if they already missed her.

With nothing left for his arms to do, Aeron held his chest tight and sobbed.

"Empty yourself of that now," Sylvia said, emerging from the trees and ducking under the twine line. "We need to be careful with what she hears first, coming back."

She held a fish by its gills with two fingers while the rest were curled around the body of a small bird. She cast them both to the soil I'd turned. Scales and feathers. Stream and sky. Crawl and walk and swim and fly. Or so it might go, were someone ever to write it with rhyme.

"You'll do it, then?" Aeron asked. Whatever he might have thought of us before, grief had made him a believer.

"Of course," Sylvia said, "if you'll pay."

Nothing was ever free. What we were about to do would cost him land, an allotment the length and breadth of Elain, multiplied by the years she'd lived before, and would again after.

Aeron nodded.

"Then dig," Sylvia said, and pointed to what I'd started for him.

He nodded again, and looked around as if he might find a shovel.

"With your hands," I told him. "You have to feel the earth, and the earth you."

Typically this was a mother's magic, but I presumed it could be a father's, too, as Sylvia didn't stop him or tell him otherwise. Aeron clawed soil from the ground and deposited it in fistfuls before realizing the better way of raking it with stiff fingers and scooping it up in cupped hands.

"Ro."

I looked at Sylvia. She had tied her hair back and was twisting it into a coil which she pinned behind her head. She nodded sideways at the shed that leant two ways at once behind a row of beans that almost kept it hidden.

I nodded.

Inside, the shed was a lot like any other. The boards were warped. Some of the roof felt was damaged enough to let rain in at one corner that remained black with damp all year round. The others were dry and cobwebby, as were the shelves. The uppermost of these were empty of all but dust while the rest held jars and plastic pots and a rusting box of old tools. A bicycle sat on flat tires, imprisoned behind a shovel, a rake, and the canes we used when planting. How our shed differed from most was in its use. It was where we cured our meats, and it was where we stored the pelts we'd scraped and dried outside. Most were rolled into bundles and tied with string made from the same creature's sinew, and these were stacked along one wall like sacks of feed or flour. The one I wanted, though, was still fresh, fleshy and wet and stretched taut across a hazel frame, ready for scraping. There was enough light left in the day to see it glisten, greasy with fat and bloody grime.

I carried the frame sideways from the shed, careful to touch only the wood now that we'd begun, and I set it down with the fur side facing Elain. I longed to stroke the downy fuzz of it, follow the direction of the nap, knowing it would be soft and ticklish under my palm. Instead, I could only admire the lustrous sheen, the tan dusking into near red and spotted white like blossoming flowers.

"Deer skin," I told Aeron. He wasn't a hunter, but he'd know the animals of this land; I only told him so he could nod, reinforcing the idea of agreement that was settling between us. Bonds between people are fickle and fragile things and require great care if they are to be kept for longer than a short while.

The same could not be said of the bond between people and the land. A promise made with the land from which you grew, in which you'd rest when dead, was as strong as any stone you could ever swear upon.

Aeron had dug a lot of soil in the short time I'd been gone, as if my absence had hastened him at the task. What had begun as little more than a turfless square was becoming something of a trench. He stared at it with misgiving.

"It's not a grave," I told him.

His hands were still in the dirt.

"Level out what you've dug so far," Sylvia said, and Aeron began sweeping at the shallow pit, moving the soil and stones around with the sides of his hands.

Elain lay on the old camper seat like somebody resting, though her hands were curled into loose fists. The berries she'd eaten would do that. Her toes would be scrunched as tight as her new shoes allowed, as well. Even a town girl would have known not to eat those fruits, but such red berries look much like many others, and accidents happen. Sometimes the land took a person young. It struck with rocks or fallen trees. It drowned them in its streams. In ages gone, it starved them. In ages to come, it might do so again.

I wanted to touch Elain's skin. I wanted to know if it was as soft as a deer's. I wanted to see how much it felt like mine. And I wanted to touch it because I knew that I shouldn't, and there is a great temptation in the taboo.

"She's yours?" Sylvia said. It required confirmation.

Aeron didn't seem to understand.

"We can't help you if she's not yours," I explained.

"She's mine."

Sylvia nodded. She tossed a thin knife to him. It landed blade first in the soil.

"Your blood, then."

He plucked the knife from the ground but only to look at it.

"Or your semen," Sylvia said.

He looked from the knife to me.

"Blood is better," I said.

Aeron nodded, like he'd always known so.

Looking at his daughter, he made a fist around the blade and drew it free. He held his palm above the ground and shook drops from it, scattering them wildly. One spot found my cheek and I recoiled with a blink, wiping it away like a tear.

"Remove the pelt," Sylvia told him. "Lay it on the soil, fur side up then fur side down."

He struggled with the knots I'd tied, and we let him, seeing how his hand still bled on the pelt, but eventually he remembered the knife and simply cut the cords. He put the skin flat on the ground.

"Press it down."

He bloodied the fur some more as he pushed the deer skin into the soil.

While Sylvia explained the rest to him, I went back to the cottage for something else we'd need.

Cottage was perhaps too grand a name for the place. It was a squat, cement block building that Sylvia had made herself and rendered smooth with a natural plaster that clumped from the wall when wet and crumbled from it when dry. The windows were crooked with ill-fitted glass. The roof was blue tarp and bark shingle that had greened with moss and sprouted here and there where birds had shit their eaten seeds. The remains of Sylvia's old camper we used as a chicken coop, and there was often a time I thought their living quarters far better than my own. We had pigs once, penned in with woven fences, but we grew too fond of them and set them free. I saw them in the woods sometimes when I went hunting but I always let them be.

In the kitchen, I removed the tin kettle from the hob and stirred the boiled plants and let them steep while I took down the hanging sticks and bent them into a new shape. Stripped of bark, they had been made pliable with steam, and I made a cross-limbed figure from them. I dipped it in a paste we'd pulped from the same poisoned berries Elain had eaten and took it outside.

Sylvia was putting batteries into an electric lantern for light to see by, while flames from three tallow candles flickered for the ritual, pushed into the soil at Elain's head and hand and foot. Aeron was undressing her, folding each garment neatly in a pile beside her. His hands lingered on her body like a mother's or lover's might, tender and trembling. Traces of his blood told of where he'd touched her, and I thought it good she wore so much of it as he folded the pelt around her, binding her in deer skin until only her face, pale, and plump as a full moon, peered from inside. I instructed Aeron where to place the offerings on her, bird and fish and bloody meat, while Sylvia walked a circle barefoot around them both. In one hand she held an elm branch, and she dragged its sharpened end through the grass and dirt to form a ring around the girl, muttering promises and prayers as she drew new power from the ground. She was as bound to the land as I was to her, and sometimes it granted her favors. Elain was going to be one of them.

"Stop!"

I looked for who called from the dark.

"*Please* stop."

Aeron said, "Caryl."

Elain's mother stumbled with an exhaustion far beyond the physical, her eyes near-closed with crying, but she found new strength at the sight of her pelt-wrapped, candle-lit girl. She stood straight. She wiped sweat and tears from her face. She said, "I don't allow it."

"She'll be all right," Aeron told her, but when he went to Caryl she backed away.

"I don't allow it."

"There's been an agreement," I told her.

"I'm her mother. I have power here, don't I?"

Sylvia watched but only walked her circles and spoke her words. Candles lit her from below, casting most of her body into shadow as she dragged the elm branch point down in the ground.

"I'll call the police," Caryl tried.

"It's a different law that holds us now," Sylvia said.

I tried to tell Caryl again that there'd been an agreement, thinking the simplicity of the statement might calm her, but she interrupted with such venomous vehemence that I feared I might be poisoned by her spit. I raised my hands to ward her off.

"I won't allow it! I *don't* allow it!"

"Mrs.—"

"I've allowed *too much.*"

With that confession she was suddenly spent. A sob wracked her. She staggered as if struck by it and collapsed. I went to her quickly and offered my hand to help her up but all she did was hold it.

Quietly, looking up at me from the ground, she said, "Why do you think she ate the damn berries?"

I looked at Elain as if the answer might be there, and in a way it was, because I saw again all the places her father's blood had marked her his.

Sylvia still busied herself with words and gestures and the moon-silvered soil, but she was looking at me, and there was a warning in her eyes.

There was a feeling in my insides like weeds that needed pulling. It was a feeling I saw mirrored in Elain's mother. It bound us, that pain, but it was too late, and I told her so.

Caryl snatched her hand from mine to grab a handful of the earth, and she threw it at her husband. He ducked from the scattered dirt. Even had it struck him, dirt thrown from Caryl's hands was still just dirt.

"*Bastard.*"

He bowed as if he agreed but made no apology for it. He watched his doe-clad daughter and waited for her to come back.

Caryl sat with her hands in the soil like she might throw more, and perhaps she drew some power from it herself because she realized something that seemed to give her substance again, made her sit up. She tossed her loose, limp hair and said, "It's my land."

It made no impression on Aeron. He shrugged her words away, the habit of a husband who thought all the world his.

Sylvia, though, understood the relevance, and though it didn't stop her—she couldn't stop, not now—I did see her falter. As if the ground had given her rocks to stumble over, or moss to slip upon.

"The land," Caryl said, "It isn't his to give."

She stood again, her strength returning with the certainty of her point.

"Caryl," Aeron warned. "We are husband and wife."

"It's a different law that holds us here."

She smiled, then. There was no malice in it. It wasn't smug or mocking or even particularly happy. It was a smile of relief, seemingly unfamiliar, and brief.

Aeron moved quickly. He grabbed her shirt into a bunch with one fist and struck her with another. Holding her up by the scruff in his grip, he hit her a second time. There would have been a third, but Sylvia got between them with her stick, striving to keep them apart while Caryl, allowed to fall, tried to crawl away. She opened her mouth to speak or groan and a tooth fell in a long glob of bloody saliva. It was pressed into the ground under Caryl's hand as she crawled, a seed for some later sprouting, while the soil, always thirsty, soaked up the blood.

Aeron broke away from Sylvia, knocking her stick aside, and drove a kick into his wife's belly. Caryl toppled with a grunt.

I ran at him, then, and had Sylvia not stopped me, had she not grabbed me round the waist as I passed, I would have killed him. I didn't remember retrieving the knife from the ground, but I had it in my hand as Sylvia turned me one way then the other in my struggle to stab the man. I was quick to temper, Sylvia had always said so. An acorn full of thunderstorms.

Caryl, on her back, began to laugh. She choked up more blood with it but cackled fit for any witch.

"Our dear girl is *free*," she said. "Nothing binds her to you now."

With that, there came a bleated, high pitched shriek from their dead Elain.

We all looked, and Elain's cry became the noise of something suddenly strangled. She writhed in her pelt, grunting her pain as she flexed and kicked within the confines of the skin. She squirmed like a worm brought from the ground by the rain, turning in the dirt in cocoon of fur until one of the tied cords snagged and snapped and she was able to unravel some of the hide binding her. She thrust one leg free. Where there had once been pale skin, where there had once

been thigh and knee and shin, there was now a tawny haunch. Where there had once been a heel and toes: a hoof. Another leg kicked, and then another, and another, and revealed in the pelt's unravelling was this new doe-eyed girl—and doe-eared, and doe-nosed—and for a moment she sat, human in her pose, forelegs like short arms in front of her. She raised her sleek, white-spotted head to the sky to give another of those bleating shrieks that had come with this new life. Then her hind legs propelled her upright and she was standing, bounding one way and then the other within a second binding, trapped inside the circle furrowed from the soil.

"What have you done?"

It was Aeron who asked. He reached for the frightened, gentle creature before him, and it turned so sharply from his hand that it fell, only to stumble upright again on the four legs it was getting used to.

"I've done nothing," Sylvia said.

No deal had bound them. The land was merely taking back what belonged to it.

"What did *you* do?" I asked Aeron.

He glared at me, and for an awful moment I was afraid because that look of his, fierce and full of violent fire, had suddenly softened into something I was still too young to ever want from a man.

Sylvia saw it, too, or maybe she simply felt the way of things like she did sometimes. She took the knife from my hand and pointed it low at Aeron. "Blood and semen," she warned him.

Behind Aeron, swollen-faced and broken, Caryl rubbed her hands through the soil, smoothing it flat. Then she sat back and waited for the deer to understand its new gift.

The circle broken, Elain turned towards the woods and bolted, her puff of tail like a shooting star in the dark, arcing towards the forest and gone. A lost wish, bounding towards a second life amongst the trees.

THERE'S NOT MUCH LEFT to tell. Sylvia continues to raise me. She teaches me things, and I learn. One day she will be gone, taken back into the land, or set free from it, depending how she wishes it to be.

Caryl and Aeron grieve, each in their own way. They work their farm on land they barely understand, and they tinker with the broken thing they have between them without ever fixing anything. I hear that Aeron has taken up hunting, though he hadn't cared for it before, and so I am extra vigilant when I am in the forest. Not because I fear him, but because I, too, am hunting, and sometimes accidents happen.

The soil is always thirsty.

Ray Cluley's work has appeared in various magazines and anthologies. It's been reprinted several times, including in Ellen Datlow's Best Horror of the Year, *Steve Berman's* Wilde Stories 2013, *and in Benoît Domis's* Ténèbres *series. He has been translated into French, Polish, Hungarian, and Chinese. He won the British Fantasy Award for Best Short Story (*"Shark! Shark!"*) and has since been nominated for Best Novella (*Water For Drowning*) and Best Collection (*Probably Monsters*). His second collection,* All That's Lost, *is available now from Black Shuck Books.*

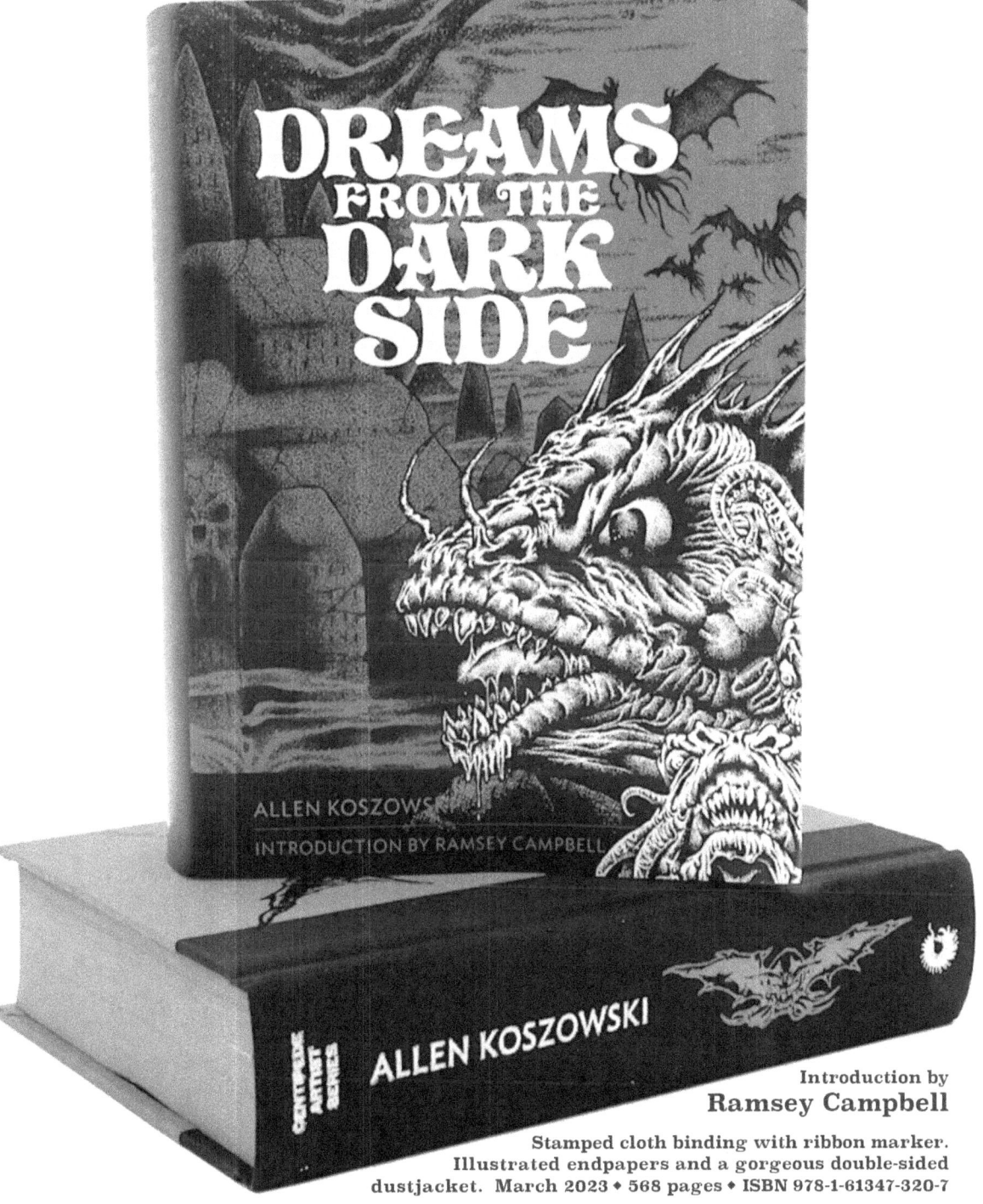

CINEMA CRYPT

A VERY BRITISH AMERICAN HORROR STORY

REVISITING *THE CITY OF THE DEAD*

UK-BASED MOVIE PRODUCING PARTNERS MILTON SUBOTSKY AND MAX J ROSENBERG WILL BE FAMILIAR TO MANY AS THE HEADS OF AMICUS PRODUCTIONS, THE COMPANY THAT CAME TO RIVAL HAMMER by making such memorable anthology pictures as *Dr Terror's House of Horrors* (1965), *Tales from the Crypt* (1971) and *Asylum* (1972). Before they formed Amicus, Subotsky and Rosenberg had a company called Vanguard Pictures. Under the Vanguard banner they were responsible for such family friendly fare as *Rock Rock Rock!* (1956) and

Disc Jockey Jamboree (1957). When the opportunity came along to make a horror film, Rosenberg created a one-off subsidiary company called Vulcan, so that if their proposed X-certificate project was an embarrassing disaster (either critically or financially) the Vanguard name wouldn't be associated with it.

Over sixty years later the entire Vanguard catalogue is now all but forgotten. However, that sole Vulcan production has increased in reputation such that it is now rightly considered a classic of horror cinema. Despite not being particularly successful either profit-wise or with critics on its initial release (perhaps Rosenberg was right after all), on re-examination it's fascinating to muse on how this unassuming little British film seems to have anticipated (and possibly influenced) the look and feel of some of the movies that were made in its imminent wake. So let's take a deeper look at 1960's *The City of the Dead*, a film that ended up being released a couple of years later in the US under the title *Horror Hotel* (and we'll discuss the reasons for that in a bit as well).

The titles open with stark black and white illustrations of a cowled and hooded figure to Douglas Gamley's music score. Gamley was the closest thing Amicus would have to an in-house composer in the early 1970s, starting with *Tales from the Crypt*, but until then this would be his only score

for the Rosenberg-Subostsky team. His frequently bombastic style of scoring horror films is somewhat in evidence here, and similarities can certainly be detected between this and his title music for one of the last Amicus horror films (co-produced with AIP), 1974's *Madhouse*. We'll talk about the

other credits as we go but Max Rosenberg isn't credited, despite his participation, with Subotsky being one of two executive producers. *City of the Dead* producer Donald Taylor is not the Don Taylor who directed *Damien – Omen II* or the other, different, Don Taylor who directed the BBC TV classic *The Exorcism*. This Donald Taylor's only other significant screen horror credit was as producer of Edmond T Greville's version of *The Hands of Orlac* (made the same year as *City of the Dead*), and which employed a number of the same personnel (and cast).

The film opens on a moodily lit, foggy exterior set. There's no date caption but we soon learn it's March 3rd, 1692, and we're in the town of Whitewood, Massachusetts. Elizabeth Selwyn (Patricia Jessel), accused of being a witch, is dragged out to the town square, tied to a stake, and burned alive. As the flames rise higher and thunder rumbles, Elizabeth makes a pact with Lucifer and curses the village "for all eternity." Amongst the angry mob is her consort, Jethrow

Keane (Valentine Dyall) who also calls on Lucifer's aid.

It's a powerful, engaging, and atmospheric opening, of a kind encountered in a number of subsequent films including Norman J Warren's *Terror* (1978). In that instance the sequence in question is subsequently revealed to be a film within a film. The movie this opening scene bears the most similarity to, however, is Mario Bava's *Black Sunday* (aka *La Maschera del Demonio*), a film which, it has been established, was made six months after *City of the Dead* had finished shooting at Shepperton. However, it has also been established that it would have been virtually impossible for Bava to have seen the film as it had yet to be released at the time of *Black Sunday*'s production. Therefore, presumably, this was just a case of a happy (and brilliantly atmospheric) coincidence.

As the villagers call for Elizabeth to burn, we transition to the present (i.e., 1959) and cut to Christopher Lee's Alan Driscoll, a

Alan Driscoll
(Christopher Lee)

And below: Nan Barlow
(Venetia Stevenson) and
Bill Maitland (Tom Naylor).
Previous: Elizabeth Selwyn
(Patricia Jessel). Opposite page:
Richard Barlow (Dennis Lotis).

history professor, shouting the very same words as part of a somewhat vigorous tutorial to a small group of assembled students. Driscoll's class is rather smaller than the one Peter Wyngarde got to teach in Sidney Hayers' subsequent *Night of the Eagle* a couple of years later, but then Vulcan/ Amicus always was a very low budget outfit. [See Mr. Probert's retrospective of *Night of the Eagle* in *Nightmare Abbey 3*.]

Every class has its wisecracker and in this case it's Bill Maitland (Tom Naylor), kicking off a long tradition of what would eventually total eight Milton Subotsky-produced films featuring a character with that surname. Oddly enough Subotsky wasn't the only UK-based American horror film producer to exhibit this particular habit. The surname Rivers seems to have been almost as popular with Herman Cohen, where it

pops up as the name of Michael Landon's character in *I was a Teenage Werewolf* (1957), Joan Crawford's in *Berserk* (1967), and in a lot of that producer's other films in between.

Bill Maitland's girlfriend is Nan Barlow (Venetia Stevenson, who gets her name spelled incorrectly in the opening credits but correctly at the end. She wasn't in a lot else, and certainly nothing as memorable as this). Driscoll asks her to stay behind after the class is dismissed so he can compliment her on her essays. Nan is so keen to excel in her chosen subject that she informs Driscoll of her desire to stay in the smallest New England towns she can find, go through all the town records, and interview all the descendants of the puritans living there. Driscoll suggests Whitewood (aha!) much to the chagrin of Nan's scientist brother Richard, who has come to pick her up. Richard is played by top-billed Dennis Lotis, who had a much higher profile career as a recording artist than as an actor (Subotsky was a keen popular music fan which likely explains his casting). Lotis's other few screen credits

include playing Alan-a-Dale in Hammer's 1960 *Sword of Sherwood Forest* and a singer in Dennis Potter's *Blackeyes* in 1989.

Richard is unimpressed that Nan now plans to cancel their planned vacation to go off to Whitewood instead, a place Driscoll also happens to know the person who owns the Raven's Inn where Nan can stay (aha again!). In fact, Richard's unimpressed with the subject matter of Driscoll's course in general, and the two have a bit of a face-off of "the science vs superstition" variety. Perhaps needless to say, in the acting stakes, poor old Dennis Lotis doesn't have much chance against Christopher Lee. Driscoll's quote of "The basis of fairy tale is reality. The basis of reality is fairy tale" isn't taken from anywhere other than George Baxt's script, in case you're wondering. Driscoll also mentions that three years after Elizabeth Selwyn was burned the daughters of her accusers were found drained of blood.

Seeing as he had already appeared in *Horror of Dracula* (1958), audiences of the time must have been wondering if with all this talk of blood their new favorite star was again playing a character up to no good, which of course he was.

The next day in Richard's apartment, Richard and Bill discuss how hard they've tried to persuade Nan not to go to Whitewood. The apartment is brightly lit and the production design is no doubt deliberately ultra-modern for 1959, all the more to contrast with the place Nan is about to encounter.

Nan drives to Whitewood, stopping along the way to get directions from the kind of gas station attendant that could have inspired the harbinger character in Drew Goddard's 2012 *Cabin in the Woods*. She gets further help from a modern-day Jethrow Keane (Dyall again) who looms imposingly out of the fog at a T-junction and begs a lift. Soon

Jethrow Keane (Valentine Dyall) joins Mrs. Newless (Patricia Jessel) at "horror hotel" (Raven's Inn).

they are both in Whitewood, which looks "just like a page out of a history book." Credit for the impressive Whitewood set has to go to both its construction by art director John Blezard (whose only other horror film credit was 1960's *The Hands of Orlac*, and that's a shame) and the way in which it is shot by cinematographer Desmond Dickinson (who worked on quite a few other horror projects for, amongst others, Tigon Films, producer Herman Cohen, and director Robert Hartford-Davis).

The Raven's Inn is right next to a graveyard "not used in 200 years," and apparently nobody visits the rundown church anymore either. The concept of the village out of time with a dilapidated church people no longer attend is also reminiscent of at least two tales by the celebrated UK ghost story writer R Chetwynd-Hayes, whose village of Loughville in the stories "The Humgoo" (1975) and "Manderville" (1978) has a similar setting, albeit populated by ghouls rather than witches.

Inside the Raven's Inn, Nan is greeted by the mute Lottie (Ann Beach, who enjoyed a lengthy and varied career on UK television) before Mrs. Newless (Patricia Jessel again) announces herself by emerging from the shadows on the stairs. With her statuesque form, sharp features and no-nonsense delivery Patricia Jessel could almost pass for Peter Wyngarde's sister, and it's surprising that she did very little horror apart from this, her other most memorable role to film fans likely being Michael Hordern's wife in Richard Lester's *A Funny Thing Happened on the Way to the Forum* (1967). The name *Newless* is a nice play on Selwyn, by the way. Presumably screenwriter George Baxt guessed audiences would work out who she really was pretty quickly.

Nan is given a room thoroughly befitting the gothic heroines of old, complete with four poster bed and a trapdoor hidden under the carpet. Meanwhile, in one of many shots nicely staged by director John Moxey, the flames of a roaring fire burn in the foreground while behind them Mrs. Newless and Jethrow discuss the forthcoming Candlemas

Reverend Russell (Norman MacOwan)

festivities. "He will be pleased," says Jethro, as Nan appears and announces she's going to explore the town. Valentine Dyall was a familiar face (and even more familiar voice) to UK viewers and radio listeners, becoming famous in the 1940s and 1950s as the "Man in Black" in the BBC's *Appointment with Fear* radio series, where each week he would introduce "a new tale of terror." He appeared in over a hundred film and television roles, including Tom Baker era *Doctor Who* (as the Black Guardian) and in the "Witchsmeller Pursuivant" episode of Rowan Atkinson and Richard Curtis's *The Black Adder*.

Did Nan's walk across the foggy town square inspire a similar scene in Roger Corman's 1963 *The Haunted Palace*? You know, I rather think it did. The church she ends up trying to get into still has a vicar, the Reverend Russell (84 year old Norman MacOwan, whose final film this was). He is blind and bars her entrance to the building, telling her that for the last 300 years Whitewood has been in the grip of the devil and "the people in it are his." He warns Nan to leave but instead she visits the local book and antique shop where the proprietor just happens to be the reverend's granddaughter Patricia (Betta St John, one of the few actual American actors playing an

Left: Russell's granddaughter Patricia (Betta St John)

American in this and soon to retire from acting). Nan leaves with a large old book about witchcraft, but not before getting a good look at the large painting of the burning of Elizabeth Selwyn that's on prominent display.

That night Nan hears chanting beneath the floor of her room, while outside in the hotel's lounge area the rest of the hotel's guests dance in and out of the shadows in a scene reminiscent of Herk Harvey's later *Carnival of Souls* (1962). Lottie brings Nan towels and tries to give her a message but is usurped by Mrs. Newless who insists Nan joins the dancing. Nan responds by telling Mrs. Newless (and us) some useful

information from her book about how on Candlemas Eve (the first of February, which also happens to be the night she's staying there) in 1692 Elizabeth and her coven sacrificed a young girl, having first marked her by stealing a personal object of value and leaving in its place a dead bird and a sprig of woodbine. Oh, and Nan's locket has gone missing.

Nan dresses as the music outside increases in volume, but opens the door onto a virtually empty room. She turns to see a dead bird has been placed on her pillow and what we presume is a sprig of woodbine on her door. A key hanging from the window opens the trapdoor and soon Nan is descending a cobwebbed set of stone steps, but not before she has observed a chanting procession, robed and cowled, entering a nearby crypt.

Nan, our viewpoint character through pretty much everything we've seen so far, is unexpectedly sacrificed by the satanists just over halfway through the film. In this respect *City of the Dead* has been likened over the years to Alfred Hitchcock's *Psycho* in both this, the fact that a sibling goes searching for her afterwards, and that we get a shot of a female corpse at the end. While the film predated the Hitchcock movie, it shouldn't be forgotten that Bloch's source

novel was published a few years earlier, and Subotsky, ever the voracious reader and provider of the original story for this, may have been inspired by elements from it.

Before Nan dies Mrs. Newless reveals, as if we didn't already know, that she is in fact Elizabeth Selwyn. Christopher Lee's Driscoll peers over her shoulder, but so riveting is Patricia Jessel's performance that it may take a second viewing before you spot him.

There's a nice transition (mirroring that of the "Burn, witch! Burn!" of the opening) to take us back to the "real world" as the descending blade becomes a knife cutting into a birthday cake. Nan has been away for two weeks and both Richard and Bill are concerned. Trying to telephone the Raven's Inn proves fruitless, while back in that very establishment Mrs. Newless returns the book Nan borrowed to Pat. As Pat leaves, Lottie hands her something. The police become involved but are told Nan checked out the day after she arrived, which in a way she kind of did.

Driscoll is busy wearing what would no doubt be a fabulous ceremonial cape if this film were in color, and sacrificing a dove at his own personal altar when Richard rings the doorbell. Richard explains his concerns and his intention to follow Nan's every step. He leaves just as Pat arrives. She wants the

address of Nan's family so she can return something that turns out to be Nan's locket, pressed into her hand by Lottie.

Pat returns to Whitewood and, just like Nan before her, picks up Jethrow on the way. When she gets there Jethrow vanishes mysteriously, just like before, and also just like before, Mrs. Newless and Jethrow deliberate behind flames that Pat would make a very good second sacrifice—"a living descendant of those who were cursed."

Richard and Bill drive to Whitewood in separate cars, getting directions from the same gas station attendant as Nan. Neither get to meet Jethrow at the T-junction, but Bill sees an image of Elizabeth Selwyn burning at the stake and laughing at him. Distracted, he crashes his car but survives, just.

After some persuasion Richard gets Mrs. Newless to give him Nan's old room at the inn. He explores the town in a scene very similar to one we saw when Nan did, but it's just so gorgeously atmospheric we're happy to be taken on the tour a second time, as well as once again encountering some of Whitewood's Lovecraftian (as in "The Case of Charles Dexter Ward") inhabitants.

Richard ends up at Pat's shop where he also gets to meet Pat's grandfather who has a familiar story to tell. The vicar also adds that it was the satanists who were responsible for him losing his sight, and that the regular sacrifices are to ensure the witches' immortality. Apart from Candlemas Eve, the other occasion on which a sacrifice needs to take place is the Witches' Sabbath, which just happens to be that very night. Meanwhile back at the inn, Lottie is caught trying to write another note and Jethrow kills her.

Richard leaves and Pat makes her grandfather some tea. She opens a drawer to find a dead bird inside and, yes, there's a sprig of woodbine on her front door. She and her

grandfather try to leave but the car won't start. Pat rings Richard at the Raven's Inn. Her phone call terminates in a scream. Richard dashes off, leaving Patricia Jessel to deliver a delicious cackle in his wake.

Pat's shop is in darkness and her grandfather has been locked in a cupboard. He tells Richard that the witches have her, and that the only thing that can destroy them is the shadow of the cross. A blood-stained Bill turns up and Richard carries him to the car. Thunder rumbles as Richard gets his gun and sees the witches' procession enter the crypt. He also finds a tombstone for "Alan Driscoll – Burned as a witch 5th December."

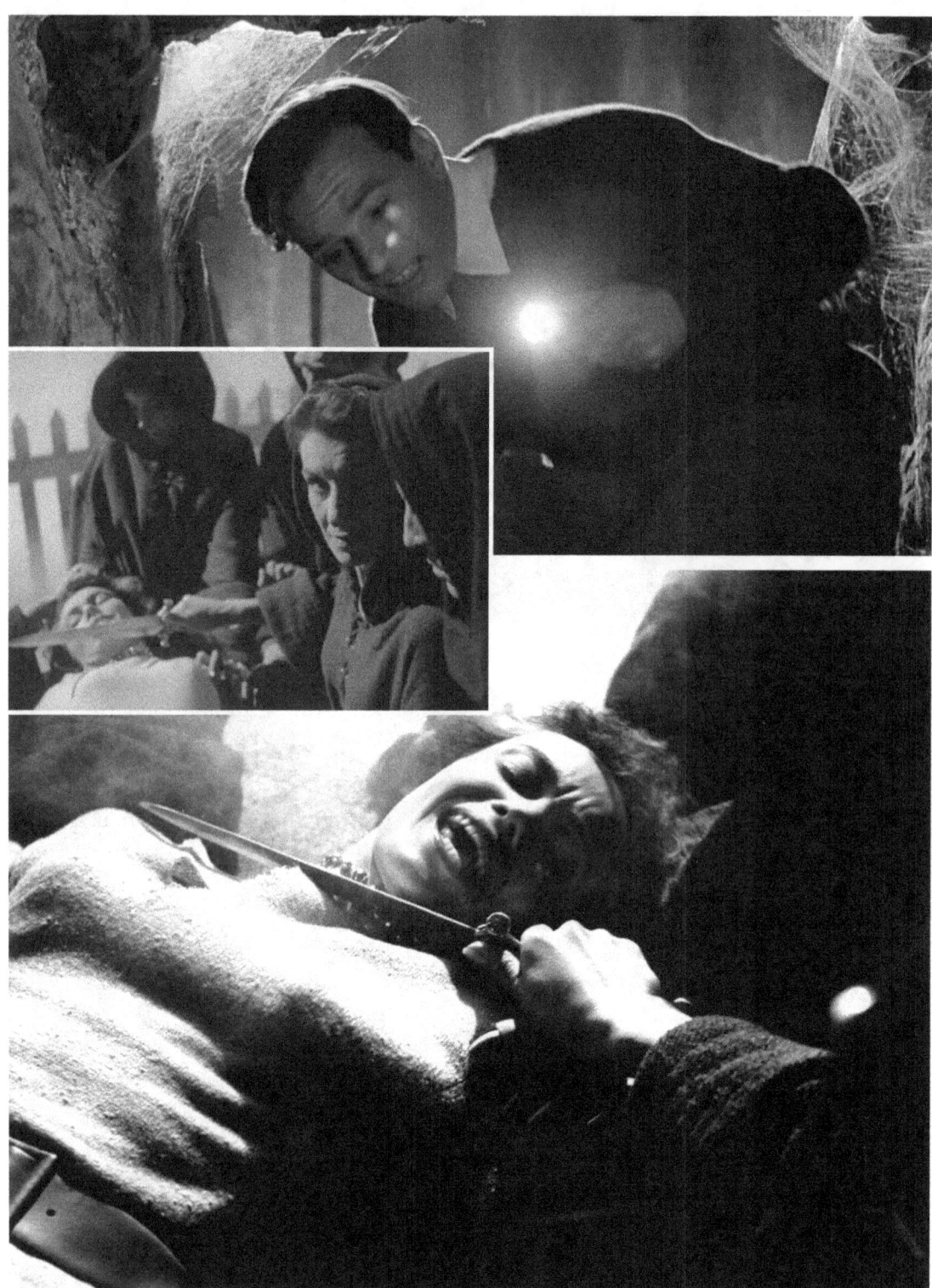

Back at the inn, Richard descends the stairs into the crypt. He discovers Lottie's dead body before confronting the witches, Driscoll among them. Bullets have no effect, but a good old fashioned shove seems to free Pat, and the two of them escape the crypt only to encounter more satanists in the graveyard. Mrs. Newless prepares to cut Pat's throat as the bell tolls, but they are thwarted by Bill who, under Richard's instruction, grabs hold of the biggest cross he can find. Even a knife

in the back can't stop him as he staggers towards them, the bell tolling midnight, the shadow of the cross in the moonlight setting the witches on fire as it falls upon them. It's a fiery, atmospheric, and extraordinarily effective climax which sees Richard saving Pat and the two of them pursuing Mrs. Newless back to the Raven's Inn. But the cloaked and cowled figure sitting behind the reservation desk is now nothing more than a burned corpse and the end credits roll to Douglas Gamley's variation on the Dies Irae, something he would employ on more than one of the Amicus anthology pictures he would score in the future.

Intended as a main attraction, *The City of the Dead* eventually went out to UK cinemas on 9th September 1960 as a second feature to Roger Corman's *The Mobster* (*I, Mobster* in the US). Reviews were middling and while the film made a profit it was small, such that Max J Rosenberg subsequently had trouble getting the film released in the US. It eventually

came out two years later almost to the day, the title having been changed by this point to *Horror Hotel* to cash in on its Psycho-like structure. In the US it also went out on a double bill, this time with the German mad doctor picture *The Head* aka *Die Nackte und der Satan* (1959). The title was not the only change. The film was several minutes shorter than its UK version, thanks mainly to US censor demands that the dialogue from Elizabeth Selwyn and Jethrow Keane at the beginning where they both call on Lucifer be severely truncated. So if you want to see the film in all its effective glory you

Here and below: A flaming ending for the Whitewood Witches past and present.

hugely successful Kolchak TV movie *The Night Stalker* (1972) as well as numerous episodes of the TV shows *Mannix*, *Kung Fu*, and the pilot episode of *Charlie's Angels* was the same man who made *City of the Dead*, the film that was his first feature. As well as some clever transition and narrative mirroring devices, Moxey uses a style of long takes, sometimes lasting a couple of minutes, choreographing the actors and the camera within the performance space but without cutting away. Such a technique must have helped immensely with the short production schedule.

While recording artist Dennis Lotis was top billed, it was undoubtedly Christopher Lee who would have been the star and box office draw on this occasion. By this stage he was already a worldwide sensation for having appeared as Dracula (1958), and *City of the Dead* was one of the films he made before reuniting with Hammer Films to make *The Mummy* (1959). That film continued the late 1950s British renaissance of horror cinema, one that *City of the Dead* was very much a part of. Even if it was not that respected at the time, this influential, atmospheric, beautifully designed and lit tale of New England witches taking revenge and continuing their practices across the centuries, can now rightfully be considered amongst the best of them.

need to watch the UK version. The film is currently available on Blu-ray in the US from VCI and the UK from Arrow. Both versions are present on both discs, and extras are the same apart from a Bruce Hallenbeck commentary on the VCI disc and a Jonathan Rigby commentary on the Arrow version. For those who are sticklers for such things (and I am), it's worth noting that the VCI transfer is slightly cropped but Arrow's disc has the film in its original aspect ratio of 1.66:1.

Director John Moxey was British but moved to California in the late 1960s where he encountered a numerologist who declared he would be much more successful if he used his middle name. Consequently, the John Llewellyn Moxey who directed the

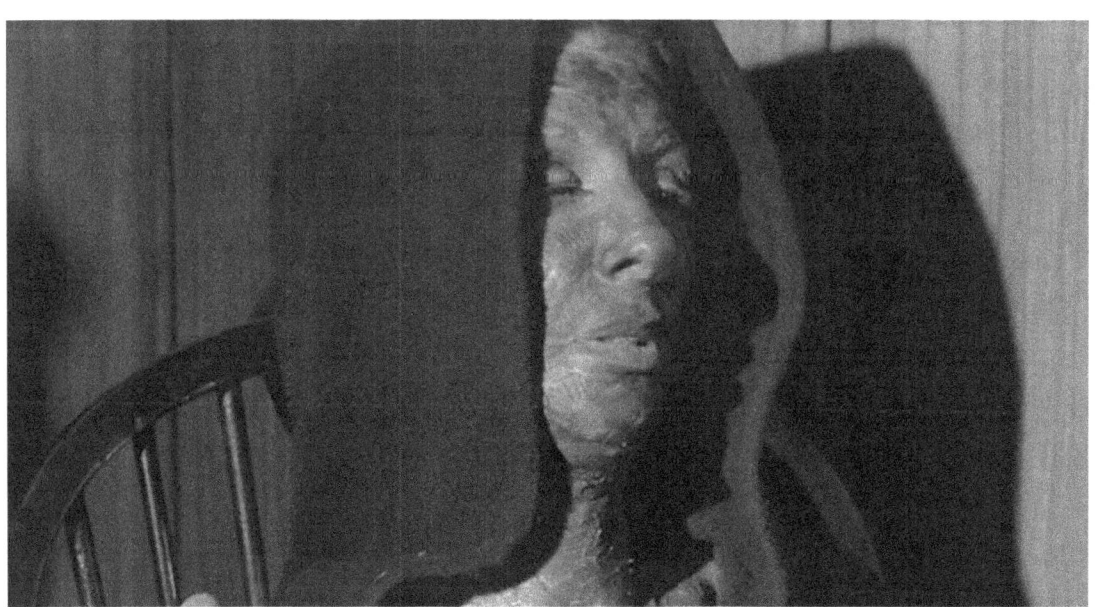

BLACK Infinity 6 INSIDIOUS INSECTS

RAMSEY CAMPBELL
ROBERT SHECKLEY
PHILIP K. DICK
JAMES DORR
TOM ENGLISH
KURT NEWTON
MURRAY LEINSTER
GREGORY L. NORRIS
MATT COWAN • VONNIE WINSLOW CRIST
JASON J. McCUISTON • ALLEN KOSZOWSKI
SPECIAL: GARY GERANI REMEMBERS THE OUTER LIMITS

BLACK Infinity STRANGE DIMENSIONS
ROCKET SCIENCE BOOK GROUP 4
STILL NOT 10c

RHYS HUGHES
CLIFFORD D. SIMAK
MARC VUN KANNON
KURT NEWTON • STEVE DITKO • ALAN E. NOURSE
PHILIP K. DICK
DOUGLAS SMITH
GREGORY L. NORRIS

WE ALSO LIKE CREEPY SCIENCE FICTION!
DON'T MISS BLACK INFINITY, NIGHTMARE ABBEY'S "SCI-FI SISTER"!

BLACK Infinity 5 DERELICTS

JAMES DORR
PHILIP K. DICK
DOUGLAS SMITH
STEWART C BAKER
GREGORY L. NORRIS
WILLIAM HOPE HODGSON
ALAN E. NOURSE • ANDRE NORTON
JACK WILLIAMSON • DAVID VonALLMEN

LOST IN SPACE REMEMBERED

BLACK Infinity 7 RENEGADE ROBOTS

A SPECIAL TRIBUTE TO ROBBY THE ROBOT

JERRY SOHL
JAMES DORR
ROG PHILLIPS
PHILIP K. DICK
HENRY SLESAR
TODD TREICHEL
MICHAEL SHAARA
ROBERT SHECKLEY
GREGORY L. NORRIS
JASON J. McCUISTON
VONNIE WINSLOW CRIST
TOM ENGLISH • MATT COWAN

VINTAGE ROBOT
COVER GALLERY

GOLDFISH

BY HELEN GRANT

WHEN HENRY CHARTERIS IMAGINED HIS REVENGE, HE SAW HIMSELF crouching on the pink onyx effect floor tiles by the lavatory, holding a tiny wriggling creature between finger and thumb. He would release it and watch it drop headfirst, like a torpedo, into the water, where it would swim frantically in circles until he depressed the lever and sent it to oblivion.

That was the idea.

In fact, it proved very difficult indeed to catch live fish in his bare hands, especially once they had taken fright. After spending some time with his arm in the fish tank as they slipped out of his grasp like mercury, he gave up and fetched a jug from the kitchen. After that it was fairly easy to scoop the fish up, carry them through into the bathroom and pour them into the gaping porcelain maw. Henry stood there for a few moments, jug in hand, relishing his sweet moment of triumph. Then he leaned forward, grasped the handle and very deliberately flushed.

After the water had stopped foaming, its smooth surface seemed to match the tranquility in his own soul. Justice had been done. When Alexis came home and saw what he'd done, she'd go berserk. She'd probably tear her hair—perhaps even grovel on the floor, screaming and pounding. Henry smirked to himself.

But, he thought suddenly, *would* she see what he'd done? There would simply be an empty tank, with nothing to indicate where the fish had gone. She might not even notice at first. After some consideration he took one of the plump rolls of quilted toilet paper and took it through to the living room, where he placed it ceremoniously on top of the aquarium cover. That, Henry thought, would make the point nicely.

He took the jug back to the kitchen, washed and dried it and returned it to the cupboard. Then he let himself out of the apartment, locking the front door with the duplicate key he had had made before returning the original one to Alexis. He slipped the key into his pocket, thinking that he had better decide what to do with it. It was incriminating evidence, after all—in the murder of a dozen expensive goldfish. The corner of his mouth twitched.

At the end of the street there was a pub, and Henry headed for that to celebrate the accomplishment of his revenge. He had quite a few drinks in the end, because there was nobody to tell him not to. Occasionally he glanced at his phone to see whether Alexis had called; he had no intention of answering, but he thought he'd enjoy listening to a few recorded messages of hysterical weeping and accusations. Some of the fish, the more unusual ones, had cost £300 each, after all. But Alexis didn't call—not then, not the next day, nor the one after that.

IT WAS A FEMALE COLLEAGUE who told him.

Henry came into the office rather late on the Friday morning, and the woman, whose name was Shirley, immediately looked up from the report she was reading. While Henry was shrugging off his jacket and sorting through the papers and other things on his desk looking for a clean coffee cup, she stood up and came over to hover at his side.

Henry ignored her at first; he had a thumping headache. Also he had a vague recollection that the woman knew Alexis, through mutual friends or something. If she'd heard about the fish she might be intending to share her opinion on the matter, and he had no desire to listen. Alexis having hysterics would be entertaining; a friend having them would simply be tiresome.

It wasn't that, however. Shirley stood there for a moment, waiting, and when it became clear that Henry didn't mean to notice her, she said, "Um, I just wanted to say how sorry I am."

Henry stopped hunting for a mug and looked at her.

"Why?" he said. "What have you done?"

Her eyes widened. "I haven't *done* anything. I meant... well, you know. You and Alexis were together for a long time, weren't you?"

"If," said Henry acerbically, "you are referring to the end of my... association with her, you needn't bother offering sympathy. It's old news."

And none of your business, he was very tempted to add.

Shirley looked bewildered, and then distressed. "It wasn't that. Of course it wasn't that. I wouldn't comment on such a thing."

"Well, what was it then?" Henry started shifting piles of documents again. Where was the bloody mug? He was dying for a cup of very strong black coffee.

"I can't believe..." began Shirley, and then stopped.

"Out with it," said Henry tersely.

"Oh my goodness—you don't know," she said, and then it came out in a rush. "Alexis is dead. I'm so, so sorry, Henry. I didn't want—"

"*Dead?*" Henry stopped what he was doing. "What do you mean, *dead*? She can't be. I spoke to her last week."

Shouted down the phone at her while drunk would have been nearer the mark, but he didn't say that.

"I'm so sorry," said Shirley again. "She really is—dead, I mean. Her sister found her on Tuesday, in her apartment." She wrung her hands, appalled to be the bearer of such bad news. "I don't think she suffered," she volunteered eventually. "They think it was her heart."

Henry didn't bother to reply. He picked up his jacket and walked straight out of the office, while Shirley wailed apologies at his retreating back. He went down the stairs, out of the building and around the corner before he allowed himself to give in to hysterical laughter. It was too delicious, he thought, as he leaned against the wall, his stomach muscles aching. On Monday afternoon he had flushed all Alexis's fish down the lavatory; pretty clearly she had come home, seen what he'd done and had a heart attack. He might as well have killed her with his own hands—except this way, they couldn't pin anything on him.

After he had indulged his bout of hilarity, something else occurred to him. His breakup with Alexis was very recent—had she even had time to change her will? Alexis had been far more organized than he was, far more diligent about administrative matters. Even so, she'd have had to think about doing it, contact her solicitor and all the rest of it. She might not even have felt there was much urgency; she hadn't expected to die, after all. If she *hadn't* done anything about it, nearly all that she owned would go to Henry.

A gloating, spiteful smile teased the corners of Henry's mouth upwards. Flushing the fish, he thought, had been a very profitable afternoon's work.

THE FOLLOWING DAY being Saturday, Henry decided to take a health-giving constitutional across the park to his favorite pub. His new apartment was much smaller and less attractive than the one he had shared with Alexis, but it had the benefit of being nearer to the watering-hole in question. He walked with a spring in his step, savoring the spring sunshine. New green leaves were sprouting on the trees, birds were singing, and Alexis was dead. All was well with the world.

As he skirted the large pond that was the park's centerpiece he saw movement out of the corner of his eye, accompanied by a *splash*. A fish had jumped right out of the water, and dropped back into it, creating rings of ripples. Henry glanced in its direction and thought he saw a flash of brilliant orange in the murky water. He shrugged and was about to walk on when the fish did it again. He saw it quite clearly this time—a sliver of bright color that described an arc in the air and audibly re-entered the pond.

Without really being sure why he did so, Henry wandered to the very edge and peered in. As he leaned forward, his reflection appeared dimly on the water's surface. A second or two later, it was churned up by a flurry of activity, and then not one but *two* fish leapt up, twisting in the air before falling back into the depths. They, too, were the color of flame.

Henry stepped back, frowning; he was vaguely disquieted. As he hurried away from the pond he heard turbulence in the water and imagined very clearly a whole shoal of tiny, copper-colored fish breaking the surface, leaping and plummeting back. Probably, he told himself, the denizens of the pond *always* came to the top when anyone leaned over; they thought they were about to be fed. All the same, his mind slid back to Alexis's goldfish going round and round the lavatory bowl before he flushed them away. Where did things go, when you flushed them?

Not into the local pond, that's for sure, he thought. There were pipes and sewers and then filters and water treatment plants. A fish couldn't get through all of that alive, and even supposing it did, it would be miles away from where it started. It definitely wouldn't be popping its scaly head out of the water in the nearest park, looking for the person who flushed it. *That* was a pure flight of fancy.

He increased his pace. The pond was soon far behind, and the pub alluringly close.

* * *

TIME DID NOT so much tick as slither by, as easily as the numerous beers which found their way down Henry's throat. He was beginning to think that he'd had enough—he had better stagger home—when he looked through the window and saw that it was raining heavily outside. Henry shrugged and ordered another drink.

Much later, when he emerged from the pub, it had stopped raining but everything was slick and wet, shining in the re-emergent sunshine. Henry could *hear* that it had been raining, too, from the hiss of tires on wet tarmac, and the gurgling of water running along the gutters. He glanced blearily towards the park but decided he'd go the longer way round, along the street; the fish thing had been peculiar, and besides, he thought he might stop off for a takeaway to soak up some of the booze.

He found himself meandering along the pavement, not so drunk he was actually falling over, but not proceeding in a straight line either. He looked down at his own shoes and then up again, and nearly collided with a pushchair. Henry was about to say "look out" when he saw the indignant expression on the young mother's face, and thought better of it. He swerved, then lurched and put one foot in the gutter. Instantly he felt cold water running over and into his shoe.

Henry cursed, which got him another outraged look, and stared dully down at his foot ankle-deep in the flow. He was about to move it when a flicker of color and motion caught his eye. There was something in the water, something as bright as a new penny, and weirdly, it seemed to be moving *up-stream*, towards the toe of his shoe. Not very much further down there was a drain, and the rainwater was pouring towards and into that with some force, but the brilliantly gleaming object was speeding against the current like a tiny torpedo.

Henry hauled his foot out of the gutter with alacrity. A second later, a small and vibrantly orange fish leapt into the air, hung there for an instant, and dropped back into the water with a splash. The stream took it, and very shortly it had vanished into the drain.

Henry stood there open-mouthed.

"I don't believe it," he said aloud. "That did *not* just happen."

Then he realized that people were looking at him, and not in a friendly way. The partner of the woman with the push-chair shook his head, and someone said, "Disgusting. At this time of day!"

Henry consigned them all to perdition, and then he stumbled off up the street, his wet foot squelching as he went.

THE FOLLOWING DAY Henry got up late and went into the kitchen in the t-shirt and boxers he habitually wore to bed. There was a slight pulsing in his temple but other-wise he was not too disastrously hungover. He opened the fridge and surveyed the contents. There were three pulpy-looking tomatoes and some yellowing salad leaves, none of which looked appetizing, half a can of baked beans, and—thankfully—some butter and milk, both just within date. He made himself several slices of toast and a huge mug of coffee, and went to sit at the little formica-topped table by the window. It was raining again, and water was streaming down the outside of the glass. The rain obscured the scene outside, turning the streets and the park into an impressionistic blur.

Henry nursed his coffee and looked at that rain. He'd never been the hearty sort of person who goes out cheerfully in all weathers, but today he really didn't fancy it. The pond in the park would be full to over-flowing, the gutters would be streaming again, and there would be puddles every-where. The incidents with the goldfish the day before twisted and darted in his memory; he felt both incredulous and uneasy.

After a while the rain slackened off, and he could see out of the window more clearly. Not far below it, there was a small trapezium-shaped section of roof over the projecting front window of the flat down-stairs. Water habitually collected there when it rained, and it had now; there was perhaps a couple of centimeters of it, with a single brown leaf from the previous autumn float-ing in it. It would not normally have grasped Henry's attention except perhaps as another instance of the infuriatingly inferior quality of his current lodgings. But now, as he idly gazed down, he distinctly saw a small bright orange shape appear. It really *did* appear—Henry actually saw it coalesce. First the spot where it appeared was a middling grey color, like the rest of the little roof, then it seemed to become somehow darker and denser, and finally it seemed to segue from grey into that familiar flame color. For a second it was perfectly still, and Henry saw, in spite of the distance, that it was a small fish. The next instant, it flicked its tail and shot across the little pool. Back and forth it went, while Henry's knuckles turned white around the handle of the mug and his face dropped into slack astonishment. Then, as though it had been working up the impetus with its furious movements, the fish suddenly erupted up out of the water in a leap which brought it right up to the level of the window. It smacked into the glass and Henry recoiled, slopping warm coffee down himself. Then it tumbled down, and with one hand Henry grabbed the toggle and drew down the blind, blocking the view.

Henry's heart was racing and he found that he was trembling. He stood up and stepped away from the window, the mug still in his hand. He waited for the fish to hit the window again, for the slap of another impact. Nothing came. He waited, while the plastic third hand of the kitchen clock ticked once around its face, then twice; still nothing. It occurred to him that he should go over and peer around the edge of the blind, but his nerve failed him. In the end he went into the bedroom to change out of the coffee-stained t-shirt.

This is not happening, he told himself. *It's a delusion. It's delirium tremens.*

He didn't really believe that; he liked a drink, but not *that* much. Perhaps, he thought, it was guilt, or some kind of weird grief reaction to Alexis's death. He examined himself, as though he were checking every limb for breaks after a near-miss accident. He did not *think* he felt guilty about flushing Alexis's goldfish; he'd been provoked beyond all endurance, after all. Nor did he think he felt particularly sorry about her death—especially not if it restored to him the apartment they had shared, with its elegant proportions and high ceilings. All the same, perhaps the mere fact of her demise after years of shared history was significant enough to disturb his equilibrium. He decided it must be that. The slap of the goldfish against the window had sounded alarmingly corporeal, but Henry supposed it wouldn't be a delusion if it weren't entirely convincing.

For the rest of the day, he kept the blind down, and avoided the kitchen as much as possible. He had food delivered for dinner, and left the takeaway boxes on the table in the sitting room.

MONDAY MORNING dawned bright and clear; by the time Henry set off for work, leaving the kitchen blind still firmly down, the puddles had all evaporated and the gutters were dry. He did not go through the park. When he arrived at the office, Shirley and the others treated him with earnest solicitude, not saying anything directly about Alexis but clearly assuming that he was laboring under a heavy burden of grief. Henry didn't disabuse them of this notion; he did a little light work with the air of one bravely soldiering on, and then went home early.

In the kitchen the blind was still down. Henry had a sprawling dinner that was more alcoholic than nutritious, watched a film without much interest, and made a few rough calculations on the back of an envelope, trying to work out how much he'd net if Alexis hadn't changed her will. It was all speculation though, until he'd heard from her solicitor, so eventually he gave up and went to run a bath. He put the plug in and turned both taps; as water came thundering into the tub he went off to get into his dressing-gown. Then he brushed his teeth, rinsed and spat, and after that he relieved himself at some length, his bare toes flexing on the tiles as he stood before the lavatory. He leaned over the bath and turned the taps off and he was just about to put a hand into the water to check the temperature when he froze.

There were fish in the water.

Henry gaped at them, blinked and gaped some more. As the ripples smoothed out, he saw them very clearly. They were small—just a few centimeters long—and a hot, vibrant orange in color. Goldfish, in fact. Back and forth they swam, tails lashing furiously, and Henry drew back, remembering the one outside the window, which had worked itself up to a mighty leap. Movement caught his eye, and he saw that another of the fish was oozing out of the faucet, as though gravity were slowly forcing it through an aperture a little too tight for it. It hung for a moment by its tail, then plummeted into the water and began to swim about with the others.

"No," said Henry aloud. "No, no."

He pushed back the sleeve of his dressing gown and plunged his hand into the hot water, intending to pull out the plug, which had no chain. He managed the task, but the next instant he was yelling. All the fish had turned swiftly in the bath water and streaked towards his bare arm; he drew it out as fast as he could but not before two of them had bitten him. The pain was instant and excruciating, as though hot irons had been applied to his skin. Henry shook his arm wildly. The two fish clung on like leeches and the others leapt out of the water, as though desperate to take their share of his flesh. Something hot was running down Henry's arm, and as he wrenched the biting creatures free with his other hand, blood spurted into the water, forming crimson clouds.

Henry staggered back until he was pressed up against the sink, his eyes round with horror. He was holding onto his forearm, and blood was oozing between his fingers. After a moment he dared to relax his grip and examine his insulted flesh, and then he nearly fainted. The fish had bitten chunks out of his arm, leaving ragged pits which wept red and stung hideously. He grabbed the hand towel and wrapped it around the wounds, gibbering with shock. Then he crashed his way out of the bathroom, in search of bandages and brandy.

Much later, he went gingerly back in with a heavy pan in his good hand, ready to flatten any fish that remained, but they had all gone, drained away with the bathwater. There were streaks and splashes all over the floor and walls, congealing to an unappealing shade of brown. His face a mask of revulsion, Henry mopped them all up, dry heaving as he wrung the cloth out in the sink. Afterwards, he threw it out.

He dared not try running another bath. He looked up at the shower head and couldn't face that either; he imagined standing underneath it, the water cascading down his body, and something moving inside it, rattling the chrome fixture, pressing itself tight against the holes so that tiny orange domes protruded through them. Perhaps miniscule golden scales would flake off... Henry pressed the back of his hand to his mouth. In the end he didn't wash at all; feeling grubby but unable to face any quantity of water, he sprayed liberal amounts of deodorant under his arms and went to bed.

HENRY AWOKE EARLY after a very poor night's sleep; the throbbing of his injured arm woke him whenever he put any weight on it. He went into the bathroom and while he was standing at the lavatory he spotted a fine spray of maroon liquid on the tiles, that he had missed the night before. Feeling queasy, he looked down instead, at the pan.

Fish. There was a fish in it.

Henry uttered a strangled oath. The goldfish circled furiously in the limited space, every movement expressing savagery in spite of its size. Henry knew what would come next. He reached out, dropped the lid shut, and pressed the handle down hard to flush. He was trembling.

Part of him, straining to be rational, said that this was a delusion: goldfish couldn't possibly be materializing in stretches of water around him. Certainly they couldn't be *targeting* him. He had heard of small fish coming out of taps in very rural places, where the water supply came straight from a river—but that was long ago. It must be impossible now, with modern treatment plants and filters. And it was completely, utterly out of the question that some specific fish—Alexis's goldfish—could do that.

However, the ache in his arm, and the faint brown stains on the bandages, told him that the bites were real. Henry touched the gauze gingerly and felt a thrill of pain.

A local infestation, he said to himself. *Someone released some kind of carnivorous tropical fish into the water around here. I should complain—to the water company, to the council, to the landlord...*

But he knew that he wouldn't. They'd think he'd gone out of his mind. And besides, he was pretty sure only one person in the neighborhood had released pet fish into the water system.

The trouble was, at some point he'd *really* need to wash, and at some point he'd need to use the lavatory again. He supposed if absolutely put to it, he could pee outdoors somewhere—an alley, behind a bush in the park. But if he had to do anything *else*, which he inevitably would... It was impossible not to think of it from the fish's eye view—the plump, unmissable target that would be presented so temptingly. Henry winced.

Eventually, he set off for the office, unwashed and unshaven. If the phenomenon *was* a local one, he reasoned, perhaps the fish wouldn't appear there. He could use the lavatory in peace—perhaps even have a sneaky squaddie wash. And if the problem was himself—if he was slowly going right out of his mind—the company of other people might make him rally. It was worth a try.

WHEN HENRY ARRIVED at the office he found Shirley in Reception, talking to the girl behind the desk. When he came in, they both fell silent and looked at him. Henry saw Shirley's eyes widen. He opened his mouth to make a cutting remark, but remembered just in time that he was meant to be grieving. Whatever they found so singular in his appearance would probably be put down to that. He put up a hand and went past them without a word.

In the mens', where he stopped off first, the water in the toilet bowl, though a startling shade of blue, was entirely undisturbed by goldfish. Henry stood there and gazed at it for a full two minutes, and nothing happened. He did what he had to, washed his hands without incident, and went out again, feeling somewhat jauntier than before. Aside from the occasional throb in his arm, he might have imagined the whole thing with the fish. Perhaps he had, he thought. Perhaps it had been some kind of peculiar fever dream and he had injured himself in some other way while under its influence.

For the rest of the morning he toyed with a few unavoidable tasks, and wondered about Alexis's will. How soon would it be before he heard anything? And would they telephone or write, if he was still the beneficiary? If they phoned him at work, he thought, and told him he'd inherited the lot, he'd take the rest of the day off. In fact, he might not go back at all. He could live for a long time on Alexis's savings account. He might take a cruise. Pleasing images filled his head: a lounger on a sun-drenched deck; a brilliantly-colored drink with a cocktail umbrella in it; a voluptuous girl almost spilling out of her bikini top, smiling at him…

The thought of the drink prompted thirst; he hadn't had a thing all morning. There was a half-full bottle of Evian on his desk, so without really thinking about it he unscrewed the lid and took a huge swig.

The next second, he was on his feet, screaming incoherently. A small golden fish swung from his upper lip, its razor-sharp teeth buried in his tender flesh. Crimson globules splattered onto the desk, the wall, the floor.

in the bottle it was in the bottle

Henry's hands frantically beat the air in front of his face, but he was afraid to yank the fish off, remembering the oozing pits the last bites had left. He bolted for the men's room, clumsy in his panic, knocking over a chair on the way past. People were on their feet, asking him what the matter was, gasping at the sight of blood.

"…nosebleed?" said someone.

The door of the men's room slapped shut behind him and Henry stumbled over to the sink, breathing hoarsely. When he looked in the mirror, he nearly fainted. There was blood streaming down his chin. His collar and the front of his shirt were drenched scarlet with it. The fish writhed against his lip, and every movement was exquisite agony; it was biting more deeply, securing its grip.

Henry made an inchoate sound. His hands fluttered to his lip and with infinitesimal care he touched the fish, feeling gently around the spot where its jaws met his skin. As he tried to ease his fingers underneath it to prise it away from his lip, the fish abruptly let go and sank its teeth deep into the pad of his thumb. Henry let out a bubbling, choking scream. There was blood in his mouth, hot and coppery, and agonizing pain in his hand. He flapped it uselessly in the air. The fish would not be dislodged. At last he took it by the tail with his other hand and ripped it off with main force, taking a chunk of his own flesh with it.

As he carried the struggling creature into the nearest cubicle, it swung wildly back and forth in his grip, fighting to sink its fangs into his hand again. It had a protruding lower jaw and teeth like no goldfish Henry had ever seen: small, yes, but wickedly pointed and as sharp as butcher's knives. Bloodied shreds of Henry's skin clung to them.

Henry dropped the fish into the pan and flushed once, twice. Red and gold circulated briefly and vanished in a froth of water. He realized that he was panting as if he had been running hard. His uninjured hand was still on the flush handle and there were bloody prints on the surrounding porcelain.

When he left the cubicle, he could hardly believe what he saw. Was all that gore *his*? It looked as though someone had been murdered in the men's room. There were pools of it on the floor and in the sink, and red streaks and droplets all over the walls. His own reflection in the mirror was a hideous crimson effigy baring bloodstained teeth.

Henry was unable to think how he might explain any of this to his colleagues, particularly with the twin agonies of lip and hand screaming at him. He barged his way out through a door stamped with bloody handprints, and made for the nearest exit.

When he got to street level he saw people's reactions—the widening eyes, the open mouths, the recoiling. He swore at them, trembling, but he didn't hang about; it occurred to him that someone might call the police, thinking he had committed a crime. He stumbled away, leaving a sporadic trail of red droplets behind him.

Home, he thought.

* * *

WHEN HENRY REACHED his flat, he peeled off the soaked shirt that was adhering disgustingly to his skin and dropped it in the bath. He actually had his hand out, about to turn on the taps on the sink, when he caught himself. Water, yes, he needed water to wash himself, but what else would come out of the faucet, sharp-toothed and wriggling?

After some deliberation he found a pack of moist toilet wipes and cleaned himself up as best he could with those. He used the entire pack and still the effect was inadequate. He did his best to clean around the wound on his lip, dabbing ineffectually; touching it simply seemed to make the blood run again, so in the end he abandoned the attempt. The bite in his hand was as bad as the ones still throbbing under the bandages on his arm. He put antiseptic on it and uttered a smothered shriek at the pain, but he dared not run any water to clean it properly.

When he had done the best he could, Henry went into the kitchen, found the whisky and poured himself a very large measure. He peered into the glass for a long time, but it seemed that alcohol was not conducive to the appearance of fish. He knocked back the whole lot in one go and fairly soon he felt its steadying effect. He poured himself a second one, and took it through into the small living room, where he sat down to think.

Whether the fish were a figment of his imagination or a genuinely corporeal phenomenon, the effect was all too physical. Water was, it seemed, his enemy, at least until he found some way of stopping what was happening. Henry couldn't think of anything. He couldn't *unflush* Alexis's fish, nor could he make things up with her, since she was dead. In the meantime, how was he to live? Whisky was all very well, but he was fairly sure you couldn't manage with alcohol as your only liquid intake.

Orange juice, he thought; he couldn't imagine fish manifesting themselves in that opaque, acidic fluid. There was some in the fridge at that very moment; he might make the experiment. He went back into the kitchen, took the carton out and wrenched open the top so that he could look inside.

The carton was half full, and for a few moments Henry stared down at smooth and perfectly undisturbed orange liquid. Then a ripple appeared in the surface, and another, and a second later he was gazing down at juice that foamed and frothed with tiny golden bodies confined in a small space.

Henry pinched the carton closed and put it back in the fridge. As he closed the door he heard it thump softly against the back of the shelf with the vigorous movement inside it. He sat down at the little table by the window still concealed by the blind, and leaned his head on his good hand. Feelings of desperation warred within him against a sense of terrible unfairness.

Why?! he wanted to scream. *All I did was flush a few goldfish. Whatever this is, it's—it's—disproportionate.*

Then he thought about Alexis, seeing the empty tank, and understanding, and then slumping to the floor, perhaps clutching at her chest.

"I couldn't have known that would happen," he said aloud. Then he raised his voice. "Do you hear me? I couldn't have known!"

There was a second or two of silence before he heard one of his near neighbors knocking on the wall, telling him to shut up. Henry shouted an obscenity back, which provoked more knocking. The fight went out of him after that. The reality of the situation was sinking in. He couldn't wash, he couldn't use the lavatory, he couldn't drink anything unless it had a hefty amount of alcohol in it. And whatever was happening was closing in on him: first it had manifested itself in a pond, then in the gutter on a city street, after that in a bath, and finally in small containers of water and juice. What next? He'd have hung his head and cried, except he was beginning to be afraid of *all* water—even tears.

That night, Henry didn't bother to clean his teeth, since he dared not rinse his mouth. He put out all the lights that were still on, and got into bed. He thought he could smell himself in the warmth under the covers: a mixture of sweaty, unwashed body and the metallic tang of blood. He was dreadfully thirsty.

There was a crack between the curtains, and as he lay there he could see the strip of light it created on the ceiling and wall, thrown by the streetlamp outside. It began to rain, softly at first and then more heavily, and soon the lamp's radiance was filtered through water running down the outside of the window, so that it seemed to flow across the ceiling like liquid. Henry gazed up at it, sleeplessly, and longed for something to drink. He could almost *taste* water in his parched mouth.

That made him think about something else. The human body was, he recalled, about sixty percent water. There was more in some parts of it than others—less in the bones, more in the brain—but still, the majority of the body was water. All those organs, and blood vessels, and cells, simply bursting with water. Supposing that was the next place the fish appeared?

The more Henry thought about that, the more terrified he became. He thought about those tiny fish, about the hideously sharp fangs they had, the searing agony of the bites—he thought about them taking shape in the aqueous parts of his body. Perhaps they could not even form entirely inside a human being; they might simply materialize as tiny, savage jaws, as blade-sharp teeth, snapping mindlessly, burying themselves in whatever bodily structures were nearest, forcing their way in, champing, gnawing...

He thought then that he could *feel* them. It began as a feeling of pressure, in a score of tiny points within himself, and then it flowered into a strident chafing sensation.

It was all over him; Henry screamed and slapped and scratched at himself, pushing back the bedclothes, but the feeling was buried so deep within his flesh that he couldn't get at it. The next moment it exploded into excruciating pain in a hundred different places in his body. Henry shrieked; he could feel them biting into him, ravening, eating him up from the inside. He could feel their teeth *everywhere*.

The neighbor next door began knocking on the wall again in response to the commotion, but Henry didn't hear him. He was consumed with the deep red agony of his own disintegration.

IT WAS QUITE a long while before anyone found Henry. He didn't have many close friends, after all; a lot of the people he and Alexis had known as a couple had sided with Alexis, and dropped him when they broke up. He wasn't close to any of his colleagues, either—or not close enough for anyone to come knocking when he failed to turn up at work again. Finally the landlord called round because other tenants had persistently complained about a strange smell; he wouldn't have been sorry to find a reason to boot Henry out, since he was consistently late with the rent.

He found Henry on his bed, amongst disordered sheets. There was no obvious sign of injury. It was not until a postmortem had been conducted that they were able to conclude that he had died of dehydration.

Helen Grant writes Gothic novels and short supernatural fiction. Her new novel *Jump Cut*, about a notorious lost movie, was published in September 2023 by Fledgling Press. *The Independent* described it as "a chilling, highly atmospheric tale."

Helen's short stories have appeared in *Weird Tales*, *Supernatural Tales*, *All Hallows* and various anthologies including Egaeus Press's acclaimed *Crooked Houses*, Swan River Press's *Uncertainties 2* and Titan Books' dark academia volume *In These Hallowed Halls*. Joyce Carol Oates has described her as "a brilliant chronicler of the uncanny as only those who dwell in places of dripping, graylit beauty can be." A lifelong fan of M.R. James, she has spoken at two M.R. James conferences.

"Goldfish" came about because Helen was considering what the most innocuous topic for a story might be, and whether it would be possible to make it terrifying...

ALWAYS KNOW WHERE YOU ARE

BY
DAVID
SURFACE

I N BILLY'S DREAM, THE MEN WERE COMING TO KILL HIM. He could hear them walking through the rubble, stepping over broken concrete and twisted metal. Something bad had happened—Billy could tell, because of the smoldering ruins, the bodies of men and women, even children like him scattered all around. The smell of burning things choked him, but he couldn't cough. If he coughed, the men would hear him. Then they would find him.

Billy tried to stay as still as he could, laying sprawled across chunks of broken stone and steel. He could hear the men coming. Every few seconds, he heard them stop, then the sound of gunshots—one, two. Always two. They were looking for survivors and killing them. They were shooting the dead ones too. One shot in each eye, just to make sure. Soon they would find him, and it wouldn't matter how long he held his breath, or how still he was. He wondered if it would hurt, or if he'd be dead before he could feel it.

Billy heard two more shots—one, two, very close, then the men's footsteps. It was too late to run. There was nothing he could do … except wake up.

That was all he had to do. Wake up.

Wake up, he screamed silently. *Wake up.*

Billy opened his eyes and saw the faded upholstery of the car roof just inches away from his face. He'd been sleeping in the back of the family station wagon on top of the suitcases, the hard edges cutting into his back like the steel girders and broken concrete in his dream.

"Billy, wake up," his mom was calling from the front seat. "We're almost there…"

Almost there… Billy couldn't remember what that meant or where they were going. The rumble and hum of the car engine had worked its way through his skull into his brain and was now part of him. He couldn't feel his legs, or remember how long they'd been driving.

Voices were blaring from the radio—it was one of those talk shows his dad listened to all the time. It was hard to hear what the voices were saying, but the tone was always the same. Urgent and angry.

"Bastards..." his dad growled.

"Henry..." Billy knew that voice—it was the same voice his mom used whenever he'd done something wrong.

"This goddamn country's got to wake up," his dad said. "It's got to wake up real fast..." Billy didn't understand—why did his dad listen to those people talking on the radio when all it did was make him angry?

"Can't we just listen to some music for a while?" his mom asked.

Billy's dad sighed and started pushing buttons on the radio—quick bursts of raw static, strange music, and different voices, one after another. Finally he twisted a dial, and all the noises stopped.

"That's better," his mom said. "Let's just have a little peace and quiet."

They drove along for several minutes, not talking. It was quiet, Billy thought, but it didn't feel peaceful.

"It's amazing how *huge* this country is," his dad suddenly said, breaking the silence. "Know how many Europe's you can fit inside the United States? Something like two or three."

Mom was already flipping through screens on her Smartphone. "One."

"One what?"

"Europe. It says only one Europe will fit inside the United States. Only like ninety percent of it. That leaves a whole ten percent that won't even fit."

Billy's dad was silent for a moment. "Well," he said, "You can't believe everything you see on the internet these days." Looking out the driver's window at the brown fields scrolling past, he waved his hand like a priest making the sign of the cross. "Look at that," he said reverently. "Why would you ever want to go anywhere else?"

Billy looked out the window again. Same brown fields. Same bare wires passing overhead, not even one bird sitting on them. He scanned the horizon, hoping to see a scarecrow, but after a few miles he gave up on that.

"So where's this place you're looking for?" Billy's mom asked.

"Should be coming up soon..."

His mom frowned and looked down at her phone. "I don't see it. Are you sure it's still here?"

"Of course it's still here," his dad said. "You think just because you can't find something on that damn phone of yours, it doesn't exist?"

Billy saw a sign on the right side of the road. His mom sat up and watched it getting closer. "*There's* a place," she said. "Right there." Billy's dad didn't slow down, and whizzed past the exit. His mom turned and glared at his dad. "Why the hell did you do that?"

"Listen, this place I'm taking you has got the best burgers anywhere. The *best*. You don't want to miss that, do you?"

Billy's mom mumbled something Billy couldn't hear. Billy was still thinking about what he'd just heard. *A place that doesn't exist.* What did that mean? What kind of place would that be?

Suddenly his dad was sitting up straighter. "Look!" he said. "I told you!" Billy saw another sign coming up on the right. This one looked older than the last one, chipped and weathered around the edges, the letters faded and washed-out by years of harsh sunlight.

LITTLE AMERICA.

Billy's dad turned their car off at the exit. Up ahead, Billy saw a large building made of concrete blocks painted muddy brown. There were flags flying from the roof, some Billy recognized, others he didn't.

"There's a flag here for every state," Billy's dad said proudly, as if he'd hung these flags himself. "Billy... let's see you find ours."

Billy looked at all the different flags overhead, hanging limply in the still, hot air. He felt panic rise in his chest, like whenever a teacher singled him out in school, asking a question he didn't know the answer to.

"I don't know..."

"You don't know?" his dad said. "You don't know your own state flag?"

"Oh, leave the boy alone, Henry," his mom said. Billy's dad sniffed but said nothing. They drove around, looking for a parking place. The asphalt was old and broken, with weeds growing through the cracks in wild clumps.

"Look at all these cars," Billy's dad said. "You know what that means?"

"A lot of people are hungry and need to pee?" his mom said.

"It means they've got the best food anywhere. The best. Everyone knows that. Come on..."

They got out of the car and started walking across the parking lot. Billy could feel the sun beating down on the back of his neck, ricocheting back up into his face from the asphalt under his feet. His legs felt wobbly, and he could still feel the motion of the car deep in his bones. When they got closer to the building, Billy saw a sign in big red, white, and blue letters.

THE REAL HISTORY OF AMERICA: THE PEOPLE'S MUSEUM.

"We can't miss that," Billy's dad said.

Bill's mom frowned. "We're starving, Henry."

"Okay, okay," his dad grumbled, "We can catch the museum after we eat."

They entered a large room filled with orange formica tables, dozens of tired-looking tourists hunched over their plates. Their table felt dirty and stuck to Billy's elbows. The waitress, a tired-looking woman wearing a uniform that was the same muddy orange color as the tables, took their order and went away. Billy's dad leaned back and looked at him with a sickly-looking smile.

"So," he said. "You really don't know the flag of your own state."

"Henry, for God's sake...." Billy's mother whispered.

"You know, my dad used to bring us here," Billy's dad kept talking. "Every summer. He made sure I knew the names of all the states, and that I knew every one of those flags out there. Every single one of them. When I got one wrong, or said I didn't know, you know what he did?"

Billy shook his head.

"He'd take a fork and stick it in the back of my hand. One of these forks ... right here."

Billy's dad reached out carefully and touched the fork on the table in front of him with one finger. He was still smiling.

"You know what he said? He said, you gotta know where you are, son. Always know where you are. And what you belong to."

The waitress set their plates down in front of them and went away without a word. Billy's mom and dad grabbed their burgers with both hands and started chewing. Billy picked his up, but it smelled funny, the bun was soggy with some kind of greasy red liquid, so he put it back down. When he looked up, he saw a trickle of red running down his mother's left arm.

"What did I tell you?" his dad said around a mouthful of chewed-up meat and bread, "Best burgers ever!" More red liquid was running down his dad's chin, staining his white shirt. The front of his mom's dress was soaked with red too, but neither of them seemed to notice or care, so Billy said nothing.

Dad paid for their meal. When he came back from the register, he was clutching three tickets. He handed a ticket to Billy who read the big black letters printed on it.

SUNRISE IN AMERICA – SHOWINGS ON THE HOUR

"What's this?" his mom said, "Some kind of movie?"

"Better than a movie," Billy's dad said. "Wait till you see it..."

"Says it doesn't start for another twenty minutes."

"That gives us time to look around."

Billy followed his parents out of the lunchroom and toward the museum entrance. Over the door were the words: ALWAYS KNOW WHERE YOU ARE. AND WHAT YOU BELONG TO.

Billy followed his parents through the door into a big empty room. There were faded rectangular shadows on the wall, as if things that were hanging there for a long time had been taken away.

Against the far wall was a hand-painted sign with an arrow pointing toward another door covered with a dusty-looking dark red curtain.

MEET THE CRYPTID

"I don't remember this..." Billy's dad said, staring at the sign. "Must be new."

A sick sort of feeling came over Billy.

"What's wrong with you?" his dad said. "You're not scared, are you?"

"No..." Billy said, "I...I just don't feel good..."

"Well, I paid to get in here, so we're gonna see all of it. The whole damn thing..."

Billy's dad pulled the curtain aside and stood glaring at him until he made his legs move and shuffled past the red curtain into the dark room.

At first Billy couldn't see much of anything. There was a single red lightbulb in the ceiling above, but it's light was dim and didn't quite reach the ground. A terrible smell filled Billy's nose, a smell he knew. A neighbor of theirs had kept dogs for fighting. They'd gotten too dangerous to get near, so their pens were never cleaned, and the stink fouled the neighborhood. The neighbor eventually shot the dogs and buried them in his yard, but the stink had never gone away. That's what Billy was smelling right now.

Billy's eyes started to get used to the dim light. There was a big cage against the wall in front of them. Something was inside of it.

"What the hell is that?" Billy's mom said.

"Come on," his dad said, beckoning them closer. "You gotta see this."

Billy's mom held him by the shoulders and pushed him ahead of her. When they were closer to the bars, Billy closed his eyes. He didn't want to see.

"What are you, scared?" his dad's angry voice cut through. "You want to be a little coward all your life? Open your goddamn eyes!"

Billy swallowed hard, then opened his eyes.

The thing huddled on the floor of the cage was big, but hard to see. As Billy's eyes got used to the dim red light, more things started to come through—a hulking body big as a bull, legs and arms that were too long and bent the wrong way. At first Billy thought the thing had no head, then he saw the head sunken down into the massive chest. A gaping mouth filled with long needle-like teeth. Eyes like blackened red pits someone had blown out with a shotgun.

"I saw one of these in Florida one time," Billy's dad said. "They sewed a dead monkey together with an alligator, called it a mermaid..."

The thing in the cage moved.

"Oh Jesus..." Billy's mother gasped. "Oh my Jesus..." Her fingers dug hard into the soft flesh of Billy's shoulders.

The thing restlessly shifted its weight, the bars of the cage creaked. A low moaning sound rose up in the dark, like cattle lowing, dying down into a rattling hiss.

Billy's dad stepped back.

"Christ..." he said. "How do they *do* that?"

"It's *real*," Billy's mother moaned. "Can't you see? It's *real*."

"Of course it's not real!" Billy's father said, "Nothing here is real! Don't you know that?"

Billy couldn't look away from the thing's eyes, or where its eyes used to be. Even though it had to be blind, Billy felt sure that it could see him. It made another sound, a terrible sound like a donkey braying.

"I can't stay in here..." his mom said. "I can't..." She turned and shoved her way out of the little dark room. Billy and his dad followed. They found her doubled-over with her hands on her knees, taking deep, shuddering breaths. "That smell..." she was gasping, "Lord Jesus, that smell..."

Billy looked around for his dad and saw him staring at another sign on the wall. He knew it wasn't here before they went in to see the thing in the cage, but it was here now. Billy read the words on the sign.

AND GOD SAID, LET US MAKE MAN IN OUR IMAGE, AFTER OUR LIKENESS: AND LET THEM HAVE DOMINION OVER THE FISH OF THE SEA, AND OVER THE FOWL OF THE AIR, AND OVER THE CATTLE, AND OVER ALL THE EARTH, AND OVER EVERY CREEPING THING THAT CREEPETH UPON THE EARTH.

"We've got to get moving," Billy's dad said suddenly. "Show's about to start..."

Billy's dad hustled them through the last few rooms, glancing nervously at his watch. Billy was sure that his mom was either going to demand to leave, or else say something about the thing in the cage to the people who were running this place, but she didn't. She just followed behind his dad as if she'd already forgotten about it. When they passed by the lunchroom, Billy looked in and saw a man and a young boy sitting at one of the orange tables. The man was stabbing the boy in the back of the hand with a fork, again and again.

Billy felt his dad's strong hand grip his. "Come on," his dad said. "We're gonna be late..."

They joined the line of people who were shuffling slowly through a dark door covered by another thick red curtain. Over the door were the words Billy remembered from the ticket his dad had given him:

SUNRISE IN AMERICA
SHOWINGS ON THE HOUR
NO ONE WILL BE ADMITTED
DURING THE FINAL TEN MINUTES

It was pitch-dark inside the little theater, and it took them a long time to find their seats. After a while, some old scratchy-sounding music started playing over some speakers hidden somewhere, and lights started to glow in the ceiling above, very dim at first, then growing brighter and brighter.

In the center of the room, Billy saw a large table covered with dark objects arranged in geometric patterns. As the lights grew brighter, Billy saw that they were houses, each one no bigger than a shoebox. The houses were all lined up along streets that bent and connected and formed neighborhoods, and the neighborhoods joined together to make a town. Around the edges of the little town were mountains with tiny trees and white-painted snowy summits. One of the little houses looked familiar, almost like their own house. Billy looked closer and saw a tiny red bicycle like his own propped against the miniature garage door. As he watched, the whole little landscape was flooded with a warm golden light as the scratchy music grew louder and louder.

"Beautiful..." his dad was shouting to be heard over the music. "Beautiful..."

The lights flickered, the music stuttered, slowed, and dragged to a halt. Then all the lights went out. Billy heard nervous voices start to rise up around him. He reached out for his mom's hand but couldn't find it.

When the lights came back on, they were dim and red.

Billy felt a low rumbling under his seat, like a train getting nearer and nearer. The little houses in front of him started to tremble. Flames flickered inside the small plastic windows, and Billy could hear tiny screams coming from inside them. The rumbling grew stronger, and Billy saw the painted mountains crack open, thick red liquid bubbling up from inside them, spilling down their sides and running into the streets.

The door at one end of the theater opened, and Billy saw the twisted hulking body of the cryptid silhouetted against the light, bigger than it looked inside the cage. Then it stepped into the room and started tearing people's arms and legs off, the way he'd seen his dad pull a roasted chicken apart with his bare hands before sucking the meat from its bones. People screamed, but no one ran. They all sat frozen in their seats while the thing kept coming closer and closer, tearing people into bloody pieces. It was going to happen to his mom and dad. It was going to happen to him too.

Unless he could wake up.

Always know where you are...

That's when Billy realized—every single person in this room was having the same nightmare he was having.

There was only one way out. They all had to wake up.

Wake up, he kept screaming inside his head. *Wake up.*

Billy shut his eyes and kept screaming, even when he felt the thing's breath on his face.

He wondered if it would hurt.

David Surface is the author of the collection Terrible Things *from Black Shuck Books. His stories have appeared in* Shadows & Tall Trees, Supernatural Tales, Nightscript, The Tenth Black Book of Horror, Phantom Drift, Morpheus Tales, Twisted Book of Shadows, Uncertainties III, *and* The Best Horror of the Year, Volume 13. *A YA supernatural suspense novel co-written with Julia Rust,* Angel Falls, *is now available from Haverhill House Publishing's YAP imprint. David is also the author of the newsletter STRANGE LITTLE STORIES. To learn more about David and his writing, visit davidsurface.net*

SEEN AND NOT HEARD

BY SEAN HOGAN

T*HERE ARE ALWAYS GOING TO BE A FEW UNWELCOME SURPRISES IN A NEW HOUSE,* **FRAN THOUGHT.**

Busily trying to convince herself of the truth of this, she pushed the bedroom door aside, banishing the spiteful words from view. Leaning out into the hallway, she shouted, "Will, can you come up here, please?"

There was silence downstairs for a few moments, followed by her husband's muffled reply, the muted quality of which did not manage to disguise its extreme reluctance. "Um, I've kind of got my hands full..."

"*Now*, please!"

Fran waited. After a suitably protracted interval, she heard Will's footsteps clomping slowly up the bare boards of the staircase, unavoidably putting her in mind of a recalcitrant child being summoned to swallow a dose of medicine.

The top of his head edged into view. Will peered at her through the balustrades,

grasping them like prison bars. "What is it?"

Fran tried to suppress her mounting irritation. "Come here. I need to show you something."

She heard her husband give a long-suffering sigh before he resumed his reluctant ascent of the stairs. Fran retreated back into the bedroom, signaling that Will should join her.

Once they were both inside, she reached out and closed the door, revealing the message crudely carved into its upper panel. "There," Fran told him.

Will took a step forward and peered at the graffiti. "Huh," he muttered.

"Is that all you've got to say?"

He turned and blinked owlishly at her. "What do you want me to say? Okay, it's a bit weird."

"Weird? It's *horrible*."

Will's gaze returned to the carved message. "*i am going to kill u trudi,*" he said, reading it aloud.

"You can't tell me that isn't awful, Will."

Her husband's face grew thoughtful. "I wonder if he did kill her?" A pause. "Or she."

Fran folded her arms. "Only a man would write something as nasty as that."

Another sigh. "Maybe it was just a stupid joke, babe. This used to be a student house, remember? I did plenty of stupid shit when I was a student."

"Stupid like making death threats?"

He tutted. "No, of course not. But people say all sorts of things they don't mean. You know, things just slip out in the heat of the moment sometimes."

Fran took a step towards the door, her finger jabbing angrily at the message. "*This* was not in the heat of the moment," she snapped. "Someone took the time to carve this into the door. It didn't just 'slip out'." Doesn't that tell you something?"

Will shrugged helplessly. Turning away from her, he sat heavily down upon one of the sealed cardboard boxes piled in the corner of the room. "Don't you think you're overreacting just a little bit?" he said quietly. "We knew the place needed work when we bought it. That was the whole bloody point."

We bought it. We. Fran briefly considered pointing out the obvious fallacy in her husband's statement, but soon thought better of it. The truth of it was, her parents had loaned them most of the necessary funds to secure the house, with Fran chipping in what meager savings she had. All of Will's own money had already gone into starting his video production business, and as for his parents, well, he hadn't spoken to them in several years. Some family falling-out that he refused to talk about.

She and Will had always been renters, ever since they first got together at university. However, when Fran unexpectedly became pregnant with their son Toby, everyone agreed that a young family needed some proper security behind them. Her parents had, she believed, been more than generous with their financial support, but Will had doggedly insisted upon remaining close to the city, claiming that moving too far away would

be a huge impediment to his work. With housing prices being what they were, this had severely limited their options, resulting in their eventual purchase of this very property: a cramped two-bedroom terraced house. Its previous owner—now deceased—had let it out as student accommodation for several years, meaning that the general level of upkeep had been cursory at best. There was a long list of minor repairs crying out to be made (not to mention one or two major ones), and the house's décor was a ghastly patchwork of cheap and cheerful mixed with some eye-watering experiments in garish form and color; just the sort of thing a gang of inebriated art students might come up with after sufficient quantities of weed and cider.

When they'd first looked at the property, Fran's initial instinct had been to run a mile, preferably at record-breaking speed, but Will had somehow managed to talk her round. *It's got good bones,* he'd said of the house. *Just imagine the potential.* Nothing but meaningless clichés, really. In retrospect, she'd come to quietly believe it might all have been stuff he'd heard on daytime DIY programs and carefully filed away for future use. But at the time, Fran had only just given birth to Toby; and, riven with the exhaustion borne of a dozen sleepless nights, not to mention the needling insecurity of a first-time mother, found herself desperate to believe him.

And so here they were, busily trying to juggle moving their belongings into the house with the looming demands of making it remotely habitable. In the run-up to the move, Fran had vainly attempted to convince herself that they were doing the right thing, that it would all work out in the end. *Six months of stress and hard work. Maybe a year to get the house exactly as we want it. Then it'll all be fine.*

But ever since they'd moved in earlier that same week, she'd struggled to believe that this ramshackle building could ever truly be their home. There was just so much to do; an insurmountable cliff face of unpacking and painting and decorating and never-ending repairs. Added to which, Fran secretly felt as though the house was resisting them, that it somehow resented them living there. *No one has ever actually owned this place,* she thought. *The people who lived here never stayed, and the actual owner barely set foot in it. It's like a feral cat, it doesn't want to belong to anyone.*

And while she understood that such fears were entirely illogical, her discovery of this vicious piece of graffiti had now brought all her misgivings bubbling violently to the surface.

Fran struggled not to lose her temper. "I'm *not* overreacting," she told Will flatly. "Think about it, for Christ's sake. I suddenly find this…"—she stopped to search for the exact right word, the perfect adjective to express the disgust she felt roiling in her stomach—"*abhorrent* thing written right here in my home, on the door of the bedroom where our *son* is going to sleep, and you don't think I have a right to be upset? I mean, how do you expect me to react, exactly?"

Will ran his hands through his unruly shock of hair. "We can fix it, Fran," he murmured placatingly. "A quick once-over with some sandpaper and it'll be like it was never even there. It's on my to-do list, okay? The moment I clocked it, I made a mental note. So, given that you're so upset, I'll just bump it to the top…"

She stared at him, incredulous. "Wait, what?" You mean you'd already *seen* it?"

He shrugged again. "Well, yeah. I noticed it when we first came to look round the house."

"And you didn't think to even *tell* me?"

Climbing to his feet, Will moved to embrace her. "Look, I really didn't think it was that important, babe," he said. "It's a bit creepy, sure, but whoever wrote it isn't here anymore, and it's not like they're ever coming back, is it?"

Fran pulled away, unable to suppress the anger she felt any longer. "Jesus *Christ,* Will!"

They stared at each other silently, neither willing to speak first, each of them realizing that whatever they said next would only serve to blow fresh oxygen over the smoldering flames of their argument.

In the end, the stalemate was only broken by the sound of their son bursting into tears in the next room. Visibly grateful for the interruption, Will's eyes darted over towards the doorway. "Shall I go, or…?"

Fran shook her head. Without uttering another word, she moved towards the doorway, trying not to look at the loathsome statement scrawled there. As she opened the door to leave, she made a despairing, half-hearted gesture in the air, unable to think of anything else to say. What use were words? All they ever seemed to do was wound or belittle, threaten and terrify. Sometimes it was far better to say nothing at all.

In the end, Will spoke for her. She heard him call out behind her as she exited the room. "I'll get rid of it, babe. Promise. Next thing I do."

BUT HE DIDN'T, of course. Before Fran could raise the subject again the next morning, Will left to film a corporate town hall meeting, the sort of tedious assignment that had very quickly become his bread and butter. She remembered their early days together at university, when her future husband had been filled with a feverish passion to make his own movies, staying up all night to write scripts and roping Fran and their friends into appearing in his short films. Now, it seemed he no longer had the time; his days were entirely taken up by corporate dullards reciting scripted inanities to camera.

No, there was no longer any time left for passion; scarcely any for her and Toby, even.

And certainly none left for any annoying little jobs around the house. When Fran had finished giving the baby his breakfast and started making her way up the stairs towards the spare bedroom, Toby cradled over one shoulder, she already knew what she would find.

Upon entering the room, Fran pushed the door closed and once again read the words she found carved there, her lips instinctively mouthing the vile shapes and sounds of them.

i am going to kill u trudi

She wondered who Trudi might possibly be. Had this person ever seen the graffiti? Was she a student who'd lived in the house? Had this been her bedroom? Fran wished she could somehow speak to the girl and discover the full story behind the message. If she could only be reassured that it had been nothing more than a tasteless prank, then perhaps the words would come to seem like less of a blight on her new home, a foul infection that threatened to spread throughout the bricks and mortar of the building and rot it from within.

But that was impossible, of course. The previous owner was dead, and she had no way of tracing any of the earlier tenants, assuming it was even legal to try and do so.

Growing irritated with herself, Fran pushed such thoughts away. She was overthinking it, she knew. Will's blithe inability to understand why the message had upset her so greatly had admittedly been infuriating, but he'd been right inasmuch as the words could easily be eradicated with just a few minutes' work. Eradicated, and speedily forgotten, like so many of the other minor unpleasantries one encountered during the day-to-day life of any semi-functional marriage.

After fetching some sandpaper, she deposited Toby into his baby seat and set to work. He goggled mutely up at her as she began to briskly rub the sandpaper over the wooden surface of the door. "Mummy's going to make the bad words go away," she told him. "And don't ever let me catch you growing up to say such horrible things, you hear?"

Toby's mouth opened wide, as if forming a reply. He was old enough now that his first words must surely be imminent, but as yet, his vocabulary was still restricted to the usual childish moans and chortles. "Mmmm," he said, his eyes bright.

Fran flashed him an encouraging smile. "Yes, 'Mummy.' Say 'Mummy' for me, Toby. *Mummy.*"

"Meeeeeoooom," the baby gurgled, a glistening saliva bubble forming upon his lips. Rapidly losing interest in their fledgling conversation, he looked away and began to slap enthusiastically at one of the plastic toys affixed to the baby seat.

"Yes, well," Fran said. "We'll get there eventually." Turning away from her son, she went back to her task, attacking the graffiti with increased vigor. Gritting her teeth, she rubbed the sandpaper back and forth for

over a minute, obscuring the message under a patina of accumulated dust.

Finally she stopped, feeling quite satisfied with her efforts. "There," Fran murmured.

She reached up to wipe the surface of the door clean, then froze.

i am going to kill u trudi

The graffiti was still there, seemingly untouched. Annoyed and not a little bemused, Fran ran her fingertips over the individual letters, trying to ascertain how deeply they had been scored into the wood. The marks didn't appear particularly deep—the door was fairly flimsy to begin with—but perhaps that was simply a trick of the light.

She suddenly imagined Will standing at her shoulder, judging her handiwork with a gently patronizing smile. *You just need to put a bit of elbow grease into it, babe.*

Scowling, Fran renewed her frustrated assault on the door, her right arm rapidly beginning to ache with the force of her labors. She stood there rubbing furiously at the wood for several more minutes, her face reddening with exertion.

At last, it seemed to her that the door panel must surely be about to crack and give way. Taking a weary step back, Fran tossed the worn sandpaper to the floor and wiped at her face with one sleeve. But even before she reached out to once more brush the gathered dust away, she already understood what she would find hidden underneath.

i am going to kill you trudi

Fran could feel hot tears prickling at her eyes. This was impossible, surely. With the amount of strength and effort she had expended, the carving should have grown visibly fainter, at least. But it were as though the sheer force of the hatred the message contained had somehow penetrated to the very core of the wood, leaving an indelible stain.

Cursing, Fran began to repeatedly lash out at the door with her fist, as if convinced she might be able to physically beat the lingering corruption out of the woodwork.

From his seat upon the floor, an alarmed Toby gazed up at his enraged mother, then started to howl.

* * *

IN THE AFTERMATH of the episode with the door, Fran had felt utterly wrung out, her body aching and listless. Choosing to ignore the unpacking and numerous other household tasks still clamoring for her attention, she'd instead retreated to bed, curling up beside Toby and falling fast asleep. By the time she awoke again, it was late afternoon, the shadows of dusk already starting to seep into the corners of the bedroom. Downstairs in the kitchen, she could hear Will making himself a cup of tea.

Rubbing at the grit nestling in her eyes, she decided to go and confront him about the message. Let him try and sandpaper it off. Either her husband would fail just as she had, meaning he'd be forced into agreeing with her that there was something disquietingly strange about the graffiti and taking further action; or else he would succeed in finally obliterating it from existence, in which case she would simply grit her teeth and admit that some tasks were better suited to a man after all.

But when she arrived downstairs, it was to find Will sitting before his bank of computer monitors, already absorbed in his editing work. Standing in the doorway, Fran watched as he absently doodled upon a notepad, patiently waiting for a blue loading bar to finish its steady march across the screen.

"Hey," she said quietly.

Will gave a start and dropped his pen to the floor. "Oh, hey," he replied, throwing her a brief backward glance as he reached down to retrieve it. "Did you have a nice nap?"

"Not really. I didn't feel very well."

"Oh, I'm sorry." In a vague attempt at spousal sympathy, he permitted her a slightly longer look away from the monitor. "I can make us dinner later, if you want."

"That'd be nice, thanks." Summoning a feeble smile, she moved to his side. "Actually, there was something I wanted to talk to you about."

Will glanced up at her, a distracted frown creasing his features. "Can it wait a little while?"

"Well, not really, I—"

He continued, not hearing her. "It's just that I'm expecting a call from Rob any second." Rob was Will's best friend and business partner. "We need to talk through what I shot today."

"Yeah, but—"

At that moment, Fran found herself interrupted by the familiar burbling of the Skype ringtone. "Oh, forget it, then," she sighed crossly.

Will made an apologetic gesture, then clicked on his mouse to answer the call. "Hello mate," he said, as Rob's face popped into view on the monitor.

"Yo," Rob replied, before noticing Fran in the background. "Oh, hey there Fran."

She gave him a distracted wave, her eyes suddenly drawn to the open notepad lying on Will's desk. All at once, the sound of Will and Rob's conversation seemed to drop away, isolating her in a wordless vacuum. Fran stared blankly down at the top page, her mind unable to properly process what she found written there.

Her eyes began to blink furiously, in the desperate hope that her vision might abruptly clear and reveal that the message she imagined she saw was merely an illusion, a teasing mirage borne of accumulated stress and tiredness.

But the jumble of words remained just where they were, exactly as Will had first doodled them, taunting Fran with their dreadful implications.

trudi trudi kill TRUDI
kill you kill
kill you trudi i am going to

"Babe, can you please...?"

Choking back the taste of bile in her throat, Fran at last managed to tear her eyes away from the notepad. "W-what?"

Will gestured impatiently at the screen. "We've got to work."

"Right," she croaked. Whirling around, she stumbled over towards the doorway, her hand clutched over her mouth. Behind her, Fran dimly heard Rob shout out a hasty goodbye, before the two of them burst into laughter at some shared private joke. She slammed the living room door closed and fled back to her bedroom, the sound of their mirth following her upstairs like hungry crows.

* * *

WHEN FRAN CHECKED the notepad again the next morning, the doodled words were nowhere to be seen. She even checked the wastepaper bin Will kept tucked under his desk, finding nothing.

She did not attempt to raise the subject of the graffiti with her husband again. Instead, Fran simply kept the door to the spare bedroom firmly closed, the hateful words shut safely out of sight. There was more than enough to do around the rest of the house, after all, and if Will noticed that she was deliberately avoiding entering the room, he chose not to mention it.

But in the days that followed, Fran slowly became assailed by the creeping sensation that there was someone else present in the house with them. The nature of Will's employment meant that he worked from home much of the time, and the feeling was far less prevalent then, but as soon as he left the house, Fran was instantly seized by a nagging dread that she and Toby were not alone. It was nothing she could quite put her finger on; despite the fear she felt, she saw and heard nothing out of the ordinary. Nevertheless, she was tormented by the inexplicable sense that she was being watched. At least once a day, Fran would find herself overwhelmed by an abrupt terror that someone was lurking unseen behind her, her neck prickling under the chill of their malevolent stare. Chest cramping with panic, her head would snap around to glance over her shoulder, her movements as quicksilver as a frightened sparrow.

But the outcome was always the same; she found herself standing alone in an empty room, the sensation of terror she felt rapidly being replaced by one of relief, and not a little foolishness.

Feeling even more foolish, Fran began to devour real-life haunting podcasts, dozens of breathlessly credulous investigations into the paranormal. But none of the accounts she found there matched her own experience. Time and time again, she would hear stories of eerily disembodied footsteps, crockery being hurled against walls, malign dark figures lurking at bedsides in the dead of night; the stuff of a thousand fireside ghost stories. She had nothing nearly so dramatic to offer, merely her own perpetual dread and apprehension. Fran wasn't even sure she believed she *was* truly being haunted. How could a house possibly be haunted by a handful of words carved into a door? It sounded ridiculous, even to her.

Still, one of the ideas she heard popularly discussed was the notion that heightened displays of emotion might somehow imprint themselves upon a building; that ghosts could simply be a preternatural recording of events that happened long ago, like a TikTok video looping over and over again. So perhaps the suggestion wasn't quite so ridiculous after all. What could be more emotive, Fran decided, than telling someone you were going to kill them?

Suddenly convinced she might have discovered something worth investigating, she dashed off an imploring email to one of the more popular podcasts, but never received so much as a reply. Infuriated, Fran imagined the program's researchers dismissing her as yet another fraudulent attention-seeker. *This nutcase thinks she's being haunted by a piece of graffiti. Another one for the crank file.*

Matters eventually came to a head one rainy Monday afternoon. Will was out on a job, and Toby had been cranky and out of sorts all day, constantly grizzling and refusing food. Normally, Fran might have taken him for a long walk around the local park, but the prospect of braving the cold wind and driving rain proved even less appetizing than being cooped up with her infant son's incessant squalling.

After finally succeeding in getting Toby to lie down for a nap, she decided to take a long hot bath. By now, her neck and shoulders were throbbing with tension, and lighting some scented candles and immersing herself in a steaming tub suddenly seemed like the most alluring of possibilities. If she was lucky, it might even relax her enough to grab a short siesta herself, assuming that Toby remained asleep and Will didn't return home too early.

Fran filled the bath nearly to the brim, a thick layer of bubbles sitting atop the water like whipped cream adorning a cake. Leaving the bathroom door ajar in case Toby awoke from his nap, she threw off her clothes, then eased herself into the tub with a grateful sigh.

She lay there with her eyes closed for a minute or two, allowing the hot water to slowly ease the persistent ache she felt in her muscles. Eventually her eyes opened again, drifting down to her naked torso. The dim candlelight of the bathroom did not quite manage to disguise the lingering after-effects of her pregnancy: the cobwebbed stretch marks on her belly, the baby weight she had not yet quite managed to shift. Fran stared critically down at herself, silently vowing that she would make more of an effort to get back into shape. Perhaps that would help improve relations between her and Will, who had barely even looked at her twice since the night that Toby was conceived.

A knot of tension tightened in her neck. Wincing, Fran closed her eyes again, shutting out the unwelcome sight of her own body. But the seed of disquiet had already been planted, and she found she could no longer relax. Sighing with irritation, she opened her eyes and eased herself upright.

Her gaze moved to the bathroom entrance. Through the gap in the doorway, she could see out into the corridor, and lying a few feet beyond, the door to the spare bedroom; the same door she had made such a point of keeping firmly closed in recent days.

The door that was now hanging open.

Fran felt a sudden jolt of cold spread throughout her body, a chill so potent that even the hot bathwater did nothing to dispel it. Clutching at the gooseflesh rippling across her bare arms, she stared over at the door with mounting unease, busily trying to convince herself that there was a perfectly logical explanation for it being open. A draught blowing in from the storm outside, perhaps, or maybe Will had wandered in there and left the door ajar without her noticing.

But however much she attempted to rationalize it, Fran's discovery of the open door had also ushered in another fear: the all-too familiar belief that she was being watched. However impossible it might have seemed, she now felt certain that the bedroom door had been opened from *inside*, permitting whoever or whatever had been hiding there to creep stealthily out along the hallway and lurk unseen behind the bathroom entrance.

She imagined the intruder crouching in readiness, slyly peering at her through the crack in the doorway. Leering at Fran's rosy nakedness, her helpless vulnerability.

Stifling a shriek, she scrambled out of the bathtub and half-ran, half-fell across the room. Tumbling bodily against the bathroom door, she slammed it closed with her shoulder, fingers frantically scrabbling to slide the lock into place.

Even after Fran was satisfied the door was properly secured, she remained in position for several more minutes, her naked back pressed firmly against the woodwork, legs pulled tight against her chest. Only when her paranoia gradually began to diminish did she at last notice the sharp nip of the air against her unclothed skin. Shivering, she relinquished her post and hurriedly wrapped herself in a bathrobe.

Still wary, she pressed her ear against the door and listened, hearing nothing. There was no evidence at all to suggest that there was anyone waiting in the hallway outside; of course, there never had been. If pressed, Fran knew she could not possibly argue that her fears had the slightest basis in reality, none of which lessened her fierce conviction that these fears were entirely justified.

It took her several more seconds to summon sufficient courage to unlock and open the door, and when she finally did so, she found nothing waiting for her save for an empty hallway.

The door to the spare bedroom remained tauntingly ajar, but it was just an open doorway, wasn't it? If this had been a story from one of her ghostly podcasts, she might perhaps have witnessed the door creak open of its own volition, propelled by invisible hands. But Fran could make no such claim.

However, she knew she had to do *something,* and quickly. Mind racing, she glanced back over her shoulder, her eyes falling upon the selection of lighted candles arranged around the bathtub's rim.

And then it came to her.

After putting her clothes back on, Fran dashed downstairs to fetch a box of tools. Duly equipped, she made her way back up to the spare bedroom. With some trepidation, she pushed the door the rest of the way open and craned her neck to peer inside, finding the room to be just as deserted as the hallway had been.

Stepping across the threshold, she began to rummage through the contents of the toolbox, selecting a couple of different sizes of screwdriver, and, after some consideration, a large hammer. Turning to face the door, Fran lashed out with one foot to kick it closed, bringing the repugnant message into view.

She felt something twist in her stomach, and quickly looked away.

Taking a firm grip upon the hammer, she began to violently smash it against the back of the door, rapidly reducing the cheap wood to a jagged crater. Within moments, the words scratched into its surface had been almost entirely banished from existence.

Fran told herself it was not enough.

In the next bedroom, she could hear Toby beginning to cry, his sleep rudely interrupted by the racket she was making. Fran ignored him. Dropping the hammer to the floor, she took one of the screwdrivers and set about dismantling the door's hinges.

Minutes later, the ruined door lay propped against the wall. Meanwhile, Toby continued to wail in the next room, his mother's stubborn refusal to answer his screams provoking them to ever greater levels.

"MUMMY'S BUSY!" Fran yelled.

Ignoring the resultant bellow from her son, she grabbed the edges of the door with both hands and began to maneuver it out into the hallway, heading in the direction of the nearby staircase.

"FRAN, WHAT THE HELL are you doing?" Will demanded.

She glanced away from the dancing flames to find her husband standing at her shoulder, a sniveling Toby clutched tightly in his arms. The reddish light given off by the bonfire lent Will's features a malevolent, almost demonic cast, and she instantly turned her attention back to the burning door. "What does it look like?" she replied softly.

"I get home to find Toby screaming at the top of his lungs, his nappy completely soaked, and you're nowhere to be seen! And then I find you in the bloody back garden of all places, burning a pile of god knows what!" His eyes moved to the bonfire. "Hang on, is that the bedroom *door?*"

Fran nodded absently.

"Jesus." Momentarily lost for words, Will shifted Toby to his other shoulder. "Would you mind explaining all this to me?"

She sighed. "I don't really feel like going into it right now. Long story short, you said you'd take care of it and you didn't. So I did."

"This is all about that stupid bloody graffiti?"

"It's about a lot of things." Fran could feel Will's eyes upon her back, glaring at her accusingly. If only she could escape somewhere far away from here, someplace quiet and isolated where she would not find herself being continually stared at and harried.

"And what about our son?" Will snapped. "Are these other things more important than him?"

"Look, I'm sorry about Toby," she replied wearily. "I thought he'd be okay for twenty minutes while I came outside." Fran turned to face her husband, her arms reaching out for the baby. "I can take him now."

Will took a step backwards, his arms tightening protectively around Toby. "He's fine with me," he muttered.

He thinks I'm nuts, Fran thought. *And really, why shouldn't he?*

She gave a tired shrug. "Okay."

"I just don't understand, Fran," he said, abruptly turning back towards the house. "I really don't understand any of it."

Fran considered admitting that she didn't either, but decided that might only make matters worse. So instead she said nothing, watching mutely as her husband retreated inside the house and slammed the back door, casting her out into the gathering darkness.

She and Will hardly spoke for the remainder of the evening. When Fran served up dinner, he wordlessly took his plate and went to sit over at his desk, picking disinterestedly at the meal while he worked. She ate hers in front of the television, caring little whether the background chatter of the evening news proved at all distracting to him.

By the time Toby's bedtime came around, Fran decided she'd had more than enough of the silent cold war that had taken hold of the house. After putting her son down for the night, she changed into her pajamas and crawled into bed with a book, intending to read herself to sleep.

But fifteen minutes later, just as she was considering turning the light off, the bedroom door slowly creaked open and Will tiptoed into the room. He gazed down at Fran, his face unreadable. "I thought you might be asleep," he murmured.

She closed her book. "Nearly was."

He stood there, apparently trying to decide what to say next. His eyes moved over to their sleeping son, then back to Fran. "Look, I'm sorry about the door, okay?" he told her with a sigh. "I still don't understand, but I said I'd take care of it and I didn't, and I'm sorry."

"It doesn't matter," Fran replied.

"Well, clearly it does." Will sat down on the bed beside her. "Do you want to talk about it?"

"Not really." She rubbed at her eyes. "I'd honestly rather just forget about the whole thing, if that's okay."

Fran could sense his unspoken frustration. "If you want, sure," Will said. He reached out and hesitantly took her hand. "Are you okay? Really?"

She managed a wan smile. "I am now, yeah."

"Okay, good." He leaned in and gently kissed her cheek. "Love you."

"Love you too." Reaching up to pull Will close, she kissed him on the mouth. "Very much."

They kissed again, several times. Suddenly wanting him, Fran tried to coax her husband into bed, only to find him resisting her.

"Sorry," he mumbled, pulling away from his wife's embrace. "It's been a long day. And Rob messaged to say he can't do the shoot tomorrow, so now I have to get up first thing and cover for him."

"Sure," Fran said, slumping back upon the mattress and tugging the covers over her body. "It's fine."

Will got up and ambled round to the other side of the bed. Stepping out of his jeans, he gave her an apologetic look. "Another night, okay? When we're both less tired."

"No problem," she said, reaching over to turn off the bedside light.

BUT LATER THAT NIGHT, Fran awoke to find her husband nestling closer to her back, his eager hands reaching over to caress her. As she emerged slowly from sleep, she could feel a pleasant warmth blossoming in her belly.

Fran reached behind to draw him closer, feeling the rasp of his stubble on her cheek, his warm breath ruffling her tangled hair. He kissed tenderly at her neck, his torso pressed tightly against hers. His fingers continued to explore her body, and she closed her eyes, surrendering herself to the pleasure she felt.

"Oh Will," she said.

His lips brushed her earlobe, moving to whisper into her ear.

But when Will spoke, his breath suddenly sour against her face, it was in a voice that did not remotely resemble his own.

"I am going to kill you, Trudi," he whispered.

Fran's limbs stiffened. They might have been carved from solid ice, rendering her utterly powerless, her body immovable as a glacier. She wanted to cry out, to scream for help, but her voice remained caught in the tunnel of her throat, like a penny tossed into the dark depths of a wishing well.

If he carries on touching me I might lose my mind, she thought. *It would be better if he did just kill me.*

But in the end, Will did neither. Laying a final parting kiss upon her cheek, he simply rolled over to the other side of the bed and slipped straight back into sleep. To Fran's ears, his contented snoring sounded almost like mockery.

She lay there listening to her husband breathe for the rest of the night, unable to bring herself to move for fear of disturbing him. Fran could not decide which might be worse; for Will to wake and again address her in that same hateful whisper, a borrowed sneer belonging to another man entirely; or for him to appear completely normal, thereby casting her own treacherous senses into doubt once more.

At 7am the next morning, the alarm clock commenced its steady whine, and she felt Will stir beside her. Feigning sleep, Fran kept her eyes tightly closed as he shut off the alarm and leaned over to gently kiss her forehead. Fortunately for her, Toby was not awoken by the sound of the clock, allowing Fran to safely continue her deception until her husband had dressed and gone downstairs.

After he'd exited the bedroom, she opened her eyes and lay staring at the cracks in the ceiling, wondering what on earth to do next. Remaining where she was seemed inconceivable, but what was the alternative? Quickly realizing that she was far too tired and anxious to think matters through coherently, Fran decided her only immediate option was to take Toby and flee to her parents' place on the coast. Once she was a safe distance from the house, from Will, she might be able to discern her situation more clearly.

As soon as she heard her husband leave for the day, she leapt out of bed and hurriedly dressed. Rushing to throw some clothes for her and Toby into a travel bag, she plucked her half-awake son from his crib and ferried him downstairs, where she fixed them both a cursory breakfast. As Toby grumpily began to deposit most of his own meal upon the kitchen floor, Fran attempted to phone her parents, only for the call to go to voicemail. She left them a deliberately cheery message saying that she and Toby were coming to visit for a few days, offering no explanation for the suddenness of the arrangement.

I'll think of something to tell them while we're on the train, Fran told herself.

Within a couple of hours, mother and son had arrived at the main city terminal, ready to catch their connection to the coast. After buying herself a coffee and some sweets for Toby, Fran was ready and waiting on the platform when the train pulled in, free to take her pick of the empty seats. Snatching up her bags, she beat a hasty path to the very last carriage. It had been several days since she'd last felt truly alone, and Fran found herself desperately craving solitude.

I don't want anyone to look at me or speak to me, she thought. *I just want to disappear.*

So fervent was her desire to be left alone that Fran even ignored the buzz of her mobile phone when her mother tried to return her call a few minutes later. Pocketing the phone, she turned her attention to Toby, waving a packet of chocolate buttons in front of his face. "Do you want a sweetie?" she chirruped. "I'll bet you do."

Toby eagerly reached out for the sweets, his chubby little hands clutching at the air.

Fran teasingly pulled them away. "Say 'Ta,' Toby. 'Ta.'"

"Emememememem," Toby burbled.

Fran tugged the sweet packet open and pulled out a piece of chocolate, waving it before his eyes. "Come on, you can do it. 'Ta, Mummy. *Ta.*'" She felt the train jerk into life underneath her, and gave her son a broad smile. "We're going to see Granny and Grandpa at the seaside, isn't that exciting?"

"Gogogogogogog," Toby agreed.

"That's right!" Fran exclaimed. "*Going.* You clever boy."

She popped the sweet into his mouth, watching indulgently as he messily devoured it. Feeling her phone vibrate again, she removed it from her pocket to discover a worried text message from her mother: *Is everything ok xx.*

Just fine! Fran typed, recoiling at her own dishonesty. *Looking forward to seeing u both xx*

The reply sent, her gaze drifted to the view through the rain-streaked train window, the clustered inner-city buildings dissolving into a watery blur. Soon she would be free of the city, freed from all the anxiety and anger and hostility which thrived here like poisonous fungi.

It would be fine. It *would.*

Having swallowed the morsel of chocolate, Toby promptly made another grab for the packet. Laughing, Fran tugged it away from his grasp.

"Who's a greedy little boy?" she told him. "If you want another sweetie, you have to ask politely. Say 'Ta.' 'Ta.'"

Toby frowned up at her. "Te. Te."

"Nearly, Toby! 'Ta.'"

Abruptly, a satisfied smile crept across his plump features: a smile that surely appeared much too sly for such a small child; a mere baby who, thank god, as yet knew nothing at all of malevolence or cunning.

Or so Fran vainly tried to tell herself, as she listened in horror to the next word to escape her son's lips.

"*Truuuudi*," Toby said happily.

Sean Hogan is a writer and filmmaker based in the UK. He has published several books of cinema metafiction, including England's Screaming *and its sequel* Twilight's Last Screaming *(each named as one of the five best genre novels of their year by* The Financial Times*),* Three Mothers, One Father, *and* That Fatal Shore. *His feature film credits include* The Devil's Business, The Borderlands, *the documentary* Future Shock! The Story of 2000AD, *and most recently, the critically-acclaimed folk horror* To Fire You Come at Last. *He is currently in pre-production on his next film,* Scenes From A Young Girl's Disappearance, *and his new novel* The Corpse Road *will be published in late 2024.*

GRAB NIGHTMARE ABBEY 2 — BEFORE IT GRABS YOU!

THE ORIGINAL SWAMP THING: THEODORE STURGEON'S "IT"

NIGHTMARE ABBEY

WINTER SOLSTICE 2022

②

STEVE DUFFY
HELEN GRANT
DAVID SURFACE
ALLEN KOSZOWSKI
GREGORY L. NORRIS
EDWARD LUCAS WHITE
GARY FRY ☠ JAMES DORR
JOHN LLEWELLYN PROBERT   GARY GERANI REMEMBERS
KURT NEWTON ☠ MATT COWAN   BORIS KARLOFF'S *THRILLER*

JOHN M. NAVROTH'S
FEAR IN FOUR COLORS

HEH! HEH! GREETINGS ALL YOU HUMAN CRITTERS! ARE YA' READY TO SLITHER AND CRAWL AROUND HERE FOR A SPELL? WELL, YUR IN LUCK SICKO'S 'CAUSE WHATCHA GOT BETWEEN YUR MOLDY MITTS IS THE NEXT *BELCH!* CHAPTER ABOUT THOSE FOUR-COLOR TOMES OF FEAR CALLED *GASP!* HORROR COMICS! FOR THE NEXT FEW OF THESE MUMMY RAGS CALLED PAGES YUR GONNA FIND OUT JES' HOW THESE PUTRID THINGS GOT *COUGH!* STARTED! AND IF YOU HAVEN'T GOTTEN REVOLTIN'LY ILL BY NOW *RETCH!* JES' START READIN'! HEE! HEE! *GAK!*

NOW, GO ON AND ENJOY THIS *CROAK!" MOLDY MISSIVE. AS YOU CAN SEE, I'VE GOT OTHER THINGS TO DO!

YOU FILTHY BEAST!

GHOSTLY

JOHN M. NAVROTH'S
FEAR IN FOUR COLORS

THE HIDEOUS HISTORY OF AMERICAN HORROR COMICS

#2- THE PRE-CODE PLAGUE

SHALL WE TIP-TOE A LITTLE DEEPER INTO THE MURKY SWAMP OF HORROR COMICS? We're still splashing around in the era known as "pre-code" horror, that period where horror comics eventually became untamed—and some would say dangerous—with their depictions of the gruesome and gory. These excesses inevitably fell under scrutiny by the government and medical profession's "decency police" that were running rampant at the time, eventually causing horror comics to be summarily dispatched with an unbending stake of morality through their blood-soaked pages.

Master of Monsters" was another mad scientist who, in his first episode, experimented with glandular transplants to make an ape-like monster out of a man, reminiscent of Bela Lugosi's Dr. Mirakle in Universal Pictures' 1932 shocker, *The Murders in the Rue Morgue*. After a second story in *Prize Comics* #6, the evil doctor disappeared from its pages, even with a last-panel teaser announcing his return. The stories were scripted by an unknown writer, but the artwork was prominently

BEFORE WE CROSS the moss-covered planks of Deadman's Bridge, there are a couple more items floating around in the muck to cover from our last trip.

Dick Briefer's Frankenstein stories were discussed last issue, but *Prize Comics* had another horror series quietly tucked away between its covers. In issue #5 (July 1940) a new villain was introduced in what was initially planned as a continuing series. Much like Jack Kirby's "The Diary of Dr. Hayward" in *Jumbo Comics*, "Dr. Dekkar,

signed by "Cardwell." Unlike most of the other artists mentioned here who worked for years or their entire career in the field, Cardwell Higgins worked for only a short time in comics and his entire output was with Prize. Besides drawing the two Dr. Dekkar entries, he illustrated just a few *Secret Agent M-11* stories. He showed promise as a comic book artist, but the career-minded Mr. Cardwell preferred to turn his talents to the more lucrative fields of advertising, glamour, and pinup art.

More of a fantasy/adventure comic than a horror comic, *Mask Comics* lured readers to their short-lived title with two mind-bending, and one might say psychedelic, covers from the masterful brush of L.B. Cole. Both issues were published by Rural Home Publishing Co. in 1945.

Now, it's time to cross that bridge into the next pool of ooze. Careful of your shaking knees...

It is often stated that Entertaining Comics (EC) published the first-ever horror comic books, but that is incorrect, as you will soon see. Regardless of that assumption, it was only inevitable that the day would come when someone would think to publish a cover-to-cover horror comic that didn't rely on books from dead authors, pulp fiction, or radio shows for their content. The day came less than two years after the end of the Second World War when an up-and-coming book publisher took up the challenge.

Acknowledged as the first all-new, all-horror comic that contained all original stories, *Eerie Comics* was published in January 1947 by the comic book division of Avon Books and cost a dime. Using simple lines, the effective cover by Bob Fujitani depicts a malicious-looking monk-like figure approaching an archetypal "damsel in distress" with a (sacrificial?) dagger grasped in his hand. The pretty brunette (in a red cocktail dress, no less) is swooning before him, fearfully anticipating her fate. Some have commented that the image shows her in a bondage pose, however, under closer inspection the arrangement of her body and the way the "restraints" are positioned renders the suggestion ambiguous. As a result, it may have been an attempt (or a possible edit) by the artist to instead, cleverly *imply* bondage. Granted, it's not a hard assumption to make as numerous horror comic covers and interior panels (and crime comics, too) not only depicted bondage scenes, but were clearly explicit about it. Even Superman co-creator Joe Shuster drew for a now-forgotten early BDSM comic named *Nights of Horror* in 1954 when he was down on his luck. Other tropes seen in the cover image are a full moon in the background that frames the villain and dilapidated columns and cracked concrete tiles that convey the scene as taking place on the grounds of an ancient mausoleum.

Bob Fujitani

Avon Books was founded in 1941 by the American News Company in New York to compete with Pocket Books, the leading publisher of paperbacks at the time. Headed by the brother and sister team of Joseph and Edna Meyers, one of their marketing strategies was to install over two hundred coin-operated vending machines in local airports, hospitals, and ferry terminals where a customer could buy a paperback on the spot for 25 cents. In 1945, they began to print comic books, and for the next decade, published over 100 titles in all the popular genres, including humor, westerns, romance, and adventure. Today, Avon comics are best remembered for their science-fiction, horror, and so-called "esoteric" titles such as *An Earthman on Venus*, *Robot Men of the Lost Planet*, *Diary of Horror*, *Phantom Witch Doctor*, *Slave Girl*, and *Gangsters and Gun Molls*. As early as the 1970s, Avon comics became a highly valuable imprint among collectors. For example, on March 30, 2023, a copy of *Eerie Comics* #1 in a sealed CGC clamshell case graded at 9.2 out of 10 sold at auction for $108,000.

The blood and gore would come later, but *Eerie* establishes some of the hallmarks of pre-code horror comics with bizarre and terrifying deaths, not unlike those seen in crime comics during the same period. As the precursor to the proliferation of horror comics titles that would be seen in a few years, it appeared six months before William Gaines became publisher of Educational Comics (later Entertaining Comics) after his father, Max Gaines, was killed in a boating accident. Moreover, it appeared three years before the EC "New Trend" titles, *Tales from the Crypt, The Vault of Horror,* and *The Haunt of Fear.*

So what's inside this landmark issue? So far as the stories go, Henry Kuttner is the only credited script writer. Kuttner and his

Joseph Meyers

wife, writer C.L. Moore were members of the "Lovecraft Circle," a group of authors who corresponded with H.P. Lovecraft in the 1920s. Besides writing many science-fiction, fantasy, and horror short stories and novels, Kuttner wrote numerous scripts for National Periodicals' (DC) *Green Lantern* comic book in the 1940s. Several prominent authors have cited Kuttner as an influence, such as science-fiction author Marion Zimmer Bradley and frequent *Weird Tales* contributor, Mary Elizabeth Counselman. Richard Matheson dedicated his 1954 vampire novel, *I Am Legend* to him, and even William S. Burroughs used direct quotes from Kuttner's novel *Fury* in one of his books.

As mentioned, Bob Fujitani is credited for the cover art, as well as penciling and inking the story that opens the issue, "The Eyes of the Tiger" (reprinted in

THE EYES OF THE TIGER

CARL CATTLER LOVED BEASTS OF THE FELINE STRIPE, AND THEY RETURNED THIS AFFECTION...FOR THE MOST PART. EVERY-THING WAS LOVEY-DOVEY UNTIL CARL MADE ONE *SERIOUS MISTAKE!* AFTER THAT, HE SAW NOTHING BUT THE *"EYES OF THE TIGER"!*

Avon's *Flying Saucers* #1, 1950). He was known as an "artist's artist" for his versatility in drawing both comic books and syndicated newspaper strips. After beginning his career as a teenager at the Eisner shop, he worked for a multitude of publishing houses, including Marvel, Dell, Harvey, MLJ, Fawcett, and Hillman. He is particularly noted as the co-creator and artist who drew the first five issues of Dell's *Dr. Solar, Man of the Atom*. He was an admirer of Alex Raymond and had the opportunity to work as his ghost artist on the *Flash Gordon* and *Rip Kirby* strips. Fujitani was Japanese-American and during the war years thought it wise to disguise his last name by signing it with his pseudonyms, Bob Fuje or Bob Wells.

Jon Small penciled the second story "Dead Man's Tale" (reprinted in Avon's *Out of This World Adventures* #2, December 1950). Born in the UK, he came across the pond to work in the US comics industry from the mid-1930s to the mid-'50s. He was the first artist to draw Bulletman, one of the very early comic book superheroes. George Roussos provided the brush work for the story. Known by the nickname of "Inky," his body of work over a long career was mainly as an inker and colorist. Roussos assisted Bob Kane with backgrounds and lettering on the *Batman* comic strip and was a part-time letterer for other titles while at DC in the 1940s. Roussos later worked on the EC titles, *Tales from the Crypt, Weird Science, Weird Fantasy* and *Crime SuspenStories*. He succeeded Marie Severin as Marvel's house colorist from the 1960s to the 1990s. In the 1970s he worked for a short time for Warren Publications, inking stories

in *Creepy, Eerie,* and *Vampirella.*

Joe Kubert penciled and inked "The Man-Eating Lizards" (reprinted in Avon's *Out of This World Adventures* #1, July 1950). Kubert was one of the most prolific and widely respected artists in comics. He began his professional career in the 1940s with Holyoke and is best remembered for his expressive and dramatic work at DC, drawing characters such as Hawkman, Sgt. Rock, and Enemy Ace. He founded The Joe Kubert School of Cartoon and Graphic Art in 1976.

Fred Kida illustrated "The Strange Case of Henpecked Harry." Kida had a comics career that spanned nearly half-a-century. Like his old classmate, Bob Fujitani, Kida was Japanese-American. (He did not opt for a name change like Fujitani.) He worked for many publishers, including the Iger Studio, Quality, Hillman, Lev Gleason, and

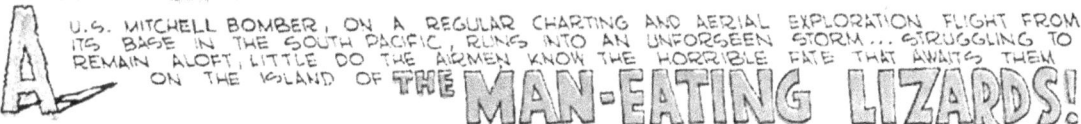

Joe Kubert

Marvel's Atlas line. Kida also worked on syndicated comic strips such as *Flash Gordon* and *Steve Canyon*. Kida died in 2014 at the age of 93, and was one of the last surviving artists from the Golden Age era of comics. "Henpecked Harry" was re-titled to the more spooky "The Subway Horror" when it was reprinted in Avon's *Eerie Comics* #15 (April-May 1954) and I.W. Publishing's *Super Comics* #12 (1964).

With the exception of a two-page humor short, "Goofy Ghost," "Mystery of Murder Manor" is the remaining story from this issue. As yet, there are no credits given to the writer and artist.

In the fall of 1948, a new comic appeared on the stands with the inviting title, *Adventures into the Unknown!* (the exclamation mark was dropped in issue #59). It has the distinction of being the first on-going, all-original, all-horror comic. Published by B&I Publications (later changed to the American Comics Group, or ACG with issue #4) they did not rely on radio shows or previously-published titles, and instead based their stories on monsters and the supernatural, especially ghosts. It seemed to catch on with readers who kept the letters page full of lively comments.

So, at this point one may ask, "Were there any EC horror comics published yet?" and the answer is no. During this same period, EC was publishing *Crime Patrol,*

Gunfighter, and *War Against Crime,* with the minor exception of a horror story that appeared in their one-and-only superhero comic, *Moon Girl* #5 (Fall 1948). The oddly-placed story, "Zombie Terror," was scripted by Richard Kraus and featured some of Johnny Craig's early work for EC. Normally overlooked by horror comic historians, Moon Girl faced a vampire in the previous issue in the story, "Vampire of the Bayous!" Rather tepid fare, it nevertheless deals with the legendary supernatural bloodsucker, but with a twist; when the creature is killed, it changes back in to its human form, a cliché that is usually reserved for a werewolf.

ACG Comics has a long and circuitous history. After a decade of selling salacious "French novels" and "medical" sex books, Benjamin W. Sangor entered the comics business when his son-in-law, Ned Pines, needed more artwork for his busy comic book company. Sangor had some friends in

Fred Kida

Hollywood who were in the cartoon animation business and he hired them to produce off-the-clock artwork to supply to Pines. He also employed a separate group of writers and artists who collectively became known as the Sangor Shop. In 1943, Sangor founded the American Comics Group and began publishing his own "funny animal" comics under the imprint Creston. In 1946, Fred Iger (no relation to Jerry), who was part owner of National Periodical Publications (DC), became part owner of Sangor's company, and assumed full ownership from 1953 until the early 1960s. At that time Harry Donenfeld (who earlier had published the first Superman and Batman comics) took over co-ownership until the company folded in 1967. One more note on Ben Sangor: described as a "distinguished-looking, pleasant man," he nevertheless published and distributed what was then considered pornography (albeit the soft type), as well as being sued more than once and tried and convicted for fraud and embezzlement. For that he spent eighteen months in jail (more details on this later in this series).

In the early 1940s, Richard E. Hughes was the co-creator of several Golden Age heroes for Pines, including The Black Terror

Ben Sangor

and Fighting Yank. He was hired as the editor and business manager of ACG from 1944 until 1967 and edited the entire 147-issue run of *Adventures into the Unknown*. An individual of many talents, he later wrote scripts for *Adventures*, as well as other ACG titles. Considered alternately a "tyrant," a "good editor" and a "friend," in many ways he was the heart and soul of the company and had a hand in nearly all aspects of guiding the many titles that were produced during his tenure. He was always even-handed with the editing of ACG's horror stories and eschewed the excessively lurid and gruesome elements that were elsewhere escalating throughout the industry. It is likely because of his "horror light" story policy that *Adventures* managed to survive the Senate Subcommittee on Juvenile Delinquency hearings of April and June 1954 and the subsequent

Harry Donenfeld

Richard E. Hughes

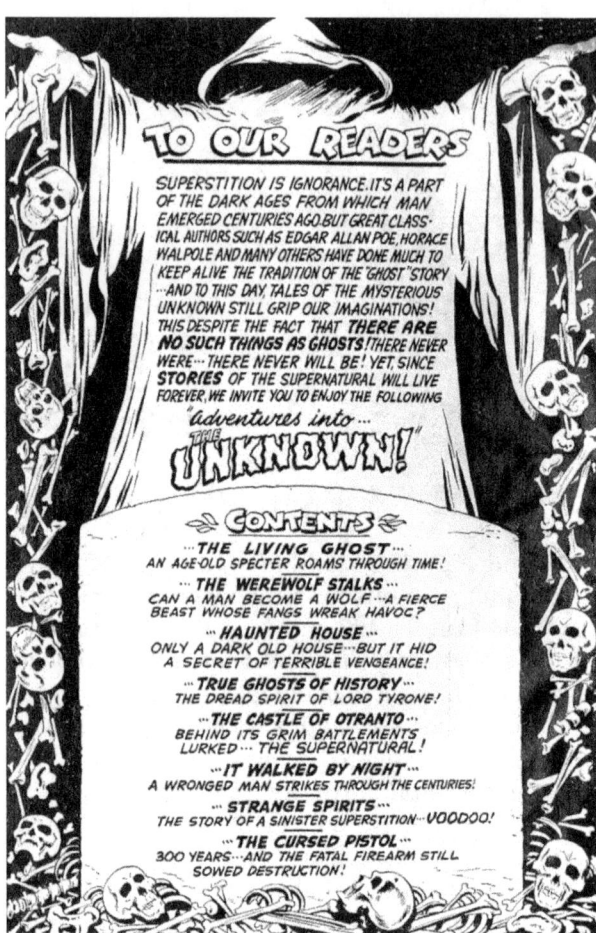

Frank Belknap Long is the only author with confirmed writing credits in the inaugural issue of *Adventures*. Long had a career that spanned 70 years. Like Kuttner, he was a close friend of H.P. Lovecraft and was one of the few people that Lovecraft personally encouraged to expand on his so-called Cthulhu Mythos cycle of stories. His first sale was to *Weird Tales* and over the years he had countless stories and novels published primarily in the science-fiction, fantasy, and weird fiction genres. He began writing for comics in the 1940s and scripted for titles such as *Superman*, *Green Lantern*, *Captain Marvel,* and *Planet Comics*. He effused to his friend and fellow Lovecraft devotee, August Derleth, by saying he thought of Hughes as a "high-grade man with knowledge of the field of horror, fantasy, and science-fiction, and that he considered ACG to be imaginative, sensitive, and discerning." It is ironic that Derleth (who coined the term "Cthulhu Mythos") had one of his stories plagiarized by an ACG writer, which appeared to have unknowingly slipped by Hughes.

purge of horror comics perpetrated by the Comics Code Authority later that same year. In his article "The American Comics Group: A Sentimental Favorite," Edwin Murray describes ACG's post-code formula that aligned them with the Code's aspirations and kept them out of trouble:

> *The main character is introduced and the first part of the story establishes his character and what his problem is. Then a fantastic element is introduced, and the rest of the story follows him as he overcomes the challenges he is faced with. It is not uncommon for the hero to win by dying a heroic death. At ACG, a near majority of the stories dealt with one of life's losers getting a chance [or a second chance] to make good.*

Hughes left comics in the 1960s and sadly he ended his otherwise brilliant career by writing replies to customer complaints for Gimbel's Department Store in New York.

Dan Gordon designed the imaginative inside front cover title page. Gordon drew comics, but for most of his career he worked in the field of cartoon animation under Max Fleischer, MGM, and Hanna-Barbera.

As a sort of disclaimer, the short preface (presumably written by Hughes) lays the template for the title's editorial philosophy and bears repeating:

> "To Our Readers: Superstition is ignorance. It's a part of the Dark Ages from which man emerged centuries ago. But great classical authors such as Edgar Allan Poe, Horace Walpole and many others have done much to keep alive the tradition of the 'ghost story'... and to this day, tales of the mysterious unknown still grip our imaginations! This despite the fact that there are no such things as ghosts! There never were... there never will be! Yet, since stories of the supernatural will live forever, we invite you to enjoy the following 'Adventures into the Unknown!'"

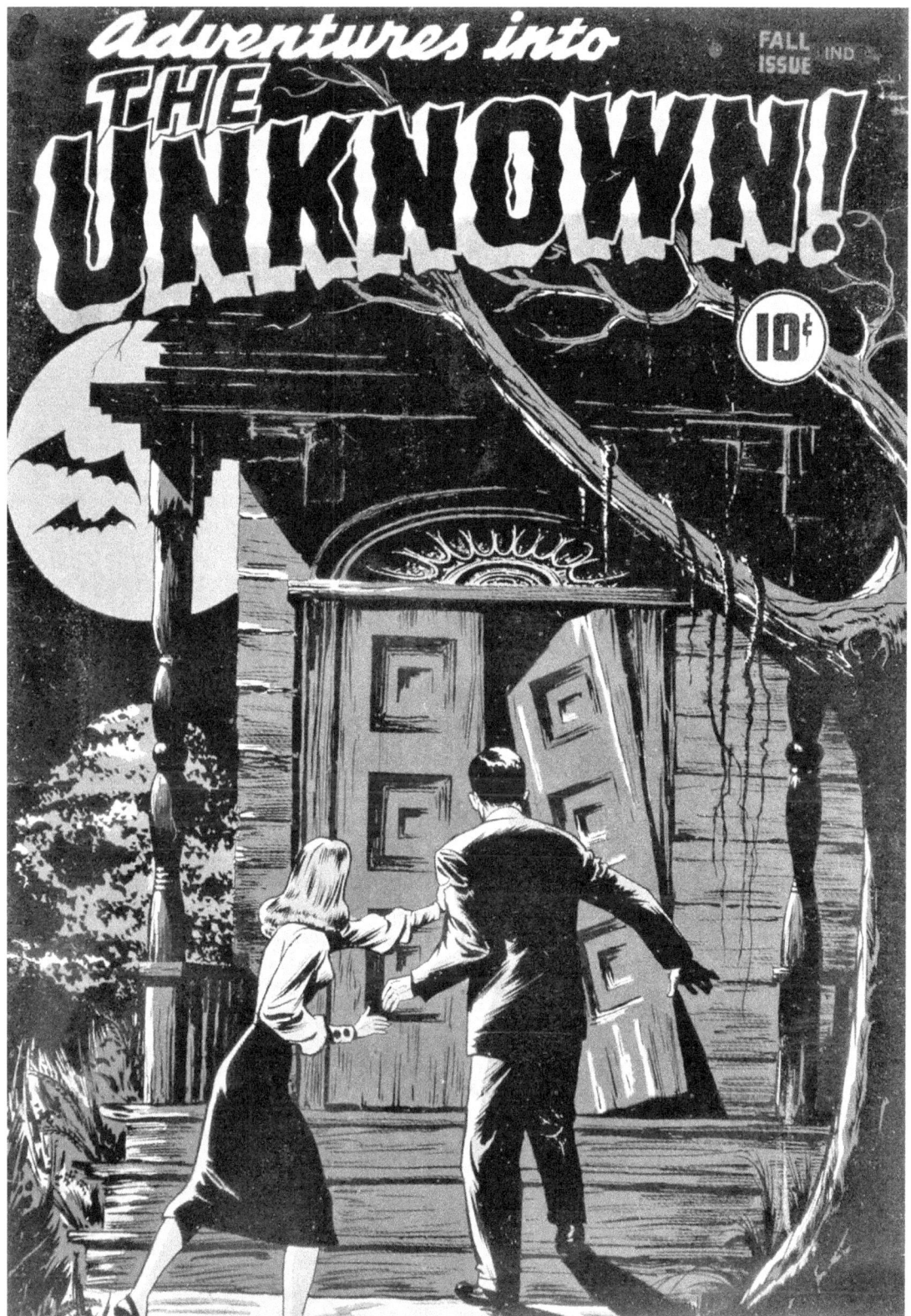

Again, it is quite possible that this long-held premise of "mild" instead of "wild" kept *Adventures* from being on the Comics Code chopping block throughout its nearly 150 issues of publication.

Edvard "Ed" Moritz penciled and inked the lead story, "The Werewolf Stalks," as well as the single-pager "The Cursed Pistol" and

The next story, "It Walked By Night" was drawn and inked by Max Elkin. Elkin worked at the Iger Shop, Quality, and Fiction House before his work with ACG.

Under the heading "Tell Me a Ghost Story" was Frank Belknap Long's adaptation of Horace Walpole's *The Castle of Otranto* (generally regarded as the first gothic novel ever written). Drawn and inked by Allen Ulmer, it suffered from being only a seven-page story of a book that has a lot going on in it. Ulmer began his art career in magazine illustration. In the 1940s, he drew numerous comics for

"The Vengeful Specter of Lord Tyrone" (under the heading "True Ghosts of History"). Moritz was a prolific comic book artist who worked primarily for Pines and ACG. In addition to horror, his subjects included superheroes, westerns, romance, and crime.

Fred Guardineer penciled and inked the second story, "The Living Ghost," a tale of Malevo, the devil's lieutenant, who walks the earth searching for a queen. Guardineer began his comics career in 1938 working for the Harry "A" Chesler shop. Among others, he also worked for Centaur, Quality, Hillman, Pines, and Lev Gleason before retiring from the field at the age of 42 and becoming a civil servant. Malevo, The Living Ghost appeared again in the second issue of *Adventures*. With the promise of a continuing series it was abruptly dropped after issue #2.

CAN A WEIRD INCANTATION PIERCE THE VEIL OF THE UNKNOWN ···BRING THE LONG-DEAD TO THE SERVICE OF A GHOSTLY MASTER!

WATCH!

MEANWHILE, TONY ISN'T GIVING UP! DESPERATELY HUNTING FOR SOME SIGN OF **THE LIVING GHOST'S** TRAIL, HE SEARCHES THE SCENE OF THE LAST MURDER! AND SUDDENLY HE SEES···

H-HOLY HANNAH! WHAT···

8.

Holyoke, Eastern Color, Hillman, Avon, and others before turning his talent to the fine arts.

The last story of the issue, "Haunted House" was penciled and inked by King Ward. Ward drew for a number of small comic book companies, but his major output was with ACG. Later in his career he became a magazine illustrator.

Besides Ed Moritz's "The Cursed Pistol," included in this issue was another one-page filler, "Strange Spirits." It covers the topic of Voodoo, although it has the usual inaccuracies and sensationalism of the period. The features "True Ghosts of History" and "Strange Spirits" would reappear occasionally after the first issue, but both eventually died on the vine.

Worth noting is another series that ran in the pages of *Adventures* titled "Spirit of Frankenstein." A modern re-imagining of Mary Shelley's original story, all episodes were penciled and inked by Charles Sultan. The series appeared in issues 5–6, 8–10, 12 and 16.

Adventures into the Unknown was published from its Fall issue in 1948 until the last cover date of August 1967. After that, ACG shuttered its doors as a publisher for good.

The next comic to surface from the swamp of horror was *Mysterious Traveler*. Published by Trans-World Publications in

November 1948, it is mentioned frequently as an early horror comic, but it was far from "horrific." Inspired by the Mutual Broadcasting Network radio show of the same name, the story is based on one of the radio scripts. Illustrated by Bob Powell it relies more on mystery elements than horror.

CONTINUED ON PAGE 99

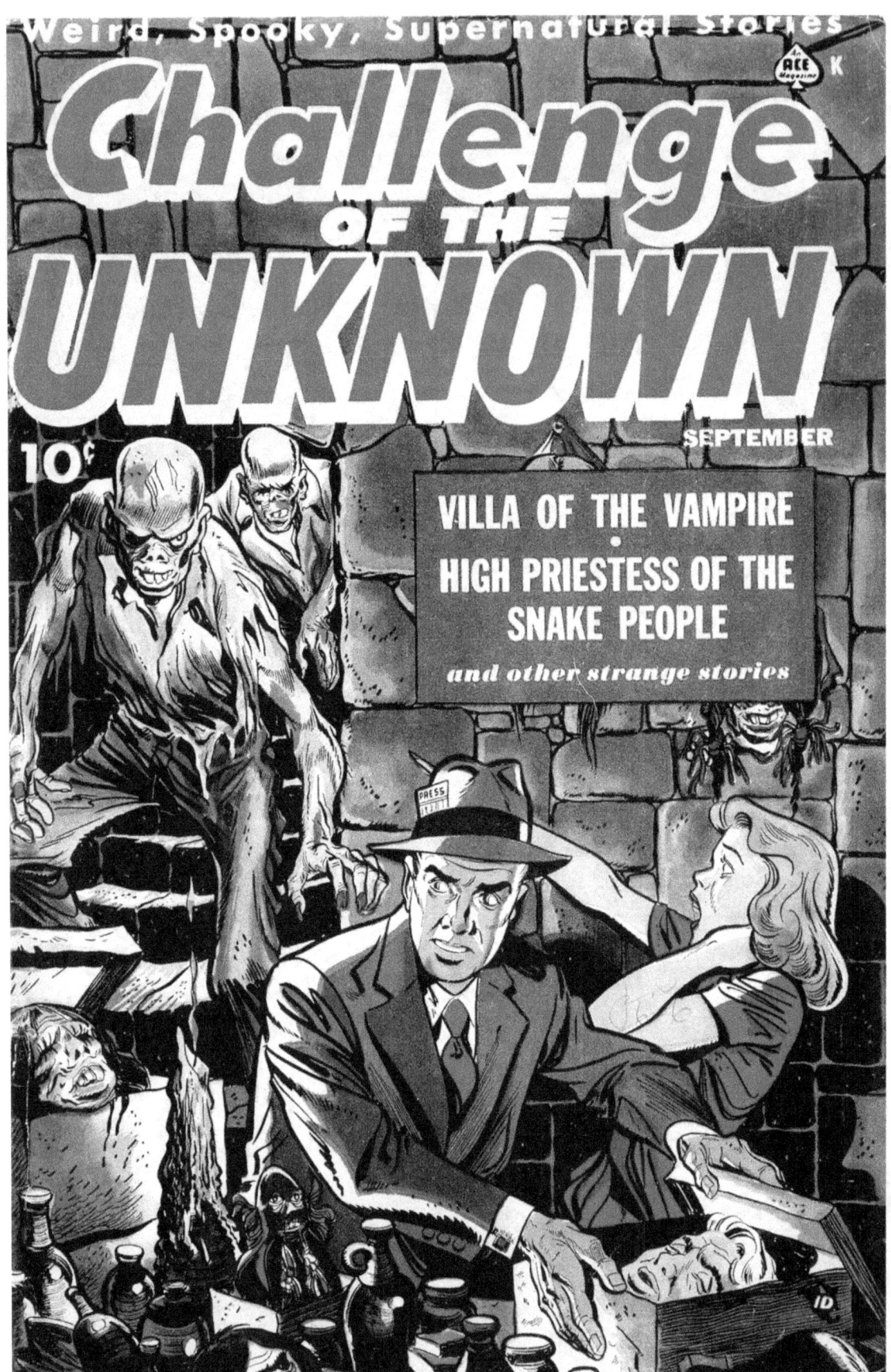

What tangentially qualifies *Mysterious Traveler* as a horror comic is the "Tales of Terror" feature in the second part of the issue that adapts Edgar Allan Poe's "The Tell-Tale Heart." If this story looks familiar, it is because it's a reprint from *Yellowjacket Comics* #6 from three years earlier (see *Nightmare Abbey* #4). Announced as a quarterly, it appears to have been an attempt by the radio network to break into the field of comics but it never made it past the first issue. Charlton would later publish a 15-issue series with original stories, *Tales of the Mysterious Traveler* from 1956 to 1985.

The one-shot *Challenge of the Unknown* (Ace, September 1950) is the next in line on the now-growing list of early horror comics. Interrupting the purple prose of the first five issues of *Love Experiences*, Ace sought to hitch their wagon to the success of ACG's *Adventures into the Unknown* introduced a year before, even going so far as to include the word "Unknown" in their title. They included the heading, "Weird, Spooky, Supernatural Stories" to inform potential buyers that this was not a typical "mystery book."

Assuming ownership of pulp-pioneer Harold Hersey's Magazine Publishers in 1928 by Aaron and Rose Wyn, the husband and wife team continued to publish a slew of pulp magazines for the next two decades. Headquartered in Springfield, Massachusetts, they launched their comics line under the colophon Ace Magazines in 1940. Their roster of superheroes was mostly run-of-the-mill with characters like Captain Victory, The Unknown Soldier, and Vulcan, which would be reborn again later under different guises by other publishers.

As early horror comics go, *Challenge* is reasonably well executed; it has an arresting cover, competent art, and stories that aren't wince-inducing by comparison. As with many comics during this fledgling period, no writing credits have yet been attributed to any of the stories here. The cover, however, establishes the graphic template for many more horror comics to come; it depicts a news reporter in a stone cellar who is in the process of opening a box containing a decapitated head. Surrounding him is a variety of occult *objets d'art*, including the first shrunken head to appear on a horror comic cover. His pretty blonde "girl Friday" is aghast, and points to a pair of decayed human monsters shambling down the steps towards them.

You've been very kind to show me your pipes, madam, but tobacco is all I'll be needing!

Perhaps then, I can do you a real service, something you will thank me for to your dying day!

"THE INSTANT I ENTERED THE TINY SWISS TOBACCO SHOP, I WAS SEIZED BY A STRANGE AND UNEXPLAINABLE SENSE OF DANGER. WAS IT BECAUSE OF THE BURNING LOOK IN THE OLD WOMAN'S EYES, OR WAS IT THE CHOKING SMELL OF DECAY AND AGE THAT BROUGHT FRIGHT TO MY HEART? HERE, IN THIS SHOP, THE FIRST LINK IN THE CHAIN OF TERROR WAS FORGED-- TO TRANSPLANT ME INTO A WORLD OF SUCH LOATHESOME HORROR, OF SUCH UNFORGETTABLE AND SINISTER FORCES, THAT DEATH ITSELF WOULD HAVE BEEN A BETTER FATE THAN ITS LIVING MEMORY!"

"PERHAPS IT WAS THE PECULIAR AROMA OF THE TOBACCO THAT GILDA GAVE ME THAT MADE ME BEHAVE IN SO STRANGE AND SUDDEN A MANNER. I CAN OFFER NO EXPLANATION FOR MY ACTION, BUT A SHARP AND IRRESISTIBLE IMPULSE COMPELLED ME TO GET OFF THAT TRAIN..."

The lead story, "High Priestess of the Snake People," is drawn and inked by Ace veteran artist Frank Giusto and tells the story of a young American mountain-climber who stops into a Swiss tobacco shop where he is persuaded to travel to a desolate peak by Gilda, the proprietor's seductive daughter. After smoking some of the tobacco given to him by the witchy brunette, he finds himself uncontrollably compelled to climb the aforementioned mountain. It turns out that inside is a cavern of serpent worshippers led by none other than Gilda herself. He escapes with the help of a local villager who blows up the cavern with dynamite. Besides being a competently written tale, this may be the first comic that uses hallucinogenic drugs as an important element of the story.

The second tale, "The Ghost in the Portrait," is drawn by another long-standing Ace artist, Kenneth Rice. It was reprinted in *Baffling Mysteries* #18 (November 1953).

Lin Streeter pencils and inks "Villa of a Vampire," and unlike *Adventures into the*

CONTINUED ON PAGE 102

THE GHOST IN THE PORTRAIT

SEE YON MANSION? IT SPEAKS OF PEACE AND HOME AND LOVE. BUT THERE IS A STORY IN THAT HOUSE, A STORY TO CURDLE YOUR BLOOD!

AN UGLY HATRED, A BURNING LUST FOR REVENGE, HIDDEN IN THE MUSTY DARKNESS OF A TRUNK IN AN ATTIC ROOM, FINDS RELEASE WHEN THE PORTRAIT OF A MAN LONG DEAD IS UNCOVERED. FOR THERE IS EVIL IN THE PAINTING, AND AWESOME HORROR FOLLOWS THE TRAIL OF THE GHOST IN THE PORTRAIT!

SEE THE GENTLE HILLS OF OUR NORTH ENGLAND COUNTRYSIDE? IT IS THE KIND OF COUNTRY WHERE A BODY SHOULD FIND PEACE. BUT THAT WASN'T SO, FOR HERE, THERE WAS ONLY TERROR AND DEATH...

"ONCE, THIS MANSION WAS LONG UNOCCUPIED, EXCEPT BY ME, THE CARETAKER. BUT THERE WERE WELCOME VISITORS ONE SEPTEMBER AFTERNOON..."

WELCOME! WELCOME YOUNG MASTER AND MISTRESS!

YES, OF COURSE! I REMEMBER NOW YOU'RE JONATHAN. IT'S BEEN YEARS SINCE I SAW YOU. I WAS A CHILD THEN.

A FULL MOON RISES OVER THE VILLA DI PINI, A SHAFT OF SILVER PENETRATES THE HIDDEN CRYPT OF A MONSTER WHO HAS SLAIN THREE VICTIMS EVERY GENERATION FOR OVER 400 YEARS! A GLEAM OF LIGHT TOUCHES THE BLACK-CLAD CORPSE. IT STIRS A RED TONGUE MOVES SLOWLY, HUNGRILY OVER DEMONISH LIPS, PARCHED FOR THE LIQUID THAT WILL SUSTAIN ITS FIENDISH LIFE FOR YET ANOTHER 25 YEARS. THE VAMPIRE OF THE VILLA DI PINI APPEARS IN THE MOONLIGHT-- IN ALL ITS HORRIFYING AWESOMENESS. NOR SHALL THE FIEND RETURN TO HIS HIDING PLACE TILL HE HAS DRAINED THE BLOOD FROM THE VEINS OF YET ANOTHER VICTIM!

Unknown's earlier claim that "superstition is ignorance," the vampire in this story is real. Numerous victims of the cursed villa fall under the creature's fangs but no blood is depicted. That would soon change as horror comics would get bolder and bloodier. Streeter worked for Archie and Pines before he volunteered for military service in 1942 where he was the staff cartoonist for his Army outfit's newspaper. This story was reprinted in Ace's *Web of Mystery* #19 (July 1953) and several times later in Myron Fass' infamous Eerie Publications' full-size magazine line of altered pre-code horror comics.

The last story of the issue is "No Grave to Hold Him," a modern take on *Frankenstein*,

possibly drawn by Mike Sekowsky. It was reprinted in *Web of Mystery* #2 (November 1953). Included in this issue were a pair of one-page "True Tales of the Supernatural" drawn by an unknown artist that emulated *Adventures'* one-pagers, "Strange Spirits" and "The Cursed Pistol."

Ace's benchmark horror comic lasted only one issue, but in some ways it was as good as or better than any that came before it. A second issue was in the planning stage with a Warren Kremer cover illustrating the story, "The Werewolf Strikes" (the image was later used for the cover of Ace's first issue of *The Beyond* with a cover date of November 1950). Unfortunately, its life as a continuing title may have been cut short as a result of the *Report of the New York State Joint Legislative Committee to Study the Publication of Comics* in March 1951. Issued several years

before *Seduction of the Innocent* (German-American psychiatrist Dr. Fredric Wertham's screed against the comic book industry), its intent was to expose "offensive and obscene" content "published and disseminated" in comics. The splash panel from "Vampire of the Villa" was one of the examples exhibited in the appendix of the report. Meekly, *Challenge* morphed back into the more socially acceptable and "wholesome" *Love Experiences*, where it ran successfully for another thirty-two issues until Ace Magazine's last gasp in 1956.

John Navroth has been a fan of comic books since he was a young lad during the Silver Age. When word got out that the same 12-cent books were becoming far more valuable than their cover price, he immediately stopped folding them over while reading them and saved up enough for a stock of plastic bags and backer boards. For readers who are interested more about vintage horror comics visit John's blog at monstermagazineworld.blogspot.com

Next: "A FLOOD OF BLOOD AND CORPSES"

Don't miss John's history of Forrest J Ackerman's **FAMOUS MONSTERS OF FILMLAND MAGAZINE** in *Black Infinity* Creature Features.

THE HIDEBEHIND

THE HIDEBEHIND

BY RHYS HUGHES

"**N**OW THIS IS THE WAY IT SHOULD BE," SAID DANNY, AND HE STRETCHED HIMSELF IN THE SADDLE AND YAWNED. They had topped the rise and down below was the wooden shack in a state of disrepair. The afternoon was changing into evening. The sun had dipped below the mountains.

"I'm listening," Burton said, and he added, "Again."

"Don't be like that," said Danny.

"We can't ride over the mountains, you told me twice already. We'll leave our horses here and continue on foot."

"Not tonight, that's my point," objected Danny.

Burton shrugged, eyes averted.

"Tomorrow night, but I don't see the point of the delay. We'll have to be out in the dark anyway. Can't avoid that, can we?" He was chewing on a piece of hardtack he had removed from a saddlebag. The valley below was wide and soft. His mouth was long and hard.

"I just want us to rest tonight," but Danny paused at this point and his look of melancholy made Burton shiver.

"To tell the rest of the story? That's the idea."

Danny nodded. "Right."

Burton sighed, finished his hardtack, thumped his chest to clear his throat of some obstruction, possibly imaginary, and said, "I've done a lot of things in my time, and I came to the conclusion long ago that I don't *need* to know more than is good for my health. And so?"

"This'll be good for your health," said Danny.

"No unnecessary details?"

"None at all. I don't inflict that kind of thing."

"Special case, huh?"

Danny nodded, jerked his heels and set off down the slope. His horse went slowly, nervously, but the gradient was gentle. The grass was long in the valley, dark green, the color of bottles on saloon shelves. Burton said, "But it's swell here," to himself and whistled a sparse tune. Danny ignored him, refusing to be baited by a melody. Then he said:

"No signs of any recent habitation. Hasn't changed since I was here last. I can say it's still a secret paradise—"

"Not on any maps yet. But that'll change soon. It always does, Danny my friend. The surveyors come and find the lost places, the rumored realms, and broadcast the knowledge to all."

"Not this one, not just yet," growled Danny.

They both dismounted.

They hitched their horses on long lines to a sunken post, allowed the mares to crop lush grass, already freshened with early evening dew, and Danny went up on the porch of the shack. It was a narrow porch, just two planks wide, and he turned the handle of the door.

The handle crumbled in his grip. The door swung open on rope hinges. It was dark inside but there was no smell of mould. Burton took a kerosene lamp out of his other saddlebag and brought it inside, together with a sack of food, a bottle of brandy tucked under his arm. Danny said, "I'll get a fire going in the hearth. The chimney might be blocked."

"Soon find that out."

Danny crouched, struck a match. He had already collected a big fistful of sticks outside. He used a paper napkin from his pocket to catch the flame. He said, once the sticks were popping, "We'd better get some decent logs. There was a dead tree back on the slope."

"Look here," said Burton, and he stamped a chair to pieces. He threw the legs and seat onto the fire. "I'll pull up the porch too. You said no one owns the shack now, nobody lives here. It's tumbling down. Might as well help it on its way. Every dog has his day, right?"

Danny shrugged but made no other objection.

They sat on the floor.

Firelight licked their grimy faces, made their expressions inscrutable but hurled their shadows onto the far wall, expanding them, turning them into the misshapen draperies of some nightmarish theatre, the curtains that would part to reveal a stage slick with blood.

"Now this is the way it should be," resumed Danny.

"Like I said, I'm listening."

Danny said, "The forest is inhabited."

Burton considered this.

"Well, that's news," he said at last. "I was under the impression it was, you know, completely devoid of human life."

"Probably it is, yes."

"That makes no good sense," Burton warned him.

"I'll tell you everything."

"You'd better," snarled Burton, but his expression was affectionate, only his voice was menacing, unhappy.

And Danny told him about the Hidebehind.

"It's like this," he began.

Burton lifted a hand to interrupt him. He said, "No, Danny, nothing is ever like this. Everything is unique."

He was always cryptic after a few swallows of brandy. Danny opened two tins of beans, positioned them near the blaze to cook them in their own casings, taking two spoons out of some deep pocket and passing one to Burton while the sauce bubbled and spat. He said:

"I met the old man in a cheap hotel in some nameless town that was dying because the newly constructed railroad skirted it. The dust swirled and it never stopped swirling. I don't understand that, to this day, tiny tornadoes, purple dust and humming as they rotated. Then—"

"He told you something and made you swear to keep it a secret? And that's exactly what you've done, Danny?"

"I'm about to share it. He had a horde of gold, he said, and he wasn't a liar, I could tell that just from listening to him. I'm a good judge of character. Then he said that he distrusted banks, he had buried his treasure in the safest place in the whole world. An undiscovered place throughout all time, but he had found it himself while prospecting. That's how he made his pile. He panned for nuggets and he'd found plenty, thousands!"

"He was drunk? Burton ventured and took a slug himself.

"That's right. But not wild."

Burton passed the bottle to Danny, who filled his mouth with the liquid, the taste burning at first then mellowing to warmth, reminding him of other lands in other autumns. He wiped his lips.

"He buried the gold near to where he found it, do you see? He'd found it in the mountains, in a river that cascaded between the peaks, and he buried it in the forest *beyond* the mountains. He built this shack and it was his base. He relaxed from his labors here, rested himself."

"How can you be certain he wasn't just a fool?"

"I followed him, that's how."

"And he didn't know you were on his trail?"

"You know how careful I can be, how stealthy," said Danny. He passed the bottle back. "It was a tortuous ride, more suited to mules than horses, the same route I guided you on, so you know what I mean; and then he arrived here, and I watched him from the top of the slope. I was concealed by a boulder. I observed him for days. When he set off into the mountains, I followed him up there too, and down the other side, into the forest. I wanted to see where he had buried his treasure. I assumed he was going back to dig it up and run his fingers through it. That's what these misers do, ain't it?"

Burton nodded. "That's what they do," he agreed.

Danny adjusted the position of the tin cans with his spoon, pushing them a few inches away from the flames.

"But I lost him. The trees were too thick, there were no paths, I felt dazed, it was very strange. Something unwholesome in the atmosphere. Like the trees didn't want me there, the atmosphere was *thick*. I shrugged off my qualms. I can blaze a trail better than anyone I know, but this defeated me. Yes, I was lost, the forest was closing in on me. I felt sick. Then I stumbled over his body. It had the worst look of terror in the eyes I've ever seen. They had retreated deep into his head, never knew that was possible, and I saw my own reflection in them, in the craters of his sockets. It was like I was confronting myself at the end of a tunnel. I wanted to laugh, a screaming laugh."

"Lying on his back?"

"No, on his front. Prone is the word. I learned the difference between prone and supine one time. Supine is on your back. Prone is face down, on your belly. Most of him was prone. But his head was twisted all the way around. And that's how he was able to stare at me."

"Imagine that! All the way."

"No need for me to imagine it. I was there, I saw. Yes, I wanted to laugh at his damn head. Twisted around."

"No accounting for that. Bears don't do that."

Danny nodded. He said:

"Beans are ready. Time to eat."

Burton pulled his tin closer with his booted foot. Danny did likewise and a lull in the conversation followed. They ate, they swigged the brandy, they licked the spoons clean, and Danny continued:

"His arms and legs broken in a dozen places each, so they was kind of very floppy. I picked him up and he was like a puppet. I soon dropped him again and I turned and I got out of there fast."

"But you were lost, you said? How did you leave?"

"Pure chance, I ran and ran."

"Lacerated by thorns, bruised by branches?"

Danny smiled. "Almost as if you were there yourself. Yes, that's true. But I almost sank on my knees in prayer when I burst out of the tree line. Climbing the mountains was like ascending to Heaven, then I was over them and descending. I rested in this shack for a few days."

"And then came to find me and recruit me?"

"Hold your horses there."

"What did you do first then, Danny?"

"Research. I went to the cities and I went to libraries and I consulted books and documents. I did a lot of reading."

"I was never one for that," said Burton ruefully.

"But I did it for you. For us. I found out what kind of thing could do that to a man, what kind of thing would want to do it. To twist a head right around. You break a man's neck, fine. But there's no call to keep twisting it and twisting it. A bear doesn't do that, a lion doesn't do that, wolves don't do that. Who does that? It's what I yearned to know."

"Some tribe not yet discovered?"

"I don't think so."

"A madman then? A hermit gone crazy?"

"Fairly certain not."

"What then, Danny? This is beginning to make me irritated. You persuade me to come all this way, for what?"

"The Hidebehind."

Burton snorted, for the word was not entirely unfamiliar to him. He knew a brace of backwoods tales, the myths that lumberjacks told each other, men who camped out in the wilds for months.

"A critter nobody has ever yet seen," he said.

"Because nobody *can*," corrected Danny. He took the brandy bottle and he filled his mouth. He gasped with relief after swallowing. "It stays always behind you, no matter which way you turn. They live in the remotest regions. And they pounce when you least expect it, even if you think you are always expecting it, a sudden leap and they are on your back, over you, *draped* is the word.

Your body convulses itself to death. Anything to avoid being dealt with by the Hidebehind. In desperation you twist your head and keep twisting it. You need to look away from the damnable thing. Look away!"

Burton said slowly, "I don't believe half of it."

"Half's more than enough."

Burton nodded. "I reckon it might be." His shoulders heaved. "So after you did this research of yours, all that reading, you came to get me. Old buddies, eh? You needed me to help you. We would go back to the valley, climb the range to the forest on the other side and seek his trove. And I am your insurance against a critter that maybe doesn't exist?"

Danny smiled in the flickering glow. "Thing is, one man is completely at the mercy of the Hidebehind, but two men?"

"That's a different proposition?"

"Altogether. Two men can look out for each other, see? Guard each other's backs, give the creature no chance to remain unseen, and it *must* remain unseen. That's its nature. If it can't remain unseen, it won't be able to come close. Two men, facing in opposite directions, sleeping back to back when camping. We'll give it no chance at all to get us."

"Makes sense, Danny, in a crazy sort of way."

"Well, that's the plan."

"Let me sleep on it and give you my answer in the morning."

"But you won't refuse?"

Burton chuckled. Danny knew him well.

And when dawn came, they were both up and taking equipment from their saddlebags, together with supplies. They didn't take much. They would be gone for one day and a night at most. That was the hope. A rifle each, long knives, a large canteen of water, pockets filled with hardtack, boxes of matches wrapped in waxed paper, a coil of rope, shovels. They left the horses grazing and began the arduous trek into the mountains.

Danny said, "The climb isn't too bad at first."

They scrambled up. At one point they saw a glint and Danny stooped to pick up a button from the ground.

"I lost this the last time I was here,"

he said.

"Keep it for luck," said Burton.

They clambered over a boulder, disturbed a hawk that flapped screeching into the rising sun, outlining itself for a moment like an ancient god. Soon they came to a stream tumbling over broken rocks and they topped up the canteen. This must have been where the old prospector had panned for nuggets. But that was hard work. Easier for them to keep going and find the horde he had buried. They reached the highest point at noon.

"And now down the other side," said Danny.

"What if?" ventured Burton.

"What if what?" queried Danny, panting, his hands sore from grasping the rocks and pulling himself upwards.

"The Hidebehind is right behind us now?"

Danny shook his head.

"They only live in forests," he said.

Burton nodded. He was a skeptic who believed in the supernatural, he told himself, which was a mighty unusual combination, or was it? He had met others who laughed at the notion of ghosts but who'd had ghostly experiences anyway. Life had no respect for the feelings of doubters, it seemed. He looked quickly at the landscape behind and below.

"But it's foolish glancing over your shoulder to catch the Hidebehind in the act. It stays always behind you."

Burton grinned. "Thanks for that advice."

"We won't ever see it. We don't *want* to see it. We want to keep it away, to deter it, to make it impossible to approach us. You'll see how safe we are when we're in the forest. It's like armor, better than armor, in fact. The Hidebehind can circle around us forever but there won't be a chink in our defences. Back-to-back. We'll rope ourselves tight."

"Our backs actually touching, yes, Danny?"

"At night, for sure. You see, we don't know how big the Hidebehind is. So if there's a gap between our backs, he might be able to sneak in there. No gaps, that's the rule. We'll bind together. The rope will save us. That damn thing will just have to be frustrated with us."

He laughed at this idea, the image in his head of something that couldn't be visualized scowling and gibbering and circling endlessly, fruitlessly, this futility for evil being a blow for justice?

They picked their way down the slopes.

It was early evening by the time they reached the forest and passed through the tree line and entered a place of silent menace, but the silence was odd, not an absence of sound but somehow made up of many sounds, all of which cancelled each other out. It was hard to explain. Whispers of different frequencies, and the frequencies had a sum of zero. Danny licked his lips. They walked sideways, so that they were always back to back.

"Slow but sure method," croaked Danny.

"But is it necessary? You said the Hidebehind doesn't come out in daylight, that it's purely a nocturnal critter."

"Purely? Nothing pure about that demon. There's a gap between our backs anyway. I am sure that gap's big enough for it to slip between us. Then it would kill us, one at a time. But all the same."

"All the same what?"

"Slow but sure method," repeated Danny.

"It's working," said Burton.

But his voice was uncertain. He blinked. He felt that some presence was in the vicinity, just out of range, hidden by the trees, but that it was circling them, a satellite orbiting a planet that itself was moving through a cosmos of fear. There was definitely *something* out there.

Frustrated, belligerent, indescribable.

They were keeping it at bay. Or was it toying with them?

Waiting for the night to come.

And it came, and the pale light that filtered between the tree trunks dropped by an octave, or so it seemed.

A silence deeper than the silence they had already been moving through. It was almost impossible to see where they were going. They had no lamp. Danny had thought it would prove useless, just make the shadows thicker. When night came they would camp and begin again at dawn, find the trove, plunder it, and be back in the mountains before it was necessary to spend a second night in the forest. The scheme was workable.

"Let's make camp then," he told Burton. Yes, it was night now.

"No fire," continued Danny, as he sank to his knees, then sat and extended his legs, and Burton did the same, and they tied the rope around themselves, too tight for comfort perhaps, but comfort wasn't what this exploit was about. They had to get through the night, is all.

Burton knotted the rope with a knot he knew that grew tighter and tighter with struggling and squirming. In the morning they would free themselves with the knife. Two pieces of rope would then be available to them for dragging back the sack of gold through the forest, one length each. Gold was heavy, like these shadows, maybe even heavier. It depended on the horde, which neither had yet seen. But the sack surely bulged.

Why would an old prospector have buried a small sack or a half-filled one? The trove would be a dream quest, a mission, but it would become a burden of delight, a beautiful responsibility.

Danny said, "Temperature dropping fast."

"Will be a cold night."

"High up, that's why. Lower than the mountains but still high. No gap at all between our backs now, none."

"Couldn't even slide a knife blade there."

"No room at all for the Hidebehind to get into. No way he can be behind us now. We don't have backs anymore."

Danny tried to remember something he had read once, or an actor told him, some fellow from a roving theatre troupe, in a resonant voice. But it was about a beast with two backs, some sort of bawdy metaphor, and he wanted to shout out that here was a beast with two fronts and no back, the opposite thing, but Burton wouldn't like it. He wouldn't get the joke. He would demand an explanation and ruin the jest, if jest it actually was.

Danny didn't know. And then a stick snapped.

It was like a gunshot.

"Could be anything, but we are safe."

A rustling of leaves.

"Maybe a bird, a squirrel, a rogue lick of wind."

They waited, tightly bound.

Silence again, that silence made from a thousand mutterings that cancelled each other out, that loud silence.

Danny said, "It's chilly tonight but your back is warm. I never imagined it was possible for a back to provide such comfort. Seriously, this is a back I will never forget, so long as I live."

They chuckled, unconvincingly, but it was a relief to move their mouths in that way, in the brooding murk.

"The same is true of yours," said Burton.

They waited, wide awake.

Danny said, "The hours will pass, I promise."

"They always do."

An hour crawled away and Burton began thinking. Or maybe his thoughts did the thinking for him. He said, "What if the Hidebehind is like a shadow, as thin as a shadow? I mean, shadows have no thickness, do they? They can't truly be said to be a thing. They are an absence, not a presence. And it occurs to me that we never see our own shadows."

"Of course we do," said Danny, but he was listening.

Burton frowned, he rubbed his cheeks, and he said, "But we never see *all* of our shadows. If we stand with our backs to the sun, the sun makes shadows of that side of us. If we are facing the sun, the sun makes shadows of the other side. Never both sides together."

Danny waited. He wished he was drunk.

Burton continued, "What if the Hidebehind is like the shadow of a man but of both sides simultaneously? A solid shadow. But thin enough not to be there. To be there and be absent at the same time. Even though we are roped together, back touching back, no gaps, as tight as tight can be, a shadow like that could slide in and come between us."

He nodded as his words carried him onwards. "That's a fact, Danny. And it makes me wonder how it would kill us. Would it expand, rise up, loom over us like a segment of night? But then how would it choose which of us to grab first? It might be indecisive, unable to make a move, wavering first one way and then another. Or might it

be able to fold itself in two directions at once? Drape both of us, smother both of us, no need to take turns. I can't believe that, Danny, it's absurd. Surely it must choose!"

He dug his heels into the soil. He wriggled a little. "What do you think? A shadow but worse than any shadow ought to be. And we can't bear to look at it in the face. Is that why we twist our heads right around? But that's not right. It jumps on our backs. Do we twist our heads right around to finally get a look at it? What's the answer, Danny?"

He joined his hands, wrung them, fingers gripping fingers. "Not possible to twist a head so far, but people do it anyway. The thing doesn't even deserve any comparison with a shadow. It's impossibly dreadful. Would it choose you or me first? What do you say? I bet it would choose me. But I'm not a gambling man, I always lose at cards, don't I?"

His teeth chattered and he bit down hard to stop them. "Why has your back gone cold, Danny? It's so cold now. It was warm before. What are you thinking about? Something jabbing me between my shoulders. Feels like your chin. That can't be true. Why don't you say something, Danny? What's wrong? Not asleep, are you? No man could sleep through this. You're dribbling on my shirt. Please stop that. Speak to me, Danny."

The rope had tightened, almost imperceptibly. He groaned. "Did it choose you first, after all? Is that why you are silent? Say my name, Danny, please just once. Anything, just once. Not even a scream? What did it do to you? What did it do? But what, Danny? What?"

Rhys Hughes has lived in many different countries and currently lives in India. He began writing at an early age and his first book, Worming the Harpy*, was published in 1995 by Tartarus Press. Since that time, he has published more than fifty other books and his work has been translated into ten languages. He recently completed an ambitious project that involved writing exactly 1000 linked narratives.*

PAST CARING

BY GARY FRY

"YOU'RE NOT GOING TO SIT THERE *ALL* DAY, ARE YOU?"** Jane called from the kitchen, cooking breakfast with one hand while holding open a textbook with the other.

"Doctor's orders, love." Tony was in the lounge, slumped in his armchair with the TV remote control beside him. "If I put my back out again, I'll have to take even more time off work."

And wouldn't that suit you just fine, Jane thought but somehow resisted saying. She set aside the chapter she'd been reading, piled fried bacon onto two breadcakes, picked up the plates, and went to distribute food to her kin.

Her husband accepted his almost without moving, simply raising his arms as a concession to her kindness. Perhaps in his vulnerable state, he'd also expect her to lift the sandwich to his mouth. But Jane had yet to lose that much sight of herself. Instead, she crossed to the foot of the steps and, over the babble of daytime television behind her, called upstairs.

"Ross! Breakfast!"

"In the middle o' summat," her son shouted back, his voice muffled by his closed bedroom door and the sounds of aliens trying to kill him. If not for the racket from his gaming console, Jane might have thought twice about entering the realm of a teenage boy in the middle o' summat. But to avoid wasting time, she hurried up the stairs, barged inside, and handed over the butty.

"When *are* you going to tidy this hellhole?" she asked, glancing around at a heart-sinking combination of grubby sheets, scattered clothing, and empty coke cans. Her son sat among the carnage, like a tramp in a dump. Apart than his thumbs, and occasionally his eyelids, he moved no more than his dad had downstairs.

"It's on my agenda," said Ross, his lips joining in the minor activity. He blinked again, presumably to combat ocular dryness caused by his hypnotic screen. "I need to beat level six first."

It's been months since you left school. What you actually need to do is start looking for work...

But Jane kept that to herself, too. She knew how tough it was in the jobs market, particularly for people without qualifications. That was at least one reason why she was determined to do well in her own studies.

"Enjoy level six," she said, and exited, went back down the stairs, grabbed her coat from a peg and struggled into it. "I'm off, love."

Above the TV he'd turned up, perhaps Tony hadn't heard her. He certainly didn't reply. But she knew better than to take offence—he wasn't a bad man and worked hard when he could.

She left the house, hugged herself against the autumn wind, and began walking to her mother's.

SHE HADN'T EXPECTED much from life, and that seemed fair, as life didn't expect much from her. She'd grown up in a similar area to the one in which she now lived—city suburbs, cramped terraced housing, kids hanging around on street corners. But she refused to bemoan such a fate. Her history course had taught her how much tougher life had been for people in the past. And however little society might welcome what she could eventually offer, she had at least the opportunity to better her prospects.

When she reached the bungalow, she let herself in with the key she'd had cut after her mother's latest fall. Wheelchair-bound until her hip operation later that month, Mum needed help each morning washing and dressing.

Jane found her in the conservatory, just sitting and watching a bird play out in the back garden. Since Dad's death last year, Jane's husband had mown the lawn and weeded the hedges, but with Tony's current back injury, Jane herself might have to do that next.

"Hi, Mum," she said, keeping her voice cheerful, despite feeling overwhelmed by so many responsibilities. "Did you sleep okay?"

"Ah, no, actually," said her mother, still dressed in the nightgown Jane had helped her into the previous evening. Her hands, misshapen by arthritis, gripped the arms of the wheelchair. "I had rather a bad dream."

"Oh yes? What about?" Feeling jaded, Jane struggled to think of anything that might disturb her the way it once had as a girl.

"It was about *you*, as it happens," said her mother, raising each arm and letting her daughter wash her with a soapy sponge.

"Me? What about me?"

The older woman fingered one temple, flattening out over seventy years of wrinkles. "My memory," she said, narrowing her eyes. "It's no fun getting old, you know."

Don't be so hard on yourself, Mum. You've already moved more this morning than my husband and son combined...

"There's years in you yet," said Jane, keeping her sarcasm to herself. "Pay no attention to silly old dreams."

The comment raised a brief frown, and then her mother glanced across at a framed photograph of her late husband on the wall, Jane's much-missed dad.

"I can't recall the details, but I think I should be glad of that. It was ... *quite horrible.*"

As she helped her mother put on a clean set of clothes, Jane experienced a shiver, one she couldn't ascribe to the chilly temperature. Central heating had always warmed the bungalow. Her father had left behind a private pension and Mum lived comfortably. Even so, something had definitely spooked her.

Having performed all her duties, Jane stepped back a pace. "Don't worry about me, Mum. I'm fine. Honest I am. Yes, I'm quite busy at the moment, but that will ease up soon. After my course is finished and Tony's back at work, we'll have only lazy Ross to sort out."

Her mother smiled. "I worry about you all, you know. Whenever I'm sat here with nothing to do. I try to resist it, but the thoughts creep in. I expect that will change once I'm right again."

"Of course it will." Still uneasy, Jane lacked confidence in her assertion, and so, having just begun to feel hungry, she checked her wristwatch. "Look, Mum, I have to go. My shift at the museum starts in half an hour and I haven't even eaten yet."

"You do too much, love. You need to get some rest now and again."

"Believe me, the minute you're back on your feet, I'm using that wheelchair myself. I'll get Tony to push me back and forth to the pub every night for at least a month."

"That'll make you twice legless," said her mother, and Jane was pleased to see her laughing again. She stepped forwards and gave her a kiss. Finally, pushing aside any residual thoughts about suffering anything "quite horrible," she left.

THE BUILDING IN WHICH she worked was one of the city's oldest houses. Built in the 1500s, it had been home to a family called the Wallers for many generations, until it had recently fallen under the stewardship of the local authority, which had turned it into a museum.

The Wallers had an admirable reputation, having been on the Royalists' side during the English Civil War and, during later periods, fully in support of economic reform, when the likes of Chartism had risen to the fore. All their money had come from farming, and the family had become responsible employers long before it became a legal necessity.

Unlocking the large front door at ten o'clock sharp, Jane again felt pride in being associated with such an historically significant building. She paced inside, her footsteps resounding on the stone floor, and then went behind the reception desk in the large entrance. She removed her coat, turned off the burglar alarm, switched on the lights, and logged into the till.

Once she'd counted out the float, she finished the sandwich she'd bought on her way here, glancing through an arched window at the car park out front. No vehicles had turned up yet, and there were no school trips booked in today. That meant Jane could take her usual stroll through the building.

She'd always been interested in history, even as a girl at such a rough school.

Agincourt, Henry VIII, the Spanish Armada, Nelson's success at Trafalgar, World Wars I and II—she'd read about these events along with many more, often outside of her lessons. Then adult life had intervened—the usual deal involving marriage, mortgage, and motherhood—before thirty years had passed with frightening haste.

She'd recently enjoyed returning to the subject, taking classes at the local college. In many ways, reading about other people's stories, however remote in time and place they were, was a welcome retreat from her own muddling existence.

The Wallers were a fascinating family, and their home was certainly special. Most of the original building had survived, though several wings had been added to it over the centuries. On the ground floor there was the kitchen, drawing room, dining hall, and a library. Upstairs were several bedrooms and a bathroom, along with various quarters used for storage.

Each room had been furnished in a specific style, representing different eras of the property's past. To add period detail, many life-sized figures made of wax and dressed in facsimile clothing had been placed around the house, as if the original occupants were engaged in historical activities.

"Good morning, Mr. Waller," said Jane, observing the first of them.

The older man sat behind a huge desk in the study, perusing important looking documents. His solemn suit hinted at an austere outlook, while his face boasted muttonchop whiskers. The skin around his eyes was sallow, just as it was on the hands that gripped a sheaf of parchment papers. Jane knew this figure was supposed to represent the nineteenth century, the sombre décor of the room around him redolent of that restrained era.

Other characters could be found elsewhere, and Jane headed for them.

The lady of the house in the master bedroom was attending to her apparel, splendidly kitted out in voluminous Elizabethan garb. Visitors could observe the expression she wore only in a mirror perched on the vanity unit where she sat. The woman was always smiling broadly. A large four-poster bed, festooned in velvet, stood behind her, and unlit lamps had been mounted on the stone walls.

Jane stepped away and wandered back downstairs to view the dolls on display there, too.

As if eternally awaiting a suitor, a young woman was dressed like the prim heroine of a Georgian novel—by Jane's namesake Austen perhaps, or maybe Henry Fielding. The room in which she stood boasted classical features, its multi-panelled wainscoting giving off a faint scent of timber.

In another room on the ground level, looking fiercely active, a young man loitered. His horse-rider's garments belonged to the early twentieth century, while the whip he wielded with one arm threatened a dog cowering at his feet, one immortalized by a skilful taxidermist.

"You let the poor young thing be, Master Waller," said Jane, and that left only one more resident to greet.

She was about to do so—this was a young woman dressed in a plain garment, climbing the stone stairs from the servants' quarters belowground—when she heard the museum's entrance open, prompting her to return to reception. As she arrived, she noticed an elderly man at the ticket desk, juggling change in his trousers with a fretful chink.

"Hello there. An admission for one, is it?"

"That would be appreciated, thank you." The man's accent wasn't local. He might come from the south, perhaps down Devon way. Tourists were common enough here, sometimes even from other countries.

"I hope you enjoy your visit," said Jane, accepting a five-pound note and handing over a ticket.

"We shall certainly see."

Just then, the hallway light overhead flickered on and off, not something Jane had ever experienced here before. But it was an old building, and its electrical wiring might need attention. At any rate, the newcomer seemed unperturbed. His ageing face—dark eyes, angular cheekbones, and irrepressible smile—never altered as he headed off to explore the property.

The job's biggest appeal was being able to work alone. It offered Jane a welcome break from looking after her family, as well as time to catch up on her reading. Sitting behind the desk, she grabbed a textbook she always left here on a shelf under the till.

Before long she was lost again in the past, learning about societies and cultures very different from her own. Sometimes she plunged so deeply into her subject that she'd grow detached from her surroundings and it would take some event to draw her back.

It was a sound of footsteps this time, pacing across the wooden floorboards upstairs. They belonged to the older man, of course, and it must be only confusion arising from Jane's divided attention that made her briefly think that *two* sets were in motion, one following the other...

But that couldn't be true. The visitor had arrived alone, and the entrance directly ahead of Jane was the only way inside the house.

About half an hour later, the man reappeared, revealing the same inscrutable face. Now she thought about it, Jane realized how fake his smile looked. She sometimes resorted to the same expression whenever she needed to control her private frustrations. But what could the sightseer possibly feel aggrieved about here?

"Did you see all you'd hope to?" she asked, setting her book aside and standing up behind the desk. Her legs felt suddenly stiff, probably after her walk earlier, but she covertly shook life back into them to lessen the discomfort.

"Not quite enough to satisfy me," the man replied, dark eyes glaring. "But now at least I have the measure of the place."

It was a strange comment, perhaps even a worrying one, and Jane couldn't help but rise to the bait. "Is there a specific reason why you visited the house?"

"That's nothing to do with me directly. But I *am* aware of someone else who has connections with it."

Jane was now much more than intrigued. The lights flickered again, just for a moment, but she didn't let that distract her.

"I know someone, my tutor at college actually, who's writing a book about the history of these parts. He might be interested in anything you have to say."

The man hesitated, as if uncertain about whether to go on. His eyes narrowed even further, making his cheekbones look all the more pronounced. Finally, with another strained smile, he capitulated.

"Well, I'm guessing you're unfamiliar with the *scandal...*"

DURING WHAT REMAINED of Jane's shift, there was a number of other visitors, most curious about the old house, having read about it in guidebooks or spotted it in widely circulated adverts.

After her colleague arrived to take over, Jane departed, catching a bus to the city centre to do a bit of shopping and get something to eat before her evening class began. She needed time to process all she'd been told earlier and must decide what to do next.

The museum's earliest visitor that day—Alan Hinderwell—was apparently related to someone who'd once worked for the Wallers, a maid back in the 1920s. It turned out that the son at the time, a headstrong nineteen-year-old, had sexually assaulted this young woman, causing an unwanted pregnancy. His parents, trying to uphold a family reputation for faultless conduct, had tried to keep it quiet. But soon after, the maid had been killed, trampled to death by out-of-control horses in the property's grounds. After investigations by police, the death had been classified as a tragic accident.

But there was a twist. The older man had claimed that, following a recent family bereavement, he'd come into possession of evidence hinting at a far less innocent conclusion. A series of letters sent by the maid to her cousin in Cornwall (Alan Hinderwell's grandmother) suggested that every member of the respectable Wallers—including even the offender's younger sister—had threatened serious consequences if she ever went public with what she'd suffered in their service. It wasn't unreasonable to assume that the maid had unwisely attempted to call their bluff.

Jane set aside her cutlery, having only picked at her salad in the Student Union café. She was unable to decide whether to pass on this new information to the lecturer running her course, an enthusiastic historian who relished unearthing knowledge about previously established matters. It wasn't that Jane believed such a scandal would damage the museum's reputation. It might even enhance it—people were always drawn to infamous aspects of the past.

All the same, she worried how the local authority that operated the business would greet the facts. The Waller family was a significant source of local pride, a long ancestral line of nationally acknowledged luminaries. Learning that it might have involved ignominious bloodshed could tarnish their former home forever.

The ache in her limbs now also creeping into her neck, Jane got up and headed for her class. She mustn't forget that an innocent woman had died and that even people lost to time had a right to be remembered, too. What was history if not an attempt to ensure that truth was separated from propaganda rooted in the past?

Persuaded by her reasoning, Jane attended her latest lecture—about feminism's first wave in the early twentieth century—and afterwards, with an incongruous memory of her workplace's lights faltering earlier that day, she upheld the standards of her discipline.

ON HER WAY HOME later in the dark, she stopped off first to attend to her mother, who appeared not to have moved very far in her wheelchair all day. Jane reminded her of the importance of keeping active and made sure she ate something before helping her wash and change for bed. At long last, she left.

It was a chilly evening which only aggravated her uncomfortable joints. As she made her way home, she wondered whether her period was likely to arrive early again; they'd been erratic lately and she'd reached the age at which menopausal symptoms wouldn't be unusual. What with the many family duties she still had to perform, that was all she needed.

After reaching her street, she heard a sound behind her, as if someone—or perhaps even several people moving together—were in pursuit, their strides every bit as taut as hers now felt. But when she turned to look, she spotted only a few kids on one street corner, limbs rigidly outstretched as if they were pretending to be robots or zombies...

Feeling suddenly tearful about her inactive son, Jane entered the house and kicked off her restrictive shoes.

Tony had fallen asleep in his armchair, as he often had lately around bedtime; the painkillers he took for his slipped disc only made that more likely. Several empty beer cans were crumpled up on the coffee table, along with a plate scraped free of what had probably been takeaway food.

At least he'd moved a few times today, Jane reflected, though a cynical part of her suspected that, in exchange for a generous tip, he'd have asked the delivery person to place the meal in front of him. In the light from the burbling television, her husband's face appeared waxen, like a mask. If not for his light snoring, she might even have fancied him dead.

Disowning a sudden troubling thought of something "quite horrible" happening to her, Jane decided to let her husband sleep. Encouraging him up to bed might aggravate his injury, and that would only increase his dependency on her. She wasn't sure how much longer she could get by without him helping out in their lives.

Up on the landing, she considered stepping into Ross's room to wish him goodnight. But he was older now, needed privacy, and besides, she could hear another video game blaring from behind the door. She wondered who was the most convincing zombie, the many digital ones he killed or her son himself.

After showering and putting on nightwear, Jane reflected on everything that had occurred today, particularly her conversation with the man at the museum which had resulted in her such spreading malicious gossip later... But these were merely bedtime thoughts, the period when everything felt edgy.

The truth was, she'd already got her tutor's permission for Alan Hinderwell to get in touch with him; she'd let the older man know tomorrow, using the telephone number he'd provided. It would be fitting to deal with the matter during her next shift at the Waller museum—*just keeping it in the family*, she couldn't help thinking with an irony that eventually pitched her into uneasy sleep.

ALMOST ALL HER BONES hurt the following morning, hinting at something worse than her menstrual cycle going haywire, maybe even a virus. She slept in later than usual, but it wasn't long before she realized that the best way of handling such an indisposition was through action. That got her out of bed and busy with chores in the house.

If Tony and Ross had contracted the same bug, neither seemed eager to do much about it; they merely complained about similar symptoms from both the armchair downstairs and the bed in her son's room. Jane rolled her eyes, wondering how she managed to tolerate such a feckless pair.

"I should have you both stuffed, the use you are to me at the moment," she said while making sandwiches in the kitchen. But she didn't mean it really; it's just that frustration got on top of her at times.

After feeding them both, she left the house to support someone seemingly more grateful for her attention.

Her mother didn't feel well, either. She claimed to have been awake most of the night, suffering various pains like "arthritis all over her body." At least that had prevented any further dark dreams, thought Jane, but diplomatically kept this to herself.

Once she'd washed, dressed, and fed her, Jane said, "I'll give you a call this afternoon to make sure you're okay. So be sure to keep your phone on you, won't you?"

"I have it right here," her mum replied, holding up the mobile she'd removed from her lap with one stiff-looking hand. It had taken Jane long enough to teach her how to operate the thing, so they might as well start making use of it.

At last, Jane was free to go to work. Her shift was a later one today—two till six pm— and that allowed her to walk slowly to the Waller house. It wasn't that she was reluctant to fulfil the promises she'd made to her visitor yesterday; rather, she now felt conflicted about the museum. If a murder had indeed occurred all those years ago, it must have been in the property's grounds, out in long-ago-demolished stables perhaps, where the car park now stood...

But frightening herself was foolish, particularly how she felt at the moment, tired and struggling to think clearly. When she eventually reached the museum, she thought she saw a figure lurking in one upper-level window, its face much sallower than any person's had any right to be... But surely that had been a reflection, the sun peering briefly out from behind raincloud, perhaps. It certainly wasn't there when at last she entered.

"Hello," Jane said to the woman who'd worked the earlier shift. "Have we been busy today?"

"Oh, you know. So so. We had a few families in earlier, and a small party of Japanese about an hour ago, but nobody since."

Which meant the person Jane thought she'd spotted up on the first floor had been nothing of the sort. Despite all the discomfort in her body, her mind settled to some degree. She exchanged places with the woman, removed her coat, and logged into the till with her own code.

"I've had a bit of a tidy up and switch around," said the woman, with a collegial smile. "That means you can get on with your college revision."

The reception desk did look cleaner, and Jane appreciated that. There were still some good people in the world, and that was worth remembering. After thanking the departing woman, she settled to her textbook.

There were visits only from a few retired couples and a small group of school pupils that afternoon, which had left Jane with plenty of time to study. Near the end of her shift, feeling much better about herself, she put down the book and decided to deal with the task she'd been postponing all day. It was unfair to make promises and not to keep them, she thought, pulling her phone from one pocket. She located the number Alan Hinderwell had given her yesterday and was about to make the call when she heard certain sounds from upstairs.

Had the lights also just briefly flickered again? But Jane didn't let that add to her unease. It was more important to wonder if someone was moving about on the next level. The noises certainly sounded like footfalls but seemed to come from different parts of the building, as if, other than herself, there were *several* people in the house...

There couldn't be any intruders here; how could they have entered without her spotting them, let alone advance to the first floor? Placing her phone on the reception desk, Jane crossed for the staircase, hesitated a moment, and then began to ascend. The wooden steps creaked, creaked, creaked as she made her way slowly up to the landing. Her role at the museum involved a duty of care. Even though dark had settled at its age-old windows, she shouldn't allow her mounting unease to stop her from checking everything was as secure as it ought to be.

"Hello? Who's there, please?"

There was no reply.

All her limbs feeling suddenly stiffer, as if whatever ailment infected her family was growing worse, she paced into the first room upstairs.

The man of the house had risen from his seat.

The wax figure had also set aside the parchment paper he'd been perusing and seemed equally unmindful of all the other documents scattered across the desk behind him. In fact, did he appear more interested now in addressing anybody who happened to enter his chambers? The way he glared at Jane, his beady eyes staring out from a face that looked a lot less sallow in the room's faux lamplight, certainly supported that conclusion...

But Jane was being ridiculous. Her mind racing, she quickly realized that her colleague must have shifted him into this position, part of the "switch around" she'd mentioned before leaving. Jane didn't think anyone in their minor role had a right to tamper with the museum's exhibits, but what other explanation made sense?

To prevent herself from dwelling on further absurdities, Jane moved quickly on to the next room, telling herself that the wax-work man's new posture was just a one-off, a presumptuous whim on the part of her colleague who'd had too much time to spare earlier today.

But it wasn't.

The woman seated in front of the vanity unit had now turned around in her chair, away from the mirror, the better to observe Jane as she entered. And she was still smiling, smiling, smiling.

The static image made Jane recoil, and she moved immediately on, assuming the dolls must have adjustable limbs which enabled easy repositioning. That at least made sense, perhaps the one thing that did right now, but Jane had more difficulty accounting for the vitality she'd detected in the older woman's skin. Had it really looked *soft* to the touch?

She was back downstairs in less than a minute, hoping not to find confirmation of any of her impressions.

But then she received that.

The younger woman, previously waiting patiently in the drawing room, had advanced all the way to its doorway, and no longer looked demure. Her rigid expression was half-alive with a complicit grin.

Letting out an involuntary gasp, Jane hurried further away, on this occasion halting in the entrance to the room occupied by the villain in the family. The young man hoisting the whip yesterday appeared to have employed it since. His stuffed dog was absent, perhaps having been subjected to as much punishment as the household's horses over a hundred years ago, which had then committed such a heinous act, trampling someone to death. The man's expression—narrowed eyes, sucked-in cheeks, pursed lips—looked as if he were just about to use the whip again.

Jane fled, her heart running faster than her legs could manage. As she went, she noted a new absence—the maid missing from the opening to the servant quarters belowground. That suggested far too much for Jane to cope with, and when she reached the museum's entrance, she suddenly didn't wish to be here anymore. Her employer surely wouldn't object if she closed early today. She was ill, should be at home in bed; she'd done far too much lately; it was having an impact on her health, and not just the physical...

Grabbing her phone and coat, she hastily cashed up, secured the float in the safe under the till, activated the burglar alarm, switched off the lights, rushed for the exit, and tried all the while to suppress a sense that other occupants of the building held a similar aspiration to leave...

Although her whole body ached unbearably, she headed rapidly in the moonlight for her mother's bungalow. She'd forgotten to call Mum earlier and had no idea if her own condition had worsened. Feeling guilty about that, Jane removed her phone, dialed the number with fingers that failed to function as freely as they should.

She received no reply, and despite the worry it caused, Jane thought that might be for the best. As she'd prepared to speak before the line connected, it had been difficult to part her lips, as if her face was growing steadily immobile.

What was going on? Was she suffering symptoms of a breakdown? Or something more sinister? In her increasingly delirious state, she wondered if the historical facts she'd been told about played some role in her derangement... Whatever the truth was, it couldn't persist. None of this had anything to do with her. If others wanted to savage longstanding reputations, she'd leave them to it.

Her hands struggling with the simple task, she sent a text to Alan Hinderwell, offering him her tutor's contact details. There. It was done. The two were hooked up. It was no longer her business.

She pushed sluggishly on, hoping she'd now be safe. But was someone following her? The closer she grew to her destination, the more she believed she heard inflexible limbs in pursuit. It was a cold evening, a forceful wind and falling rain adding to the murk. All the same, as she eventually struggled up her mother's garden path, it was difficult not to imagine several figures in her wake, their rigid forms going undetected in the deserted streets. Even children wouldn't linger outside in such inclement weather.

Thinking of her son, and also of her husband, Jane glanced up at the bungalow ahead. No wonder her mother had failed to answer her call; she hadn't even pulled on her curtains this evening. That was worrying, and it forced Jane to advance—with frustrating slowness—not for the front door but for the lounge window, where light from inside served as guidance to potential intruders. She looked through the glass.

The older woman simply sat in her wheelchair, having at least shifted from the conservatory she'd occupied that morning. But was that the only movement she'd managed all day? It seemed likely; she was frozen in a single posture, staring across at family photographs on the mantelpiece while covering her mouth with one hand, as if to keep her head upright beneath a weight of grief. Her flesh appeared as inert and as smooth as plastic. If anyone tapped it with a finger, might she even sound *hollow*?

Her mother couldn't possibly be dead. How in that case could one of her arms defy gravity like that? No, this was a stranger form of rigor mortis, one that might even exist only in Jane's fretful mind. As if to compound the problems caused by her stiffening body, Jane suddenly found herself unable to think clearly, feeling almost empty inside.

And yet one mental image lingered: whatever might remain of her family back at home, perhaps as redeemable as she might still be herself.

Offering a silent, despairing apology to her doll-like mother, Jane pushed herself away, back down the path, out into the street, and then along the streets towards home.

Several people, or at least entities with ambition to achieve that distinction, gave immediate chase, their previously stiff limbs growing—in direct contrast to her own—more audibly fluid as they came.

But Jane refused to turn and look. She kept moving, cursing the weather for keeping indoors more reliable witnesses than she might prove to be herself. Then she was at her front entrance, letting herself inside, shutting the door behind her, keying the lock, and hurrying through for the lounge.

Tony sat in exactly the same place he had the previous few days, his body matching his mother-in-law's in every static inch. He clutched the remote control for the TV, switching channels for all eternity. He'd

become little more than a waxwork version of himself.

If her mouth still worked, Jane might have spoken with hysteria—"Such a fitting image, love… It's how you'd liked to have been remembered"—but then she backed away, towards the foot of the staircase, knowing what greater horror awaited her in her son's bedroom.

Her legs hardly functioning, she climbed and climbed, a long minute at the task. Finally, she opened the bedroom door.

Her boy, her still beautiful boy, appeared every bit as immobile as life had rendered him anyway. He simply lay in bed, hands gripping his video-game controller, killing zombie after zombie forevermore.

And was *that* about to become Jane's task? Returning to the landing at an agonizingly slow speed, she heard her latest visitors gather at the house's front door. They'd had no trouble getting out of the museum, and so entry here would be as easy.

A moment later, there was a crack of wood on the ground level, and then a clank of the latch failing, and finally hinges widening with a sinuous creak.

They all scrabbled inside…were in the hallway…on the staircase…coming up…

As well as real flesh, they'd also regained their voices. And each of them—father, mother, daughter, and the monstrous son—sounded excited.

Jane, hardly capable of any movement at all, hoped she'd feel as little as her family did when the four long-dead Wallers finally laid their vengeful human hands upon her.

Gary Fry is a semi-retired academic who lives in coastal countryside in the northeast of England. He has had published around 100 short stories, a bunch of novellas, and several novels. He was the first author in PS Publishing's Showcase range, and none other than Ramsey Campbell has described him as a "master of philosophical horror." He plays piano, loves dogs, and reads a frightening number of books each year. His web presence can be found at:
https://garyfrytalks.blogspot.com

TETHER

BY IAN ROGERS

*T*HE WORLD IS FULL OF HOLES.

The woman sat on the ground and watched the leaves do cartwheels across the lawn. Occasionally they would get stuck in the tall grass and she would wait to see if the wind would pull them free or if they'd stay there trembling and trapped.

Her husband had been meaning to mow the lawn, had actually gone outside to do it before it got too dark, and that was when their son had vanished. He told her—one moment he was there, the next he was gone, disappeared into thin air.

What a strange expression, she thought. What was "thin" air? Was there such a thing as "thick" air?

She shook off these thoughts before they could take her away on a pointless tangent. She had to stay focused and keep herself together if she was going to get him back. Get them both back.

Because her husband was gone now, too.

She looked down at the rope in her hands. She let it fall into her lap and combed her fingers through the grass on either side of where she sat. It had grown long in the two weeks since they'd moved in. They had meant to cut the lawn, but other things kept coming up. Dusting and cleaning rooms that had been empty for so many years. Making the various appointments to set up the telephone, cable, and internet. Arranging for their first delivery of propane since they were too far out in the country for natural gas. And unpacking the seemingly endless number of boxes that were scattered throughout the house.

She still couldn't believe this was happening. It was so absurd, and yet in some strange way so expected that it was almost like a portent.

They had bought their dream home and it turned out to be a nightmare.

It was the story of a hundred horror movies. Only this was real and they were living it. Living *inside* it. Like a monster had swallowed them whole and there was nothing they could do now except sit and wait to be digested.

And hadn't it been a movie that had led to this?

She looked down at the rope, followed where it ran out of her lap and across the shaggy lawn in a straight line to the side of the wooden shed where it rose upward on an angle and disappeared in mid-air about three feet off the ground.

The shed was an old, decrepit thing; they had been planning to tear it down, but, like cutting the lawn, they hadn't got around to it yet. She worried that their son would get hurt playing inside it, that the patchy, rotten roof would choose that moment to collapse and fall in on top of him. She and her husband had strictly forbidden him from going into the shed, but they both knew that kids had a tendency to do the things you told them not to.

Only it turned out going inside the shed wasn't a problem. Their son had disappeared simply by walking around the side of it.

Her husband had seen it happen.

He was pushing the lawnmower out of the garage while their son was running around the backyard, dashing from one side to the other, sometimes getting close to the old shed. His father told him again not to go inside and the boy said he wouldn't, and he didn't, but he vanished anyway.

Her husband was filling the mower's gas tank, and out of the corner of his eye saw their son sprinting across the lawn, then around the side of the shed...

...and he was gone.

Her husband stood up and went around the other side, to see if the boy was behind the shed, but he wasn't there. It was like someone had spliced him out of the movie of their lives.

There she was, doing it again, going back to the movies.

It was her husband who first brought it up. The movie about the family whose daughter is taken to the other side by vengeful ghosts. They try to find help, but no one can do anything, so they go in themselves to get her back.

She and her husband knew the house had issues. The realtor—a short, fast-talking man with a penchant for ugly ties—had told them that the first time he showed it to them. That was the reason for the low price that she and her husband had initially found so enticing. They told themselves it wasn't anything they couldn't handle, and the realtor urged them along that line of reasoning.

Their son was excited about the prospect of living in a haunted house. He said that he and the ghosts would become friends. The first time they went to see the house, he spent the entire time racing from room to room, looking for spirits.

The realtor assured them the house was safe. *If it wasn't,* he said, *the feds wouldn't let me put it on the market.* But he also told them parapsychology wasn't an exact science, and things could change. Things could *escalate.* If that happened, they were to call him, and he gave them a number where he could be reached at any time, day or night. He told them if things ever got so bad that they feared for their safety, they should leave the house immediately and call another number that he gave them, a 1-800 number for the feds.

Will they take our house? her husband had asked.

If it gets to that point, the realtor told them, *then you wouldn't want to live here.*

That was the problem, the woman reflected. They loved the house, and being in love meant looking past its shortcomings. Something they knew they'd have to do if they were going to live there. They told themselves if you loved something, you didn't abandon it. You stuck with it, through thick and thin, like a marriage. Richer and poorer. Sickness and health. Till death do us part.

But her husband wasn't dead. And neither was her son. She was sure of that. As long as she held onto the rope, as long as she felt the occasional tug from the other end, she knew they were still alive.

She picked up the rope now, ran her fingers across its rough, fibrous length, and pulled on it lightly. A bit of slack came out of the empty space where the far end hung in mid-air. She waited. A few moments later, there was a small tug from the other side that drew back the rope she had drawn out and a few inches more. She watched the small amount of slack play out from the coil that remained in her lap. She wondered what would happen when it was all gone, when the rope went taut where it was tied around her waist.

She could untie it at any time, but she wouldn't do that. If you loved a person, you didn't abandon them. The same went for a place. If you loved it, you didn't leave.

Now the people she loved were trapped inside the place she loved, so leaving was completely out of the question. She would sit here and wait until... until...

She tugged on the rope—a big, doublehanded heave—and pulled a few feet worth back over to her side. Then she dropped the rope back into her lap and watched as the slack, and a little bit more, was slowly reeled back through the invisible opening next to the shed.

That was how it had been since her husband had gone in after their son.

Back and forth. Give and take.

But the other side had already taken so much from her. Why wouldn't it give them back? She loved this place, so did her husband and her son. Why didn't it love them back? Why was it hurting them so? Why did love and pain always have to come packaged together?

Was the house affecting her mind? Love could do that, too. When their son went missing, they didn't even talk about calling the police, or the 1-800 number the realtor had given them. Panic made you blind, but so did love.

The house was haunted. They weren't blind to that. But somehow they knew they had to deal with this themselves. That calling the police or the federal authorities or anyone else would mean never seeing their son again. And time was of the essence. They had to do something *now*.

She had followed her husband out to the garage. He found a long coil of rope and tied one end to the trunk of a big oak tree in the back yard. The other end he tied around his waist. He had kissed his wife and hugged her and whispered in her ear, "I'll bring him back." Then he went striding across the scruffy lawn, around the side of the shed, and vanished in mid-step. Only the rope remained, hanging in the air like a magician's trick, still reeling out into the empty space where her husband had disappeared.

She didn't know how long he had been gone. She wasn't wearing a watch and she'd left her phone in the house. The sun had set and the stars had come out. There was no moon. She was warm for a while, her body holding the heat of the day, and then it started to seep away until she was trembling. After a while the trembling stopped and all she felt was numb.

She didn't know how long the rope was, but her husband had gone far enough on the other side to stretch it almost completely taut. All that distance and he still hadn't found their son. If he had, he would have followed the rope back and come home.

She had grabbed the rope on her end and given it a series of small jerks, trying to get his attention, to get him to come back, but nothing happened. She felt resistance at the other end of the line, but it was a solid, unmovable weight. Almost like he'd tied the other end to a tree on the other side. Were there trees on the other side?

At some point she decided she couldn't keep standing there watching the rope. She had to know what was going on over there, and short of going over herself, there was only one thing to do. So she untied the rope from the tree and wound it around her waist. She tied a thick knot that rested solidly against her stomach. She thought of the day her son was born, looking down at his small purple body, his closed eyes, his tiny curled fists. She thought of the umbilical cord that ran from his navel to the spot between her upraised legs. She picked up the rope and held it in her hands. This was just like giving birth, she told herself. Only this time she'd be pulling instead of pushing.

She tugged on the rope again, and when she felt some give on the other end, she started pulling in the slack. She coiled it in her lap, drawing it slowly and steadily like she was reeling in a fishing line. She experienced a brief resistance, like the rope had caught on something on the other side, then she was able to draw it in again. She was worried about what would happen if she drew the whole thing back and her husband wasn't on the other end. What would she do then? What if the end was frayed and covered in blood? What if the rope was tied to something else? She tried not to think of these things, but it was hard not to, sitting alone in the dark.

She could barely see the shed now. There was a light on the back porch, but she hadn't turned it on when they left the house, and she couldn't reach it now. She squinted her eyes at the spot at the side of the shed where the rope vanished.

She had never seen a portal before. But then no one really had because they were invisible. She wanted to be mad at the realtor about there being a portal on the property, but he couldn't have known. Portals appeared, without rhyme or reason, and all anyone knew about them was that they led to the Black Lands and there was no way to close them. This portal might have appeared days or weeks ago. Maybe only hours.

People had stumbled upon portals in the past. Often that was how they were discovered. Sometimes the people managed to return, or were recovered by the authorities. Sometimes they weren't. It was rare for someone to happen upon a new portal, but it happened often enough that they had a term for these unfortunate people. Accidental Tourists.

She didn't want that for her husband and son. She didn't want them to be statistics in some government report. A sound bite on the six-o'clock news.

She gave a harder tug on the line and

drew in a bit more rope. At first there was nothing from the other side, then there came a responding jerk, stronger than any she felt since tying it around her waist. It snapped the rope out of her hands and left a light burn across her palms.

She watched as the line unspooled rapidly out of her lap and went snaking through the grass to disappear into the portal. The rope didn't stop moving, and she felt her breathing speed up as she realized the pile in her lap was gone and she—

Her body snapped forward and she was dragged across the ground, the grass cold and wet on her skin as it whipped across her face.

She reached out and grabbed the grass on either side of her, in an attempt to anchor herself, but the force on the other side was too strong. She felt the grass in her hands tear out of the ground and she was sliding forward again, toward the side of the shed. Toward the portal.

Suddenly the rope went slack and she was no longer moving. She lay motionless, breathing heavily, and waited for the dragging to start again.

But it didn't. She continued to lie there, sprawled out on the ground, arms spread like she was embracing the lawn. She waited until her breathing had returned to normal, then tilted her head upward.

She was only about five feet away from the spot where the rope disappeared in mid-air next to the shed. Another second or two and she would've been pulled through.

Scrambling to her feet, she backed away from the invisible doorway. Her breath was starting to quicken again, and she slowed it down with an effort. She needed to remain calm. She looked down at the rope around her waist and thought about untying it. Instead, she reached down, picked up the rope where it dangled down to the ground, and started to pull it back in. She did it slowly, until she felt the same resistance as before. Then she dropped the rope back to the ground and braced her feet, waiting for that returning pull from the other side.

It didn't come. She picked up the rope again and gave it a light tug. There was no give. How long could she keep playing this game? Back and forth. Give and take. Even if her husband was injured, or worse, dead, she wasn't strong enough to pull him back. But she had been dragged almost right through the portal. That meant he was alive, didn't it? She tried to think of him that way over there, alive and wandering through the darkness that was the Black Lands, looking for their son. She didn't want to think of something—some *thing*—that had killed him and was now dragging his body away to devour it.

She gave the rope another sharp pull and a long spool came flying out. The resistance was entirely gone. She started reeling the rope back in, thinking, *It's too light, the line has been broken, it must be, it must—*

The rope jerked in her hands and she couldn't pull back anymore. There was a returning pull from the other side, hard enough and fast enough to cut a sizzling burn across her palms. She dropped the rope and watched it disappear back into the portal.

When it seemed like it was going to keep going and start pulling her again, she prepared herself for it by kneeling down on the ground and gripping the rope directly below the knot.

But then, just as all of the slack had been taken up, the rope stopped moving.

She let out an unconscious moan—a sound of mingled frustration and denied anticipation. She slammed her fist against the ground. She couldn't keep on like this for much longer. She had to make a decision. Either untie the rope around her waist and go make the call or...

What was her other option? She couldn't draw her husband back. He might not have found their son yet. This rope was her only lifeline to them. She couldn't let it go. But she couldn't pull them back, either.

She stood up and wiped her eyes. She had started crying at some point. She didn't have time for tears. She had things to do.

She reached down to the knot resting against her stomach. She gripped the rope from either end and tightened it. She wiped her eyes again and started walking forward, picking up the slack as she went. Her choice had been made.

Right before she stepped through the portal and disappeared from this world, she reflected, there had never been any choice at all.

Ian Rogers is the author of the award-winning collection, Every House Is Haunted. *His novelette "The House on Ashley Avenue" was a finalist for the Shirley Jackson Award and is currently being adapted into a feature film produced by Sam Raimi and directed by Corin Hardy. His debut novel,* Sycamore, *the first book in the Black Lands series, is forthcoming from Cemetery Dance Publications in Fall 2024. Ian lives with his wife in Peterborough, Ontario. For more information, visit* ianrogers.ca

MATT COWAN'S HORROR DELVE:

—ALLEN K.

I RECENTLY PURCHASED TWO BOOKS WHICH I'D BEEN HIGHLY ANTICIPATING. First up was Ramsey Campbell's new novel *The Lonely Lands*. Ramsey has been my favorite author ever since I was lured in by that awesome gatefold cover adorning *Ancient Images* back in 1989. After that I continued on reading many more of his novels and story collections over the following years and I've never once been disappointed, so when a new Campbell novel comes available I order it.

After finishing *The Lonely Lands*, I moved on to the new *Terror Tales of the Mediterranean* anthology edited by Paul Finch. I love short stories and these *Terror Tales* series of anthologies have proven incredibly addictive. I buy them all!

Having now read both books, here are my thoughts on them:

RAMSEY CAMPBELL

ANCIENT IMAGES

THE LONELY LANDS
BY RAMSEY CAMPBELL

The Lonely Lands (published by Flame Tree Press, 2023) follows recent widower Joe Hunter as he struggles to cope with his life following the tragic loss of his wife Olivia from the Covid virus. As he attempts to keep the resale shop they ran together going, Joe begins to hear faint whispers from his deceased wife inside the store. In his desperation to speak to her again, he finds himself somehow able to slip into the afterlife when he sleeps to visit her. Shifting through various places and events they experienced together during their lives, he's happy to be with Olivia again, whatever form that may take. There is a dark side to this gift, however, as Joe recalls something his grandfather made him promise years before. *"Maybe you have nightmares"—"Don't have any about me or I might end up in them,"* he said. These beliefs of his uncle originated during his time as a member of The Trinity Church of the Spirit, and the theory is validated when a nightmare version of his grandfather begins stalking Joe during his dream journeys to visit Olivia, forcing him to continually try and lure his grandfather away from her. The places they move through during these cat-and-mouse escapades unfold as a miasma of twisting streets peopled by denizens who look and act strangely. Joe's grandfather isn't the only threat to Olivia either, as is discovered later on in the book.

This is an outstanding novel which deals with one man's grief and intense desire to hold onto a love taken too soon. Meanwhile, that desire also threatens her peaceful afterlife existence. I was enthralled by how expertly the dream-logic is done here. Everything seems like hazy versions of the real world during Joe's treks, just

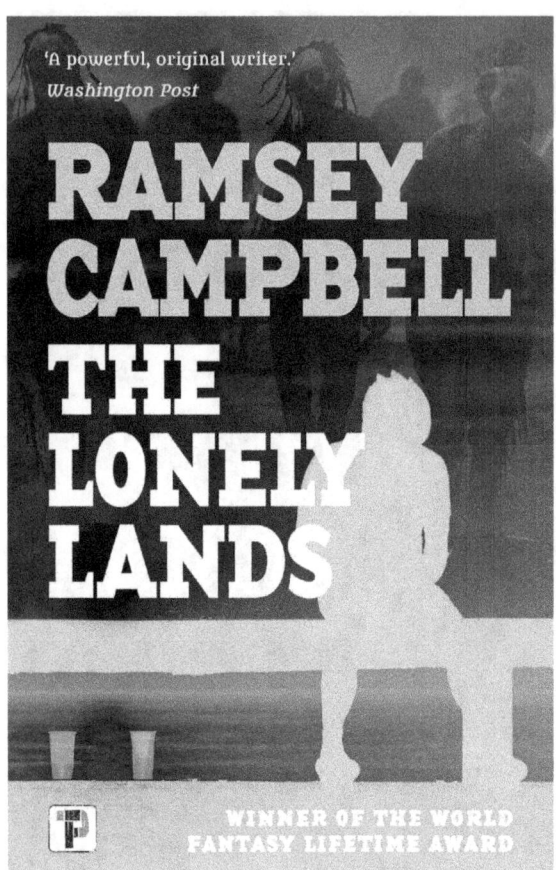

'A powerful, original writer.'
Washington Post

RAMSEY CAMPBELL

THE LONELY LANDS

WINNER OF THE WORLD
FANTASY LIFETIME AWARD

While the horrors start gradually, they mount along with the story's progression, and the surreal landscapes Ramsey crafts during the dream/nightmare scenes are masterfully portrayed here.

TERROR TALES
OF THE MEDITERRANEAN
EDITED BY PAUL FINCH

Few things bring me joy as much as adding a new horror anthology to my collection, which might explain why I have so many of them lining my bookshelves. A little while back I took a chance on one called *Terror Tales of the Seaside,* edited by Paul Finch. I immediately fell in love with it. After finishing it, I was excited to discover there were a lot more of them. I swiftly bought and read *Terror Tales of the Lakelands, ...of the Cots-wolds, ...of Cornwall, ...of the Ocean,* etc., and loved them all. So, now I make it a point to keep an eye out for new *Terror Tales* anthologies. While the previous iterations of this series have taken place in different British locales, this one moves its stories

slightly off-kilter, such as the way a street full of shopkeepers all smile too obsessively while attempting to call him over, or how the workers at a hotel only communicate by parroting his own questions back at him. Early on, Joe has a particularly eerie dream where his grandfather is sitting in a darkened room with a group of friends from The Trinity Church of the Spirit (a great callback to Christian Noble and his church from Ramsey's superb Three Births of Doaloth trilogy). When Joe turns on the light, he's greeted by a nightmarish scene only a writer as skilled as Ramsey could evoke.

Aside from these dream sojourns, Joe also has plenty of real-life struggles to deal with, such as intrusions from Olivia's self-centered parents or his attempts to ensure the person who purposely infected his wife with Covid sees justice. More subtle trials arise for Joe as well, in the form of his often clumsy efforts to hide everything he's experiencing from his supportive neighbor Abigail who tries to help him through his despair. I highly recommend this novel.

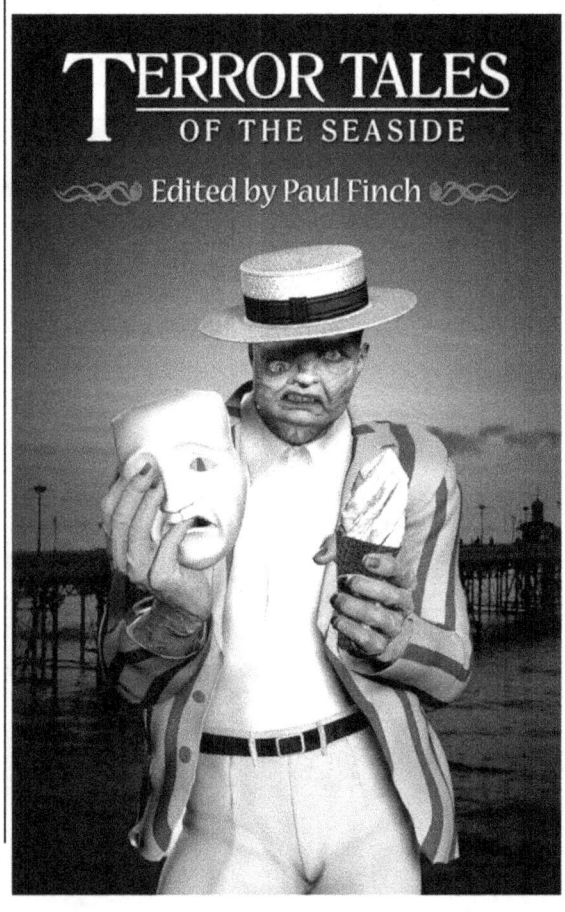

TERROR TALES
OF THE SEASIDE
Edited by Paul Finch

to the Mediterranean. These fourteen short stories take place in locales such as Greece, Rome, Crete, Spain, Turkey, and the like. As an added bonus, interspersed between each of these fiction tales, Paul writes brief essays about various mythical beasts (The Cyclops and Medusa for example), demonic manifestations in the Vatican, serial killers, and occult lore birthed within the regions. I burned through this book, moving from one story to the next, always finding brilliant new treasures along the way. I can honestly say, every story here was a great read, but I did still have some favorites.

The book gets off to a roaring start with Peter Shilston's "The Catacombs," a reprint which follows a tourist in Sicily who stumbles upon a church filled with blasphemous artwork. Finding himself locked inside, he's forced to seek an alternate way out, which leads him to horrors awaiting in the crypt below. The next story up is "On Our Way to the Shore" by Maxim Jakubowski. I should note that my wife and I love taking cruises, so this story about a man who encounters a mysterious woman on cruise ship who isn't what she appears to be was one of my favorites.

"Meet Me in the Middle" by Aliya Whiteley takes us to the Isle of Samos in Greece where a ticket taker for *The Tunnels of Eupalinos* is forced to enter them himself for the first time to try and locate two missing visitors, only to make a horrifying discovery within. The always magnificent Steve Duffy offers up "The Lovers," which follows an assassin with the propensity to cover his victims' faces with a cloth. He travels to Marseille only to be confronted with his past there in the Turkish Baths. This story references one of my favorite paintings by Rene Magritte which is also named "The Lovers."

In "The Wretched Thicket of Thorn" by Don Tumasonis, a couple find themselves stranded on a vacant island full of dense bramble after their rented boat dies, and unfortunately for them something monstrous resides there as well. "Vromolimi" by David J. Howe finds a couple hiking to the top of a hill during the oppressive heat of the day in Crete. From its apex, they look down upon a lake referred to as *Vromolimi*, which

means "stinky lake." Something dire lurks beneath its waves. Horror veteran Gary McMahon's "Should Not Be" sets us in Turkey where a mythic artifact called *Yabbel's Box*, said to contain the end of the world inside it, is discovered. Uncovering something such as this is bound to end tragically.

Every Reggie Oliver story is superb and "The Haunted Heaven" is no exception. Here we observe an archeology student working on the isle of Skliros to help excavate an ancient temple of the goddess *Cybele*. He likewise encounters a cult there who still follow her edicts, one of which demands her male followers to castrate themselves.

"The Quiet Woman" is a brilliantly written tale by a writer I'd not previously encountered and whom I will now seek out. This story is about a reserved woman who flees England to Ravenna, Italy to escape an abusive husband. She finds further torment, as well as redemption, there. "The Teeth of Hesperides" by Jasper Bark takes us to Morocco and a carnivorous plant that's far more insidious than *Cilia* could ever hope to be.

Editor Paul Finch also includes his own tale "Reign of Hell," where two brothers whose lives took separate paths, one becoming an archeologist, the other enlisting in the Greek military under the Nazi regime, finds themselves thrust together again but still at odds. This excellent tale has strong Lovecraftian vibes to it.

Late into this anthology we come across two of its darkest-themed stories. In "Mistral" by Mark Morris, a family vacationing in a remote French manor house acquiesce to the aggressive insistence of their hostess that they attend a special dinner prepared by her son who is a renowned chef. The banquet turns out to be a horrifying affair. Another very bleak but exquisitely written story is "Gerassimos Flamotas: A Day in the Life" by Simon Clark, where a destitute father in Greece accepts an offer to allow his young, mentally challenged daughter to spend an afternoon on a yacht with a rich man without knowing why. What follows is ghastly and heartbreaking.

I've discovered so many new-to-me authors through these *Terror Tales* anthologies, Reggie Oliver, Anna Taborska, and Steve Duffy, for example. This time I've added Maxim Jakubowski, Sean Hogan, and Carly Holmes to my list of writers to follow. Carly's story "Mammone" is about a daughter taking her aging mother on an extended vacation together that ends up in Salerno. While there, she comes across a quaint, little cafe with an affectionate cat named *Mammone*. The charismatic owner of the place informs her the cat is named after a demon. This excellent tale perfectly captures a favorite theme of mine, vacation horrors.

I give this anthology my highest possible recommendation. I relished the varied and magnificent horrors offered up by each of these tales. *Terror Tales of the Mediterranean* (Published by Telos 2023) is an exquisite feast of short horror fiction which will entice you to devour each and every morsel printed upon its pages.

💀 💀 💀

THE RETURN

BY STEVE RASNIC TEM

JOEL HADN'T BEEN BACK TO HIS HOMETOWN IN OVER FORTY YEARS, NOT SINCE HIS PARENTS' FUNERAL. His health was so poor the last couple of years, he knew this was his last chance. It wasn't a trip he wanted to make, but he believed it was a journey whose time had come.

Nothing on the map seemed familiar, not even the names of nearby towns. The topography of Southwest Virginia appeared threatening. Had there really been so many ridges, so many winding roads? It seemed unlikely any of those features would have drastically changed over the years, so the difficulty must lie within his aging memory. He might be better off ignoring his recollections completely.

He'd read that the geology of the region consisted of folded sedimentary rocks from the Paleozoic Age, limestone, dolomite, shale, and sandstone. Sinkholes riddled the karst terrain, many of them leading into the hundreds of caves lurking beneath the surface. He didn't know any of this when he was a child. But hadn't someone warned him to be careful where he stepped?

As a boy he'd isolated himself much of the time. Painfully shy, he relied on his books and comics for company. After graduation he lost contact with the few he might have called friends. A few years after his parents'

deaths the house he grew up in burned to the ground. There was nothing in that town left for him, and yet he still felt compelled to return.

If Celeste were alive she would have traveled with him. She would have made things so much easier. Throughout their marriage she'd been his go-between with the outside world. They'd made plans to come a few times, but something always came up. "Don't wait until it's too late," she said. "These memories won't last forever." She understood him all too well.

Joel took a direct flight into Knoxville Tennessee. A two-hour drive in a rental car carried him across the Virginia state line and into a wide green valley between forested ridges. The Woodland Indians camped here before the white men invaded. His grandfather took him arrowhead hunting a few times, and once to a cave on private land full of their bones. This angered his mother and the trips with grandad stopped.

There was now a better road, but it bypassed the old highway going through town. A small, weathered sign showed him the way. Another, barely readable sign indicated the area was a bird sanctuary. He recalled the large flocks of birds which filled the trees around town. The clamor they made sometimes frightened him. He'd been a fearful child. His father used to say he didn't know what to do with him.

The winding road skirted a pond and followed the complicated curves of a low-lying ridge, the lane narrowing until he wasn't sure what he'd do if he met a vehicle coming from the opposite direction.

But he confronted no such vehicle. Joel encountered no cars at all. But he remembered it was always a sleepy town. Now that the mines were gone, and so many people moved away, he imagined it was practically comatose.

It occurred to him he hadn't checked for hotels. There had been two on the edges of town when he lived here, decades ago, but the chance of them still being in business seemed remote. How could he have missed such a basic aspect of trip planning? He felt like a child again, helpless without Celeste to watch out for him.

The radio played a constant stream of bluegrass music. He wasn't used to the genre, but it was so different from the things he usually listened to, it was almost charming. During the two-plus hours he'd been listening there had been no interruptions for news, ads, or announcements of any kind. Changing the channel delivered static. Apparently this was the only choice the locals had.

So far nothing he'd seen on this trip was at all familiar to him. He gazed at the passing landscape, looking in vain for something to trigger another memory. Certainly, he grew up surrounded by neighbors, relatives, classmates, their houses, their businesses. An entire community. He hadn't spent *all* his time in his room. But this world had nothing to do with him. He'd never had a good memory for faces, and names often eluded him. But this was worse. He had only the vaguest ideas about his own parents. He couldn't remember the last time he looked at their photographs. And his beloved grandfather—was he tall, or fleshy? Did he have a beard? Joel vaguely recalled the sweet smell of tobacco, but had that been on some other old man's clothes?

Celeste was ten years gone, and she too, he had to admit, had become a bit less real, no longer a vivid part of his now. And the now was important—that's where we all lived. He had an abundance of photographs, of course, in almost every room: Celeste at various ages, in the blue Mexican dress she'd worn on their wedding day, a closeup of the marigold she'd pinned in her hair, dancing at a party, lying in bed reading, and standing in the park she'd loved so much, smiling so broadly at the camera, the same spot where he scattered her ashes.

All these images folded one into the other until they were all the same. Joel could no longer hear her voice in his head, or remember the smell of her hair, or the particular way she felt when he held her in his arms. They were no longer a part of his experience of the day, of any day.

The ditches along the roadside had been allowed to fill with weeds. It felt negligent and dangerous. He drove slowly, afraid of what might wander into the path of the car.

COMING OUT OF A long bend in the road he came upon a beautifully preserved antebellum home. He knew there were houses like this when he was a boy, but he couldn't remember any in such good condition. There were columns out front, and a second story porch above the main porch. Filigreed brackets ornamented every corner of those porches as well as the eaves. The house looked freshly painted. Flower beds flanked the sidewalk leading up to the steps, and rose bushes hid much of the stone foundation. A small sign by the front gate promised ROOMS. He pulled off the road into a narrow parking area.

The small woman behind the screen door tilted her head. "Can I help you?"

"You have rooms available?"

"Sometimes. Come inside and let me have a good look at you." She wore an old-fashioned dress with a lace collar and a print of tiny yellow flowers on a field of cream.

With her pale, papery skin, and white hair she almost disappeared into the pastel patterned wallpaper behind her. But her eyes, like dead coals resting in cloudy water, held his attention. "I taught you in school, didn't I? You were in my sixth-grade history class. Jack, or Joe, something like that."

"Joel. I grew up here, but I think I'm too old to have been one of your students."

"Nonsense. I'm not always good with names, but I know my faces. And I'm always happy to rent to a former student."

In which case Joel wasn't about to argue with her. "I'm not sure how long I'll be staying."

"Stay as long as you like. People aren't lining up to rent here. Not since they moved the county seat."

"This isn't the county seat anymore?"

"Not for over twenty years. They decommissioned the courthouse, tore it down and sold the parts to one of those architectural antique companies. There's not much left of downtown I'm afraid. I take it you've lost touch?"

"I have." It felt more than a metaphor.

"Most of Main Street is empty. We don't have a newspaper anymore, a hospital, or a school. The sun's setting fast on this old town. You should have come back sooner."

She showed him around the house. The dining and living rooms were from another era, full of antiques. The kitchen looked as if it had been last updated sometime in the Fifties.

"Lock your bedroom door. Folks around here tend to sleepwalk."

"You have other renters?"

"No. You're the first in a long time. Supper's at sunset if you're around. Breakfast at six AM. You're on your own in between." A white cat came bounding down the stairs. It halted, frozen, when it saw Joel. "Do you like to bird watch?"

"I suppose. Sometimes."

"Birds are the only things worth looking at around here." She pulled out a drawer in a sideboard and handed him a pair of binoculars. "This will help."

AFTER SETTLING INTO his room Joel came back downstairs thinking he'd drive into town

and see for himself the changes the woman talked about.

"Hello!" he called out. "Missus?" But he'd never gotten her name. He wandered downstairs looking for her but found no indication of her presence. Out of curiosity he opened the refrigerator. It was empty. He checked the cabinets. They were empty as well. Perhaps she'd gone grocery shopping? He wasn't hungry in any case. He might skip dinner if he got busy in town.

He got into the car and continued down the road. He assumed he would reach part of the town that way. If not, he could always double back.

He needn't have worried. Almost immediately he was within the town limits. Block after block of tidy little homes. White and blue were the predominant colors. This sense of perfection was spoiled now and again by a weed-filled lot, and areas where the woods took over. Tall plants and brush now filled many of the old gardens.

He had to veer away from low-lying branches, and sections where weeds and saplings grew across parts of the roadbed. Had the town given up on road maintenance?

He kept hearing the distant sound of chainsaws, but he never saw the workers using them. The sounds seemed to descend from the sky, so they may have come from miles away.

He drove up a hill with boarded buildings on either side. Suspended over the top of the hill was a single dead caution light. Joel remembered it well. It had been the only traffic light in the town, meant to warn drivers about the cross street beyond the peak of the hill. Perhaps the warning was no longer needed?

He turned right at the dead light and parked. The courthouse used to be on that corner. A few large foundation stones marked the spot. He got out of the car and looked around. There was a used furniture store across the street. It was hard to tell if it was out of business or simply poorly kept. Dust filled the windows, and the interior looked shabby. But cosmetics might not dissuade customers from looking for a bargain. He was sure the building used to house the post office. Marks on the brick indicated the lettering had been removed. He remembered as a teenager going to the post office to pick up his magazine subscriptions, the books from his mail order book club.

He began walking down the hill into the short block they'd called downtown. A pair of boarded-up law offices. An empty drugstore. He didn't remember this building exactly, but he recalled sitting at an old-fashioned soda counter and browsing the paperback racks. This could have been that place. He pressed his face against the glass. A square window resolved out of the dimness in the back, a dirty PHARMACY sign. A man in a white coat leaned over the small counter, waiting for his order. The sky brightened behind Joel, glazing the window yellow, and the man was gone.

Next door was an empty lot, scraped down to a broken concrete slab littered with cans and rags. He thought there might have been a clothing store here, or was it a hardware? Two more empty stores, their windows plastered with browning newspaper. One of them might have been the old Five and Dime, but he had no idea which one.

A tall man wrapped in swaths of gray stepped out of one of the boarded entries then disappeared. No doubt some trick of the light played on Joel's aging eyes. It was unnerving to see the town empty, with no evidence of human habitation, so maybe his nerves created a presence or two.

Their family doctor had his office in a building on this block. The building was no longer there. His grandfather died in that doctor's waiting room one hot July afternoon.

Where was everyone? It wasn't even three o'clock yet. Despite its problems, this had been a good place to grow up. He could find no justice in its abandonment.

He heard the children running down the sidewalk. He used to do this with his friends, excited that classes had ended for the day, they'd raced each other to the drugstore, or the tiny newsstand attached to the barber shop, eager for a treat, or one of the new comic books. He moved closer to the wall lest they trample him. He was brittle now, frail. That was the biggest change in his life.

He had to be on his guard against falls. The right collision with a gang of eager youngsters could break him.

When he turned his head he saw it was a small dust devil carrying pebbles and grit. But what made those clomping sounds, those thrilled children's voices echoing down the walkway?

Joel hadn't thought of this street in years, or these businesses, these houses, this town. He doubted he remembered it accurately, and there were holes. But now it was crucial that he remember, that he recover every lost detail.

He allowed his fractured memories to lead him down the street and into the now-empty lots, where he prodded the rubble for clues as to what once stood at that location, to mostly empty storefronts, where he pressed his forehead against the cool shop windows, his eyes searching the shadows for either goods or occupants. Sometimes there was movement, a shift in the light, the silhouettes of forms coming and going, but nothing definitive, and nothing confirming he'd lost his senses.

Finally, he arrived beneath the grove of ancient Hickory trees on the edge of town, then wading through the tall grass he made his way to the narrow, winding creek. Everything seemed impossibly hushed. Even the shining water tumbling over the dark stones apparently felt the need to keep its voice down.

Shadows drifted and fell apart like smoke. He remembered fishing in this creek when he was a boy. He couldn't remember ever catching anything. They stocked the big stream on the other side of town with trout, but not this small branch. No one else ever fished here. That was why he preferred it.

He wondered if they still stocked the streams in the county. If anyone fished. If they bothered anymore. Everything has its time. Everything eventually dies.

He heard distant chainsaws again. He looked up. Birds were circling overhead. No. They'd made a circle, but now were motionless, frozen, suspended in midair. He never knew birds could do such a thing.

It occurred to him there were many more insects here than he was accustomed to.

They filled the air, and they were crawling all over his clothes. Had one gotten into his ear? That might explain the mysterious sound of chainsaws.

He had a moment which he experienced on every trip he'd taken as an adult, a nagging suspicion he'd forgotten something important at home. Had he turned off the stove? Did he lock the back door? He couldn't remember if he'd requested a mail hold or not. Did he tell anyone where he was going? He had no memory of those last few days before getting on the plane. He was usually so careful, obsessively so. He couldn't remember packing.

Joel returned to his lodgings just before sunset, but no dinner was evident. He went searching for her again and found no one. No matter. He was exhausted and had no appetite. He lay in bed gazing out the window until it was dark. During the night, a new assortment of bugs came out, the big moths and the lightning bugs like sparks fallen from the stars.

JOEL WOKE UP to a morning muted in both color and sound. He turned on the lights in his bedroom, but they did nothing to increase the ambient illumination. He dressed quickly, eager to get out of this silent mausoleum. The wallpaper lining the stairwell had turned sepia. He noticed some peeling. Everything revealed itself to be much shabbier than when he moved in the day before. The downstairs furniture was scarred. A gray dust had settled into the wounds. He didn't bother to call for the landlady. He was convinced she was either dead or missing. He would find other accommodations before nightfall.

When you grow up in a place, you never imagine it going away. People don't last, but it seemed to him a town should.

He drove out to the cemetery to visit his parents' graves. It was a small distance out of town, but up a steep rise which the car struggled to negotiate. He remembered as a child going with them to pick out the three plots.

The cemetery wasn't fenced so he walked right in. To his surprise his parents' graves had been well taken care of. No weeds and the grass well-trimmed. The empty space by his mother's was meant for him. The flowers in the two vases were dead but appeared to be recent additions. He went to the small office at the back of the graves to thank whoever was in charge, but the door was locked. No hours were posted.

He could hear the rain before he felt its distinct drops, on grass, on headstones, on tree leaves, on the small building's roof. He could feel it before he saw the small spots of gray, like fingers touching his shirt, his skin, before it became a rapid flutter, and then a painful scouring of his flesh. He ran to the car and got in. Even with the wipers on he couldn't see past the windshield. On the other side of the glass pale figures writhed as if suffering. He waited until it stopped, then rolled down the window to gaze at the mist rolling off the grass.

After the rain, the worms came out, fleeing the saturated ground, rising like pink, boneless fingers eager for a touch. He must have known many of those buried here, but for the life of him he couldn't remember any names. Did they ever imagine they would someday be gone and how much of their lives did they spend trying to avoid that realization?

If he gazed in a certain unfocused way between the mist and the narrow trees and the gray tombstones he could sometimes make out their faces staring at him with resignation, disappointed they no longer mattered in the world.

On the way back through town he tried to find the spot where their house had been, but as hard as he tried he couldn't remember the address. He drove back and forth through the neighborhoods for hours with no luck.

THE NEXT MORNING a scream woke him up. Of terror or bereavement Joel couldn't quite decide. He thought the voice had been female, but it might have been male. He should find out whose it was and offer help, but he had no idea where to begin such a search.

Some of the wallpaper in his bedroom had fallen off and curled into loose rolls lining the baseboards. The dried yellow paste on their undersides looked like patches of disease. The downstairs area had furthered its progression into brown. Two side tables lay collapsed due to their rotted legs.

He wasn't sure whether it was Friday or Saturday. Perhaps it wasn't even the weekend.

In the early morning light he could almost hear the sigh as the fog flowed down the mountain hollows into the flatlands below. He decided he would walk that day, but instead of going into town he turned onto a narrow gravel lane which pointed toward the distant hills. The area was farmland, but the fields were dried up and dead, the plots marked by small, ragged farmhouses missing both doors and windows.

An awful stench drifted through the air. Deeply unpleasant, and in certain pockets it was intolerable. In those moments he picked up the pace and tried to ignore it. Farm country was rife with unseemly aromas, but this stink was unfamiliar to him.

Joel thought he saw a man walking through a distant stretch of amber-colored grass. He started walking in that direction, calling out a strained *hello*. But the closer he got, the more distant the man became. He had to give up and returned to the gravel road.

He came to an apple orchard. The trees sagged with heavy, bright red apples. He hadn't eaten in a couple of days, so he thought he should be eager to eat one, but he was not. He didn't feel hungry at all. He should eat something anyway, at least to nourish his body. He walked into the trees and reached for an especially beautiful apple, but couldn't make himself pick it.

Joel thought he saw a woman high in the next tree. He walked around the trunk, looking up to get a better view. He saw part of her back, an arm, a portion of one leg, but he could never quite apprehend her face. "Hello, do you need help?" he asked. She said nothing. He tried repeatedly, rephrasing the question each time. But she refused to speak to him, even when he was as polite and apologetic as possible. He gave up and moved on.

Most of the fog lifted by mid-morning, leaving dew on the grass and brightening the bark of the trees. The sun rose higher and by lunch it looked glorious, inviting anyone living to come out and enjoy the day. He was eager to witness this. He remembered the town and its surroundings as always an unusually sunny place. But he saw no one, and supposed the downtown area was as empty as it had been since he arrived. He couldn't figure it out. Someone must live here, more than a few since many of the lawns in town were mowed and the bushes trimmed. And someone had taken care of the gravesites in the cemetery.

THE NEXT MORNING Joel woke up with no memory of the walk back to the woman's lodging house, or what he might have done with himself the previous evening. There was a sourness in the air, and he thought maybe it was him, because he'd neglected to take a shower since he'd been here. Not on purpose—he simply forgot. He slipped into his bathrobe and walked down the hall to the bathroom.

He looked at himself in the mirror. The glass was hazy, and appeared as if it hadn't had a good cleaning in years. But there were clear areas, and in those areas his face was pale, unhealthy, and the skin had a broken, crepey appearance, which he thought was new, although he might be mistaken.

There was no shower, just a tub. He bent down and stuck the cracked black rubber stopper into the green-stained drain, then turned the faucet handle. A hollow sucking sound erupted accompanied by a rattle in the pipe, but no water. Then a long-legged black spider crawled out of the spout, over the handle, and back into the wall through a narrow gap. He tried the sink faucet with no better luck. At some point he would have to figure out how to wash.

After getting into the last of his clean clothes Joel started down the staircase, pausing halfway because of all the cracking sounds. He looked down. Several of the treads had split. The ones below him looked rotted. He stepped carefully onto the more solid-looking bits for the rest of the way down. Downstairs the walls were painted with mold. When he got back he would retrieve his luggage and find somewhere else to sleep.

He drove in town for a while taking the long way around the back, then through the alleys, and the narrow streets of the outlying neighborhoods. He saw no one, not even a cat or a dog. Areas were impassable because of downed trees or bushes growing through the pavement. The sidewalks were practically destroyed. Some houses had burned. A few leaned so badly a moderate wind might knock them flat. He saw none he would have considered intact.

He chanced upon a familiar backroad he remembered led out to his grandfather's farm. It wound upwards into the ridges and through a series of wide valleys. He passed several abandoned farmhouses. In some their walls had fallen inwards making them resemble crushed skulls. A few barns had been left partially disassembled. He remembered there used to be a market for gray barnwood. Many landowners sold their old outbuildings to feed the demand.

Joel found no signs of people, but birds were now plentiful, roosting on telephone lines, filling the branches of trees, soaring overhead in great flights of migration. Their overlapping wings made Escher-like patterns in the sky. But they made no sound, which he found bitterly disappointing. He would have given anything to hear a disruption in the dead silence, even if it were a scream.

The sun was high overhead yet provided no warmth. This didn't make much sense in summer, but was it still summer? He couldn't remember the name of the month when he had flown in. It would be on his return ticket. He had a return ticket, although he had no idea where it was.

He gave up looking for his grandfather's farm. He may have passed it without recognition, or it wasn't on this road at all. On his way back into town he found a high place overlooking downtown. He parked and grabbed the binoculars off the back seat.

He used them to take in the distant views: the side of a cliff, hay bales arranged artfully in an empty field, old farmhouses with peeling paint. He still looked for signs of human life. It was impossible he was the only one. But there was nothing, or worse than nothing, as among those brief glimpses of beauty he could see plentiful evidence of extensive loss and decay.

We are slight, he thought, *and temporary.*

JOEL DROVE BACK to that once lovely antebellum home to pick up his luggage and find someplace safer, or at least more intact, to sleep. He wondered if he should leave money on the kitchen table for the lady in case she ever returned. He hadn't yet paid her anything and he owed her *something.*

The question was moot. He couldn't find the place. He drove from one end of town to the other and beyond, trying every road, sometimes driving at a crawl to make sure he didn't miss it, and found no indication of its existence.

Joel couldn't think of anything logical to explain this omission, or what a next reasonable step might be. He went back through town and parked near the Hickory grove at the end. He was uneasy about the prospect of sleeping in any of these abandoned buildings, and it would be too uncomfortable sleeping in the car. But it was warm. He would stretch out beneath these trees and think about what he could do tomorrow about his situation. His search for the woman's house would be more successful with a rested pair of eyes. If all else failed he had his wallet with him. He could drive to Knoxville tomorrow and find an actual, normal hotel. He could stay there until he got a new plane ticket home.

He was alone beneath the trees and the moon, the scatter of stars from one end of the darkness to the other. He knew there were things which once made him happy, but he could not remember what they were. He remembered there was pleasure, when he was young, in simply being alive, but he could not remember any of the particulars. He remembered wanting to be married. He couldn't remember if he ever asked her, and he couldn't remember her name or whatever happened to her. A wife would have made all this much easier. But if he had learned anything during his lifetime it was that we all face death alone, trapped inside that secret self which can never be shared.

He could hear a distant storm, a crackle of electricity like a chainsaw inside his head.

Lightning filled the air above the trees. He felt the hairs on his arms stand up and knew how incredibly lucky he was to be surrounded by such a terrible beauty.

He awakened as the sun peeked above the distant hills. He knew he had much walking to do. Why hadn't he rented a car? He was too old to be doing so much walking. He raised his head to look around. There was a road, and fields of rubble on either side, and nothing else. The world was perfectly quiet. He remembered he'd wanted to visit his hometown one last time before he died. He couldn't remember how he'd lost that opportunity.

He could remember nothing else and knew that what he could remember only yesterday had faded away. The morning came up all silver, and he was aware that something new was about to begin.

💀 💀 💀

Steve Rasnic Tem is a past winner of the Bram Stoker, World Fantasy, and British Fantasy Awards. His novel Ubo *(Solaris Books), a finalist for the Bram Stoker Award, is a dark science fictional tale about violence and its origins, featuring such historical viewpoint characters as Jack the Ripper, Stalin, and Heinrich Himmler. He has published over 500 short stories in his 45+ year career. Some of his best are collected in* Thanatrauma *and* Figures Unseen *from Valancourt Books, and in* The Night Doctor & Other Tales *from Macabre Ink. You can visit his home on the web at* www.stevetem.com

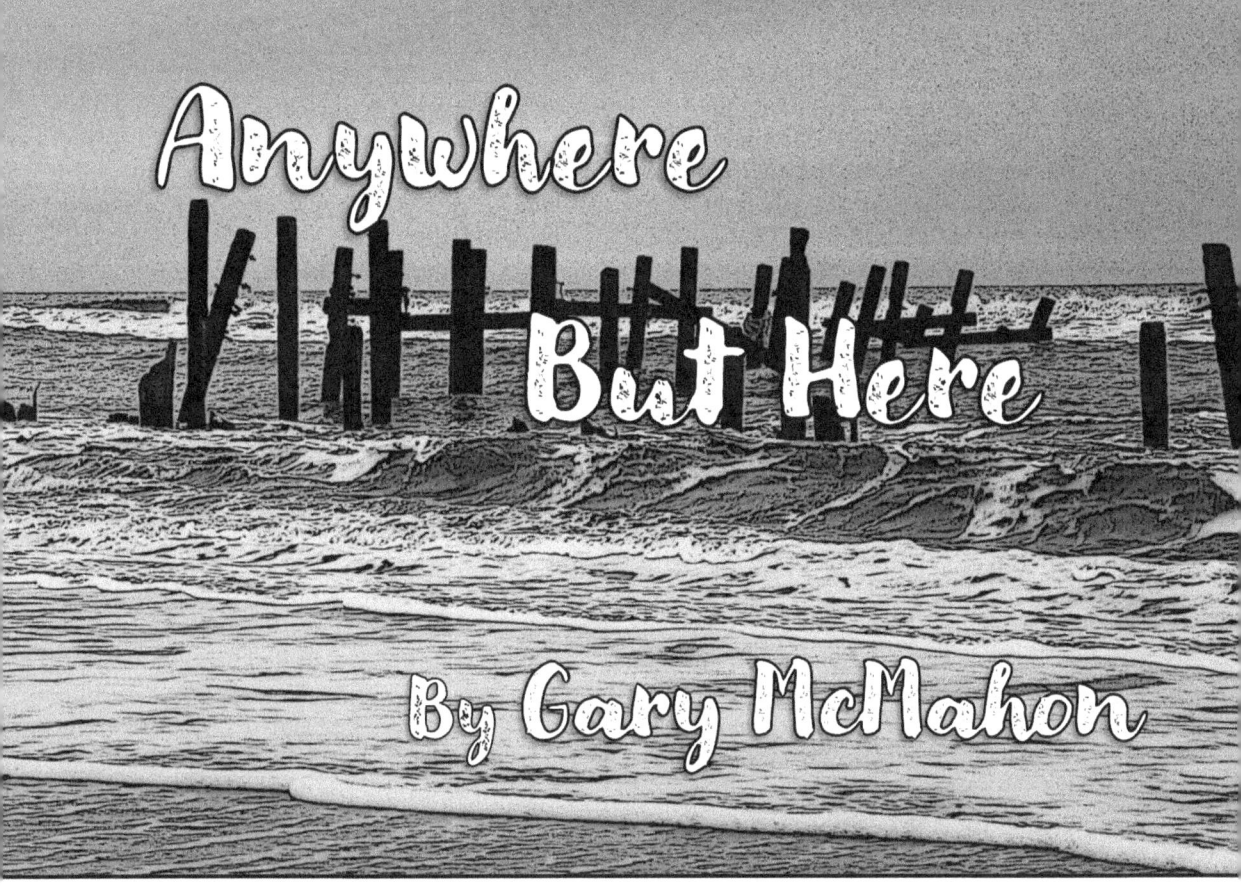

Anywhere But Here

By Gary McMahon

ON THE NORFOLK COAST, A FEW MILES EAST OF HUNSTANTON, accessed along narrow lanes originally meant for horse-drawn carts and through tiny villages whose streets seem deserted outside of the summer months, is the place where my mother asked me to scatter her ashes.

In Victorian times, Lynnburgh had enjoyed some modest popularity as a quiet tourist destination for those seeking a more subdued alternative to the main resorts further along the coast. These days, it doesn't even draw the attention of the occasional day-tripper to its sallow, barren little bay and forlorn beach of grey sand and slate chippings.

I don't blame the tourists for staying away. I don't blame them at all. The place isn't unattractive or unwelcoming as such; there hangs above it a sort of pall, a sense of sadness that never seems to shift.

In my imagination, I return to Lynnburgh often. In reality, I have been there only once.

"JESUS," SAID CATE as I switched off the car's engine. "It's a bit…dismal, isn't it?"

"Yeah. I have no idea what mum saw in this place. All she ever told me was, as a child, she'd spent a wonderful summer holiday here, crabbing in the bay and riding a bicycle along the sea front."

Cate glanced at me. The fading sunlight flared in the lenses of her glasses. "One summer? That's it?"

"That's it," I agreed.

We got out of the car and looked towards the beach. I was stiff from driving, so I bent over to touch my toes and loosen my hamstrings. Cate took her battered leather suitcase from the back seat and slammed the door. I hadn't seen that old case in years; it used to belong to our mother.

"Very limber," she said, watching me and smiling. She smiled a lot. I wished I could do the same.

I straightened, bent over as far as I could

backwards, enjoying the sensation of my muscles uncoiling and lengthening.

The slight breeze ruffled Cate's hair. Her cheeks were pale. She tugged at her hoodie, pulling it up over her head, and hugged herself. The smell of fish and chips hung on the breeze. A whiff of sea air. Salt and vinegar.

"How many people do you think live here? It looks desolate…empty. Like a ghost town."

Slowly, I turned to survey the tiny high street, with its budget supermarket outlet, charity shops, and a pub called The King's Hat. "Not many. It doesn't even have a Wikipedia page."

Cate pressed up against me, threading her arm through the crook of my elbow. "I doubt the locals even know what the Internet is, dear brother," she said, shuffling her feet on the gravel car park.

We walked slowly downhill, towards the high street, arm in arm, and stepped carefully over the knee-high fence forming the perimeter of the car park.

A bus shelter on the opposite side of the road looked as if it was gathering dust; a few of the shops behind it had boarded windows and CLOSED signs taped to the inside of their doors.

"Not exactly a picture postcard, is it?" said Cate. "I'm sure it was pretty…once."

We crossed the road and headed down towards the sea. Only a few cars passed us on the road as we made our way along weed-strewn paths between dead grass verges. The big Norfolk sky was slate-grey and oppressive. Gulls called high overhead, looking for food. The doors of a kebab takeaway shop swung open and a tall, pudgy youth emerged balancing three pizza boxes across one forearm as he spoke quietly into a mobile phone. He climbed into a battered red Ford Fiesta parked at the curb outside the takeaway. It took three goes to start the engine, and then the car pulled away belching black smoke from a rattling exhaust pipe.

We stood on the cracked concrete promenade and looked out at the sea. The waves were irritable; the water was choppy and aggressive. The sea-worn tops of timber groynes were visible in rows above the surface, leading out from the darkening shore.

The water looked grey and silty.

"Surf's up," said Cate, squeezing my arm.

I smiled. She could always, eventually, make me smile. She was the only one who ever could.

We headed east along the promenade, looking for the B&B I'd booked us into for the night. Cate was still linking my arm. We fell into step as we walked. Everything seemed normal, but with a layer of fragility, a veneer that felt as if it might crack at any given moment to reveal the rot inside.

As we walked, I tried to picture my mother's face, but all I could remember was the coldness in her eyes. For some reason, memory failed me, and all I was able to summon was the mental image of a short, stooped woman in a dull floral housecoat with a grey smudge for a face. But within the scribble where her features should have been, a cold fire burned; a coldness that lived on even now that she was dead.

The guesthouse wasn't far from where we'd parked the car. Another half a mile along the front, as promised in the email confirmation I'd received from the landlady.

As we walked, it began to rain. Light spatters, but cold.

"There it is," said Cate, halting and gesturing across the road with her free hand.

A narrow doorway with a colorful stained-glass inset. "Vacancies" announced a handwritten cardboard sign hanging on the inside of the glass. The guesthouse's name—Lynn House—was proclaimed in delicate font on a tiled plaque set into a shallow alcove above the door.

"Here goes nothing." Cate pulled me across the road, her trademark fatalism never far from the surface.

She stepped up to the door and rang the bell, which sounded shrilly somewhere deep inside the house.

I inspected the brick and flint façade—a traditional local construction method—and wondered how long these buildings had stood here, braced against the elements, welcoming travelers who rarely came.

Presently, I heard someone approaching in heavy shoes across bare boards, and before long, the door opened.

Standing on the doorstep was a tall, thin woman with a stern posture and steel-grey hair pulled back into a severe ponytail. Standing in the dimness of the doorway as she was, I couldn't make out her face, and was reminded of the image of my mother I'd struggled to picture earlier.

"Good afternoon," said a pleasant voice. "Can I help you?" She stepped forward to reveal a pinched yet kindly face, and I was immediately put at ease.

"Yes," said Cate. "We have a booking. It's under the name…Anderson." She stumbled over her maiden name, almost forgetting her married surname had been stripped from her in the divorce proceedings.

The woman had a blank look. I wondered if she was confused.

"Daniel Anderson?" I said. "The booking is in my name."

The woman smiled and took a small step backwards. "Ah, yes. Please come inside."

We followed her along a wide hallway. Polished wooden boards underfoot. Walls hung with landscapes and portraits that looked as if they were painted by a decent amateur rather than a professional artist. Nautical-themed knickknacks displayed on narrow shelves. The lights were low. Shadows gathered in the corners. The place looked clean but cluttered, like most guesthouses I'd stayed in.

Under the stairs, there was a little wooden desk crammed into a space far too small to comfortably accommodate it. She squeezed behind the desk, opened a drawer, and took out what I assumed were our room keys. "If you'll just sign the register, I'll show you upstairs."

Cate winked at me as I leaned over to sign the old-fashioned paper register. I caught sight of a dusty visitor's book next to it on the desk.

Cate's room was next to mine. There was no adjoining door, but it was okay. I'm sure she felt safe enough in the house.

I unpacked my clothes and put my toiletry bag in a drawer under the window. When I glanced outside, I had a good view of the sea, but it did nothing to reassure me. There was something prancing on the sand. A small figure with sticklike limbs, it kept doing clumsy cartwheels and somersaults in the low dunes. My mouth went dry and I felt a dull pressure growing behind my eyes.

It took me several minutes to realize I was merely watching the broken and twisted remains of a kite, perhaps abandoned on the beach by a child earlier that day. The wind eventually dragged it away; I watched for a while longer as it cavorted towards the early evening surf, before closing the curtains on the view.

There was a knock on my door: three sharp raps. "You ready?"

I opened the door and felt relief at the sight of Cate, standing in her skinny jeans, black hoodie, and holding a thin raincoat over her arm.

"Ready to go?"

"Yeah…erm, just let me get them. The ashes."

She stood in the doorway as I retrieved the small plastic urn from my suitcase, checking that the lid was still screwed on tight.

"The sooner we do this, the sooner we can get something to eat. I'm starving." She walked towards the stairs, clearly hurrying me up.

I locked the door and followed her, feeling as if I'd forgotten something. Whenever I leave a room, there's always a nagging doubt that I've left something behind, or a small task undone. A tiny anxiety, but one with teeth.

Back on the promenade, the wind was stronger than before. I scanned the beach but there was no sign of the dancing corpse of the kite. "I'm not sure exactly where we should do this."

"Didn't she say? Not even in her will?"

I shook my head and realized Cate wasn't looking at me. "No…no, there were no specific instructions. She just wanted them scattered here. I'm guessing she meant in the sea."

"Let's go, then. I'm getting cold." She strode ahead of me, towards a gap in the sea wall, and stepped onto the beach. Stones grated underfoot; the wind tugged at her hair. Her face was turned away from me, lost for a moment in shadow. It felt like a warning, or perhaps a premonition. Then the moment was gone, taken by the wind.

"Wait," I called, speeding up to catch her.

We strode together across the beach, towards the sea. There was nobody else around. The sky was darker now; the clouds had gone black and the spaces between them were the color of dirty slate. The moon was pale, like a poor reflection of itself, and there were not yet many stars.

The sound of the sea grew louder as we approached. It was like a distant crowd, applauding, urging us to action. When we reached the harsh white surf, Cate stopped short of the water, not wanting to get her feet wet.

"Do it," she said, softly but with an edge to her voice "Do it now, quickly."

I struggled to get the lid off the container, but eventually it came free. "Should I say something? Like, a few kind words?"

"Why? She never had any for anyone else, so why should we give her any?"

That stung, but I didn't know why. Mum had always treated Cate badly, even when she was a child. And once Cate escaped across the country, starting a new life in London, that ill-treatment had turned swiftly and easily to resentment, and finally hatred.

"Do it. Toss them in."

I fumbled with the urn, almost dropping it, spilling some of the ashes in my haste. Rescuing the situation, I simply threw everything—ashes and urn together—into the sea as hard and as far as I could. At that moment, the sound of the wind over the water was like a woman calling out wordlessly.

When I turned to look at Cate, she was weeping silently. I didn't know what to say so I simply stood there, feeling the wind and the salt spray on my face, wishing I was anywhere but here.

Later, in the restaurant, the mood between us softened. A few drinks, some decent seafood, and the sharing of what few good memories we had of our childhood.

The place was empty apart from us and another couple at a table near the door. They kept reaching out for each other across the table, and whenever the waiter approached, they'd quickly pull back their hands, as if afraid to be seen sharing such an intimate moment.

"They're having an affair," said Cate, grinning.

"How do you know?"

"Because that's how I acted when I had mine." The grin faded; her eyes lost some of their light.

"Listen, I know you and Mum had your issues, but it doesn't mean *we* ever stopped loving each other." I raised my glass. "You're my sister, and nothing can ever change that fact. Wherever you live, wherever *I* live… we're still family, and I'm always here if you need me."

We clinked glasses. Cate emptied hers, so I poured her another glass of Malbec.

"There's so much you don't know." Her cheeks were red now from the alcohol. "So much I've never told you."

"About you and Mum?"

She nodded, then shook her head. "Yes, no, maybe. About everything, really. Me and Mum. The mess I made of my marriage. The affairs. The miscarriages. All of it."

I took a long drink from my own glass.

"I'm sorry. Are you shocked?"

I set my glass on the table. "No, not shocked. Surprised, maybe, that you never felt you could tell me any of it. I kind of guessed about a lot of what went on, but I was always waiting for you to open up and tell me yourself."

The waiter ghosted past our table. He gave me a funny, unreadable look but didn't approach us. Perhaps he sensed this was not the right time to interrupt.

"I know, and I'm sorry. Sometimes… I dunno. I suppose I forget that I'm loved, and I go deep inside myself. I try to hurt myself by keeping it all inside." She looked at me with an expression I couldn't identify: I wasn't sure if she was about to cry or burst into laughter. In the end, she did neither.

"Sometimes the ghosts that haunt us are barely-glimpsed figures, shades and phantoms rattling their chains in the night. Often, they're simply noises in the dark." She paused, taking another drink of wine. "And occasionally we're haunted by the ghosts of people who were never really there."

It was warm inside the restaurant, but I felt cold, as if someone had opened a door directly behind me and let in a chill. "What do you mean?"

Right then, she did laugh, but it was a horrible, truncated thing: a throaty, still-born sound I never want to hear again as long as I live. "Nothing," she said. "Sod it. Let's get drunk."

"Okay. What shall we drink to?"

Cate raised her glass in the air, as if she were about to pour out her drink on the table. "To Mum," she said. "The bitch."

I have no idea how many bottles of wine we went through that night, but I didn't care how drunk we got and how bad we would feel in the morning. Those scant few hours are some of the best I'd ever spent with my sister. We didn't deconstruct the past; there were no painful conversations about how badly our lives had come apart: we drank and laughed, and sang—oh, how we sang—and in the end, the waiter had to nervously ask us to leave so he could close the place for the night. He seemed wary of us, afraid even, but I wasn't sure why.

Staggering back along the promenade, the black sea at our left and the dark town to our right, we kept on singing. When we ran out of songs, we sat on the sea wall and composed an impromptu sea shanty, finishing off the bottle of wine we'd brought with us from the restaurant.

I remember Cate having to hold me up as we climbed the stairs in the guest house, trying, and failing, to keep quiet so we didn't wake anyone.

"But there isn't anyone else," I remember Cate saying, through whispery giggles. "We're the only ones here!"

At the door to her room, I hugged her hard, as if I didn't want to let her go. And I didn't: I wanted to stay there, holding her, forever, or at least until the sun came up and the hangover kicked in.

"I need to sleep, baby brother," she said, pulling away from me but still holding my hand. "Full English in the morning, to soak up all this booze." She grinned; the skin of her nose crinkled; her eyes didn't quite light up but at the time, it didn't seem to matter.

"G'night," I said, tripping on the carpet as I backed up towards my room.

The last thing I saw as she closed her door was the darkness swallowing her up.

Darkness, like a hungry mouth.

I woke in darkness, too. I had no idea what time it was, or what had awakened me, but there was somebody standing at the foot of my bed. I stared at the figure, trying to focus my eyes. The wine, the night, the sense of not knowing where I was.

"Who's there?"

The figure didn't move.

"Cate?"

In the darkness, its head slowly turned, looking away from the bed. Then, even more slowly, it turned back to look directly at me. I couldn't see the face, because it was nothing but a dark smudge, but I knew the eyes were upon me. Cold, harsh eyes. A cold fire, seeking me out, pinning me there, against the mattress. Then, blinking on like lights, I saw twin white circles where those eyes should be.

"Mum? Cate? Who is that?"

But she was already gone.

In her place was a familiar skeletal shape, with a ragged torso and too many thin, spiked limbs sticking out at odd angles. The tatters of its central core rustled slightly, as if in a breeze, but otherwise it remained motionless. Watching me.

A kite, I thought. *It's just a child's kite.*

I could feel its icy, fathoms-deep gaze upon me, willing me to get out of bed and approach it. I felt that by doing so, I would cause it to spring into motion; but if I stayed here, still and quiet and afraid, it would be unable to dance.

Battling against my fear, I somehow managed to close my eyes. I wanted to open them to see if the thing had come any closer, was even now leaning over me, but I kept them shut. Not long afterwards, I must have fallen back to sleep.

The next day, I got out of bed much later than I'd planned. The curtains were still closed, so the daylight had failed to wake me. I didn't care; it was the best night's sleep I'd had in years. My usual insomnia had not bothered me, even after the weird nightmare with the figure in my room.

I put on my clothes, thinking I'd shower after breakfast, before we checked out, and went to knock on Cate's door. She didn't answer. I figured she was either deep into a hangover sleep or downstairs already, tucking into breakfast because she didn't want to wake me.

The landlady was in her little cubbyhole under the stairs, tidying some papers.

"Morning," I said, but not too loudly. A headache was brewing behind my eyes.

"Good morning, sir. I'm afraid you're a little late for breakfast, but I could do you some eggs and a pot of coffee if you'd like."

"Oh, has my sister already eaten?"

She looked at me oddly, her face expressing what I could only call confusion. "Your sister?"

"Yes, Cate. My sister. The person I arrived with."

"I'm sorry, sir... but you arrived here alone."

A sudden memory from last night: *darkness, like a hungry mouth...*

"No. I was with my sister. We checked in together ... came here to scatter our mother's ashes. We ate out last night... came in a bit late, I'm afraid."

Slowly, she shook her head. "I'm sorry..." She glanced down at the desk top. She was pushing the guest register towards me, still open to yesterday's date.

I knew what I'd see before I even read the entry. My own name, the date. Nothing else. Only me, on my own. Always on my own.

"I don't understand..." The headache began to bloom in full; light mushroomed before my eyes, and I reached out to steady myself against the underside of the stairs.

Her voice in my head, repeating the words: *And occasionally we're haunted by the ghosts of people who were never really there.*

But she *had* been there, throughout my entire life. I had the memories to prove it. We'd grown up together, and even after she went away, she was always there on the other end of the phone, and, later, an email or a text message.

Last night, I hadn't been drinking and singing alone. She'd been with me. We'd sung sung together, making up the words when we couldn't remember them.

She was my sister; she was there.

Hours later, after the police had questioned me and I was finally allowed to leave, I walked along the promenade and stopped when I was level with the spot where I'd so clumsily scattered my mother's ashes.

The tide was out. The exposed beach looked bleak and unwelcoming.

Standing knee deep in the shallows, holding hands, were two figures. Both women. Both looking my way. As I watched, they turned their backs on me and waded together out to sea, returning to the silty depths...

* * *

...but no, it didn't end that way at all. Not this story.

It happens in my dreams, and in my thoughts, but it never played out like that in real life. What really happened was, I stood staring at the sea, wishing that someone or something would appear: a trite, soothing vision to offer me some kind of closure. Anything to give me solace and rid me of confusion.

That was when I spotted something on the sand, a few yards up from the white-frothed shoreline. It was far enough away that I couldn't make out any specifics, but it looked like a battered leather suitcase. Sitting on the sand.

I have no evidence to support this, but I knew it was hers. It was Cate's case. I don't know why it was there. It just was.

I stood there for a long time, watching the suitcase until it became meaningless: a vague image of something I might once have recognized. Several times, it looked to me as if the suitcase was bulging, a movement that might have been caused by something moving inside. I knew it was nonsense, but the image was at once shocking and oddly comforting.

I suppose my mind must have wandered for a while, because at some point late in the afternoon, I realized the suitcase was no longer there. Nobody had come along and picked it up. The tide hadn't come in to wash it away or bury it in the wet sand. It had simply vanished.

In some ways, I feel as if I'm still standing on that beach now, watching and waiting. But nothing ever comes creeping into view. The suitcase does not fall open to reveal what is writhing inside. Nobody walks out of the waves and the darkness to help me make sense of the rest of my life.

They never do. Never did. Never will.

———

"What is all this love for if we have to go out into the dark?"

—M.R. James

Gary McMahon writes intensely personal horror stories. His short fiction has appeared in countless anthologies and magazines and has been reprinted in The Best Horror of the Year, The Year's Best Fantasy & Horror *and and* Best New Horror. *He's been nominated for several awards and even won a couple of obscure ones. He is the author of the* Thomas Usher *novels,* The Concrete Grove *trilogy.* The End, The Bones of You, *and his novella* The Grieving Stones *was recently adapted into a feature film. He lives with his family in Yorkshire, UK, where he reads, writes, watches far too many films, lifts weights, and trains in Shotokan karate.*

WE HOPE YOU RETURN TO NIGHTMARE ABBEY—

WE'RE DYING TO HANG OUT WITH YOU AGAIN.

Now available at AMAZON and other online venues:
BLACK INFINITY: CREATURE FEATURES

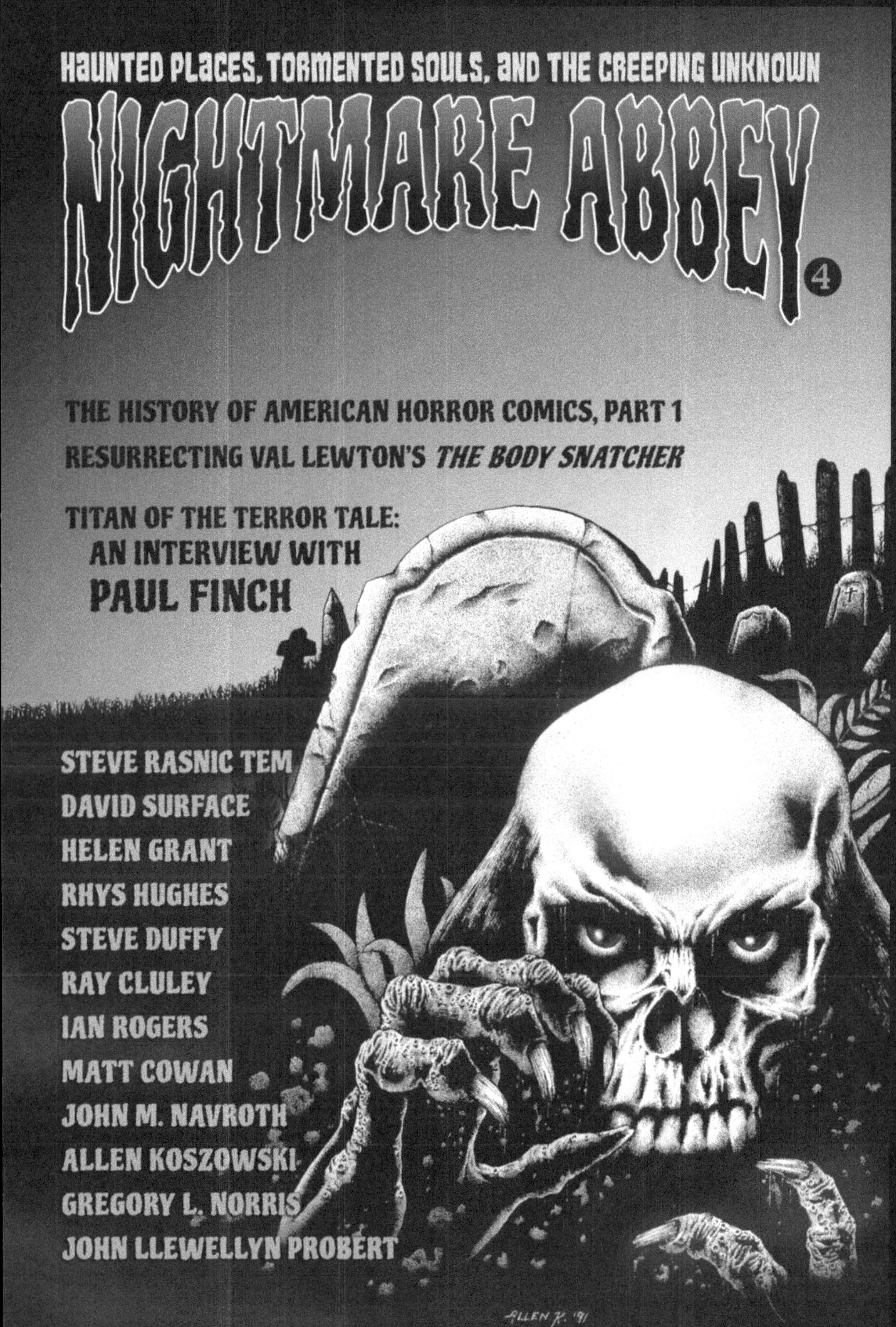

HAUNTED PLACES, TORMENTED SOULS, AND THE CREEPING UNKNOWN

NIGHTMARE ABBEY

④

THE HISTORY OF AMERICAN HORROR COMICS, PART 1

RESURRECTING VAL LEWTON'S *THE BODY SNATCHER*

**TITAN OF THE TERROR TALE:
AN INTERVIEW WITH
PAUL FINCH**

STEVE RASNIC TEM

DAVID SURFACE

HELEN GRANT

RHYS HUGHES

STEVE DUFFY

RAY CLULEY

IAN ROGERS

MATT COWAN

JOHN M. NAVROTH

ALLEN KOSZOWSKI

GREGORY L. NORRIS

JOHN LLEWELLYN PROBERT

ALLEN K. '91